# ROGUE RAIDERS

## Book 18 of the Rogue Submarine Series

## By John R. Monteith

# BRAVESHIP BOOKS

## PROLOG 1

Seated behind the desk of his study, Pierre Renard examined the digitized map of the Mediterranean Sea's eastern shore.

He pondered ways he could oppose terrorists stealing aid destined for those enduring unrest in Damascus, but his de facto agent in Israeli intelligence–Lieutenant Colonel Ariella Dahan–had warned him that railgun rounds overflying Lebanese airspace would strain relations between the neighboring countries.

Damascus, Syria was beyond reach.

While pondering if his forces could counter atrocities committed within reach of coastal Syria, he glanced across the room.

His closest friend and confidant examined a computer screen, searching for opportunities to bring relief to people suffering under Ortega's Nicaraguan tyranny.

"Henri?"

"Yes, my friend?"

"Any luck?"

The silver-haired assistant leaned back in his chair, folded his arms, and shook his head. "We could cover a good deal of Nicaragua with railguns, especially if we put the *Xerxes* and *Goliath* on either side of it."

"I suppose the Panamanians would allow use of their canal."

"But Ortega's restricted himself to mostly nonviolent oppression thus far."

Renard pondered the situation. "I see. He can't be seen as a terrorist to his own people, even though I'm sure most Nicaraguans know the difference."

"They might, but nobody's opposing him. Only at that point might it flare to violence worthy of our intercession."

"Is that what you're seeing in your research?"

"Yeah. I think it's a dead end for this year."

Days earlier, Renard had welcomed 2023 wondering if events at the end of 2022 would cost his friend, Jake Slate, his life. The thought of the *Specter's* comatose commander still battling for existence in a hospital bed under his roof saddened him.

"Pierre?"

"Yeah. Sorry. Divert your attention from Nicaragua to Myanmar."

"Myanmar? Do you still have spies there?"

The question made Renard reflect upon using people as objects. Over the years, he'd scaled back his spy network, partially by relying upon the CIA instead and then more so by shifting his focus to humanitarian missions.

He found that people wanted to help with humanitarian missions and didn't require threats or rewards to do so, and he found abandoning such manipulation comforting.

And humanitarian missions kept the fleet's interventions public. People could approach him or receive him in confidence based upon his public track record, such as in Yemen and Nigeria, and he could work through formal channels without the need for espionage.

But limited time and energy reduced his private spy network, leaving Myanmar void of clandestine links. He confessed. "No, I don't. If we need to intervene, we can knock on someone's door."

"Which 'someone'?"

Admitting to himself he doubted they'd find an opportunity in the beleaguered Southeast Asian country, Renard again confessed. "I'm not sure. I'll leave it to you to find potential allies, if you can first find people in need of our services."

Dutifully, Henri lowered his head to his screen. "I'll see what I can find in Myanmar."

In silence, Renard admired his friend's loyal diligence. Then he felt compelled to say something, although in a rare moment of verbal uncertainty, he wasn't sure how to express himself. "Henri?"

"Yes, my friend?"

"Should I retire?" Renard reconsidered their mutual dependence and rephrased his question. "Should we retire?"

The submarine mechanic thought and then offered a sarcastic

smile. "I thought this was our retirement."

Henri's retort stung, but Renard was unsure why.

During the next hour, he tried to find his next mission, but he spent more time tormenting himself with thoughts of dissolving his fleet. Henri Lanier had been his earliest confidant and assistant, and he represented the fate of all his employees.

Renard realized he'd made them prisoners through loyalty, rewards, and addiction to adventure.

As age dragged the fleet's founder towards thoughts of a life beyond arms dealing and world shaping, the phone on his desk chimed with a call from the Director of Business Development at France's military manufacturing juggernaut, the Naval Group.

He shared an inquisitive look with Henri while answering. "Director Pompidou. To what do I owe the pleasure?"

"Our ambassador in Indonesia just called me. There's been a coup, or rather one is brewing and seems unavoidable, and President Widodo wishes to speak to you."

Dossiers of world leaders flickered through Renard's mind until settling upon the island nation's leader. Joko Widodo, nicknamed Jokowi, was a progressive Muslim ruling the largest and most religiously tolerant Muslim nation, and he'd entered politics late in life after a business career.

Hearing about interest from Widodo triggered Renard's curiosity. "Jokowi himself wishes to speak to me?"

"He's not one for pomp and formality when working in private. The ambassador assures me he says what he means and means what he says, at least more so than most politicians."

Renard appreciated France's ambassadors considering his mercenary navy's abilities and keeping the Naval Group director's phone number handy. "That aligns with my understanding. However, I'm missing one submarine commander. Before I'd waste the president's time, does he know that?"

"I've informed all the ambassadors of your operational status, and I'm assured President Widodo's staff has considered this."

While gathering his next thoughts, the fleet's leader glanced at Henri, who angled his monitor for his companion's viewing while pointing at a Wikipedia article about Widodo. Renard nodded the silent order for his assistant to switch to the new subject of research. "Did he say when he wanted to talk?"

The Naval Group director replied. "Three o'clock our time."

Renard checked his clock. "That's only ninety minutes away, and Jakarta is six hours ahead of us. So, he's sensing an urgent need, and he's dedicating his late evening to this."

"He's dedicating his late evening to solving a crisis. He and his staff will be up late tonight."

"Understood. Where's the crisis?"

"Papua. Again. Only, this looks larger and better organized than the 2019 protests."

The Frenchman recalled that the western half of the island of New Guinea bordered the country of Papua New Guinea and marked the eastern end of Indonesia. Racial unrest had plagued the half-island in the recent past. "Will you give me a moment?"

"Of course."

Renard muted the director and stared at his confessor. "Henri?"

"My friend?"

"If I take this call, I'll draw us into whatever agenda is on Jokowi's mind. We'll yield the independence we've gained in Yemen and Nigeria if we're under his employ."

"Hearing a man's request is hardly agreeing to fulfill it."

Renard sighed. "But I know incremental recruitment, and I know myself. He'll put something tempting in front of me, and I don't see myself refusing a well-formed request."

"Then don't. We're coming up empty here with our research."

"I appreciate your wisdom, my friend." Renard unmuted the director. "I would be honored to hear from President Widodo at three o'clock."

"It'll be a video conference. I'll verify and then send you the secure link. At that point, I'll recuse myself from the transaction."

"Understood." Renard hung up and folded his arms. "Let's check for unrest in Papua Indonesia."

"I'm on it, boss."

Ten minutes later, a confirmation of the meeting arrived on Renard's phone, and he felt butterflies in his stomach.

Wondering how he'd react to the stress of serving yet another nation's leader, he heard his study's door open.

His wife, Marie, ogled him. "Pierre?"

"You surprised me, my love. What is it?"

"Come quick! Jake's awake."

## PROLOG 2

As Renard outpaced Marie and Henri to the room he'd dedicated two weeks earlier to his comatose friend, rising hopes shaved thirty years off his aging body's movement. After passing through the doorway, he darted past a nurse, crouched, and folded himself over Jake's torso, capturing Linda's arm underneath him.

Weakly, Jake protested. "I thought you hated hugs."

Gathering himself, Renard stood and replied in English for Linda's understanding. "I make rare exceptions, and today I am quite thrilled to make one."

"Thanks. I feel like shit."

"You look like shit, to be truthful."

Henri replied while folding himself into his turn at hugging. "You've traumatized Pierre to the point of saying silly things, like insulting you minutes after you awake."

"Yeah. That wasn't nice, Pierre. But Linda's already told me I look like shit."

Henri stood. "A wife can say that. A friend should not."

Renard examined his friend's face to assess his demeanor. He seemed distant and more relaxed than usual. "You feel terrible, but how's your mind?"

"Working, I think."

In French, the nurse interjected. "He needs his rest."

Renard nodded. "Right. Of course." He switched back to English. "Henri and I have a conference call in an hour, and we should be preparing for it. But I also want to enjoy this moment."

Jake's voice remained weak. "I'll be fine, Pierre. And I'm not going anywhere."

"No. I imagine not."

"Are we getting ready for a new mission?"

Renard knew his friend was useless for Indonesia. "We are. You're not. Your next mission, while in my employ, is to appreciate your wife. She's hardly left your side."

Linda mouthed a quiet thank you as Renard led Henri out the

door and back to the study.

At three o'clock, Renard invoked his conference call and sensed Henri rolling his chair beside him. Though unsurprised, he was disappointed when an Indonesian man appeared who looked more like a smiling politician than Widodo. "Hello, sir. I am Pierre Renard, and this is my assistant, Henri Lanier."

Educated at George Washington University, the speaker's accented English was perfect. "It's a pleasure, Misters Renard and Lanier. I am Luhut Panjaitan, President Widodo's chief of staff. Thank you for taking my call on short notice."

"It is our pleasure, Mister Panjaitan, or shall I address you as General Panjaitan?"

"Mister Panjaitan is fine, but thank you for acknowledging my military service."

"Of course." Already, Renard sensed himself subjected to statecraft and gamesmanship. He was off-balance, expecting to meet with a leader but instead getting his underling. "I was invited to meet with President Widodo. I assume he's been detained?"

"That's correct. I'm sure you understand, we're working feverishly to counter the pending insurgency."

"I knew you had unrest, but I was unaware of an insurgency. Is there a government in waiting?"

"Unfortunately, there is, at least in four of the six provinces. The governors of Central Papua and Highland Papua remain loyal, but the other four are siding with a rogue army officer."

Renard showed off his recent research. "You have two major generals in Papua, one each for your fifteenth and sixteenth regional military commands. I suspect one of them?"

"You suspect correctly. One of them is seeking to establish an independent nation under himself. The other is dead."

"A major general is dead? I hadn't heard."

"Killed earlier today. I suspect that Major General George Santoso will be the first of many casualties."

"So, we know who's in charge."

"Yes. Major General Djoko Purnomo heads our fifteenth regional command in Western Papua. The four rebel governors are aligned with him."

"What about other flag officers and other services?"

"Purnomo befriended Rear Admiral Mego Hakim during an interservice assignment, and he's delegated all but the army to Hakim, who he's picked to become his future military chief. As for other flag officers, we have off-island assignments and two suspected murders removing Purnomo's opposition from all sources."

Renard tallied the cost. "With an uprising on a distant island, you've lost an eighth of your army, a sixth of your air force, and a third of your navy. You've lost one of your three fleets."

"Roughly, yes. Purnomo has spent three and a half years since the Papua Conflict bullying local politicians and flag officers of the other branches to follow him. They, in turn, have been indoctrinating recruits for his cause. To echo public cries for independence, they'll speak of racism and indigenous rights, but Purnomo and his junta act for themselves."

"As do all tyrants. That's nothing new in history."

"But his influence is terrifying."

Renard chewed on the meaning. "A charismatic godman?"

"Yes. And frighteningly so. His passion and zeal in person are becoming the stuff of legend. It's being said that he can incite anyone to anything."

The Frenchman compared the man mentally to Hitler, who'd turned German rage against vulnerable minorities to increase his power. "Such charisma usually requires fanning the flames of hatred against someone."

"The numerous dividing lines between ethnicities and religions give Purnomo more than enough ammunition for his rhetoric."

"Understood." Renard pivoted back to tactics. "Even after losing an entire naval fleet, your remaining forces are enough to overcome the rebels. So, how may I assist you?"

"The president requests your assistance in crippling, but not sinking, his rebellious ships and defending a troop landing."

With his navy's less-than-lethal maritime combat experience, the Frenchman had expected the crippling request, but the landing support posed an obstacle. "I understand why you want our help softening your rebel fleet. Our railgun and slow-kill weapons can neutralize but preserve the stolen combatants for reunification when this is done."

"Precisely. And President Widodo is ready to offer clemency to rebels who might come to their senses."

Renard drew breath to inquire of the amphibious landing.

But Panjaitan continued. "He's offering you a handsome sum."

"You have my attention."

Widodo's chief of staff spoke a number of euros more than five times greater than Renard's expectations.

The Frenchman stopped breathing.

"Mister Renard?"

The mercenary leader exchanged a look of shock with Henri and then replied. "Yes. To be clear, that was..." He repeated the number.

"That's correct, Mister Renard. But it assumes you leave his ships without any damage beyond that of your sub-lethal weapons."

As the dreamlike sum settled in his understanding, the Frenchman found himself framing a compensation schedule based upon milestones of partial mission accomplishment, along with future penalties for unforeseen shortcomings. "If I must sink a ship, would I incur the cost? That would all but defeat the profit motive."

"I won't bore you with details now, Mister Renard, but there would be modest subtractions from your payment if you must sink our ships. We could do that ourselves, as you insinuated."

"For the sake of expediency, I'll trust that your payment schedule is fair and will examine it later."

"Thank you, Mister Renard. Time is critical."

"But what of scuttlings? I could damage a ship and keep it salvageable, but a rogue crew may sink it to avoid capture."

"We can raise them and replace corroded components faster and for less cost than procuring new ships. But a scuttling would be a terrible loss we wish to avoid. We're contracting with you to keep our enemy's ships impotent but afloat." Panjaitan looked away. "Ah, here he is now."

His skin sagging, Widodo spoke English in a thick Malay accent. "It's a pleasure to meet you, Misters Renard and Lanier."

"The pleasure is ours, President Widodo."

"I trust that Mister Panjaitan has explained my needs."

"Quite eloquently, Mister President."

"Mister Renard, can you imagine being a soldier, airman, or sailor in Papua? Their leaders are tyrants, but to young men they appear more legitimate than my government thousands of miles away. I must use minimal force to stop them, so that I can offer them a peaceful return to ordered lives."

"Understandable, Mister President. I'm quite sure I can help."

Widodo was direct. "How fast can you reach Jakarta?"

"It's roughly seven thousand miles. I'll need fifteen days, assuming I can use the Suez Canal."

"I can protect your use of the Suez."

Renard's objections evaporated. "That would help."

"I'll also send you escort combatants and pay for your refueling at Port Said, Socotra, and Sri Lanka. Would that speed your arrival?"

Mentally bumping his fleet's speed to its maximum, Renard adjusted the timing. "That would reduce it to thirteen days."

"I'll send you a downpayment to compensate you for mobilizing. Assuming you'll agree to the details within the next forty-eight hours, may I schedule your first refueling in Port Said?"

"I can get the *Xerxes* and *Wraith* there in three days. The *Goliath* will be a day behind, after its release from its dry dock. As you know, the *Specter* is out of commission due to an extended upkeep." He omitted the submarine's wounded commanding officer.

"I'll have a team in Port Said in three days to oversee logistics.

The escorts will meet you in Socotra. Is this to your liking?"

"Yes, Mister President."

"I've familiarized myself with details of your fleet to show how important I consider nonlethal force. But now that we've agreed directionally, I ask you to discuss details with my chief of staff."

"Of course."

Widodo excused himself, leaving Panjaitan. "Mister Renard, shall we reconvene tomorrow morning at eight o'clock your time to develop plans and agree to compensation schedules?"

"That would be great, Mister Panjaitan."

"I look forward to our next meeting then. Thank you, and good night, Mister Renard."

"Good night." The screen went dark.

Renard faced his assistant. "Did I just get bought?"

"Bought. Bedazzled. Steamrolled. You couldn't have refused."

"I've never been so overpowered in a negotiation. I entirely forgot to question the troop landing."

Henri shrugged. "They're still probably planning it."

"I imagine so. But that number placed me off kilter."

"Yeah, you looked flatfooted. But for that amount, do you care?"

Renard guffawed. "Not one bit! I'm positively giddy!" But reality settled in. "We need to get the crews traveling to the ships, and we need to get the ships mobilized. Tonight."

# CHAPTER 1

The next morning, Rear Admiral Mego Hakim stepped aboard his flagship, the first hull of the *Martadinata*-class frigate.

The vessel's commanding officer saluted. "Welcome aboard, Admiral Hakim."

Hakim returned the salute. Since the combatant was the last to abandon the Indonesian fleet for his navy, he wanted to see and be seen by its sailors. "Is this ship ready to join my navy?"

"Yes, sir. I've recruited a loyal crew ready to fight for Papua."

"You proved that when you abandoned the quarantine."

"I surprised them, sir. The Indonesians threatened me as I defected, but not a single shot was fired. I helped them establish their quarantine, and then I gave them its first gap when I surprised them by defecting. They had no response."

Hakim smirked. "They expect to break our spirits and recapture their ships, and this error makes them docile. If you and the other commanders stay loyal, we'll continue to prove them wrong."

"The sun is rising on our righteous nation, and it will have a strong defense from its birth."

"Well said. Welcome to the Papuan Navy, Commander Basarah."

"Thank you, admiral. Would you like to inspect the ship?"

"I would. Lead on."

An hour of touring revealed the rebel crew's diligence in having cleaned the *Martadinata's* innards for its new navy.

A beautiful frigate, approaching its sixth birthday since commissioning, was the jewel of Hakim's new country, his new fleet, and his new squadron of ten surface combatants.

New. New. New.

Rebirth.

After his tour, Hakim flew back to his headquarters.

A day ago, the Sorong Main Naval Base had been home to the Indonesian Third Fleet. Now, after three and a half years of reassigning personnel loyal to Jakarta far from his command and bringing in those sympathetic to Papuan independence, Hakim made Sorong his navy's headquarters.

He expected more attention and authority after his pending installation as General Purnomo's chairman of Papua's complete military. With an army general as acting president and a nation surrounded by water on three sides, a naval chief would offer a balanced perspective to a fledgling junta's cabinet.

But his immediate need was protecting the new country's shores and, more important to him, assuring loyalty of his underlings who surrounded the table.

Checking the uniform collars around him, he liked being the only flag officer. He'd sent his loyalist chief of staff, a one-star admiral, to Jakarta on a bogus assignment as exile.

Among his maritime rebels, he stood alone as the leader. His chest swelled as he announced his latest victory. "As you're all aware, the *Martadinata* has escaped our former imperialist oppressors and is at our disposal."

Gestures of obedience pasted smirks on nodding heads. Across the wall behind Hakim's subordinates hung the coat of arms of Western New Guinea, the Morning Star flag, which had replaced the Indonesian standards sewn into the warriors' uniforms.

Hakim continued. "We have ten large surface combatants with air support, one submarine, seventy patrol craft, and all the utility ships we need to operate a strong fleet."

Additional obedient gestures acknowledged the report.

Hakim addressed his marine corps leader. "Colonel Pardi. The land war status?"

A lean, grizzly officer aimed a stylus at the digitized map covering the table. "Sir, we're on schedule to end martial law in the four free provinces. I've got half my marines interspersed with the army to assure cooperation during policing operations."

Hakim pointed at the colonel. "And to make sure the people see the marines alongside the army in their liberation. They love the general, and we need our forces seen beside his."

"Of course, sir. The people are also obeying General Purnomo's advisory to conserve fuel, and the army controls the utilities."

"The civilians are wise to embrace austerity measures. But how are civilian casualties?"

"Only sixty dead thus far, sir. Below our predictions."

"That's hardly more than the 2019 protests."

"The people are proving receptive to our junta. Most would-be loyalists throw down their arms and come to their senses when they see their neighbors accepting us."

A known confidant of the junta's leader, the admiral praised himself by praising his boss. "General Purnomo was insightful in his timing. He's giving the citizens what they want."

Parroting a rebel paradigm, Colonel Pardi glorified the general. "History will remember him well."

"How about our casualties and detainees?"

"Sir, I've lost two marines, and the army has lost sixteen soldiers, half of whom died retaking a loyalist fuel depot in South Papua. Most detainees came from that depot, thirty-one of the total fifty-eight across all military branches."

"These detainees are being treated well? We must show goodwill to strengthen our position in independence talks."

"They eat the same food my marines eat, sir."

"Good." Hakim locked eyes with his staff one by one. "Make sure your sailors, airmen, and marines know that as of this moment, there are no more detainees–only traitors, traitors to the People's Republic of Papua. And they will be executed for treason."

Faces tightened as heads nodded.

The admiral continued his inquiry. "What of our borders?"

"The army's guarding the borders to Central Papua and

Highland Papua, and they have insurgents stirring riots. That will keep the loyalists busy with peacekeeping and unable to challenge our provinces, and they'll be weakened for future taking."

"Very well." The admiral eyed a short air force officer. With General Purnomo wanting his army air corps supporting his troops' ground efforts, he'd delegated the rest to Hakim. The admiral welcomed the personnel, and he let his highest-ranking Indonesian Air Force officer manage anti-air and, with a few naval subordinates to assure competency, maritime air assets. "Colonel Soebijakto, the maritime air status?"

"I've placed a helicopter on each combatant that can hold one."

"But they're not conducting flight operations?"

"No, sir. To conserve fuel, and because my naval advisors assure me we don't expect hostile submarine intervention yet. I've got one patrol aircraft around the clock for maritime surveillance. That's a three-section rotation with three aircraft, and it's where I'm burning most of my fuel."

"Good. And our defense of the air?"

"Looking skyward for airborne threats, sir, but mostly from ground radar stations and two airborne drones. We're conserving fuel, too, although four fighters are in an Alert-Five status. Indonesian aircraft are still respecting our airspace."

The admiral bragged. "With five anti-air capable surface combatants deployed, I'd avoid our airspace, too."

Haughty expressions embraced his bragging.

He continued. "How about the airports?"

"We've taken over security. Most flights remain canceled, but we're letting some women and children fly to domestic cities."

Hakim judged the policy wise. "Fewer mouths to feed. Less medical supplies needed. And we appear magnanimous compared to the human rights violations the Indonesians committed in 2019."

"Yes, sir. Especially to the sympathetic media outlets whose reporters we're allowing in."

"Good." Hakim faced a pudgy officer. "Captain Moeljadi. The

surface war status?"

"You're not interested in the undersea status, sir?"

Hakim sniffed. "No. Like Colonel Soebijakto said, Indonesian submarines couldn't have reached us yet. And don't we have undersea drones deployed?"

"Yes. Two, sir. One on the north shore, one on the south. However, the Chinese are shipping us six more."

"Good. And this blockade? The so-called quarantine?"

"With the *Martadinata* joining us, that leaves only eight large Indonesian combatants in the quarantine, but they're plugging the holes with patrol craft. Nothing passes unchallenged."

Hakim dismissed the blockade. "But we can run it if needed."

Captain Moeljadi challenged the admiral. "Our combatants, yes. But not merchant ships."

"Understood." The admiral considered Moeljadi his ideal underling. A bureaucrat, he'd dedicate his career's waning years to serving Hakim in exchange for a solitary admiral's star. And he'd buffer Hakim against the ambitious commanders and captains. "But the Indonesians are allowing food and medical supplies through."

"I'm concerned about fuel, sir. Even with our conservation measures, we'll run out within months, and the civilians will feel the pressure. We'll need their ongoing favor."

Hakim trumped the challenge. "Then we'll run the quarantine to prove we can. We'll use my new flagship to make the point, and I'll be on the *Martadinata's* bridge when it happens."

The *Martadinata's* commander revealed his courage. "It would be an honor, sir. When shall I get underway?"

"In one hour."

The bureaucratic captain's eyes held pleading fear. "You'll want me here, running operations in your absence, sir?"

"Of course. I need you coordinating the fleet while I'm busy." Hakim watched fear fall from the pudgy coward's face.

"You can count on me, sir."

Hakim eyed the marine. "Colonel Pardi, I want marines on the *Martadinata* to repel borders if the Indonesians attempt to board us."

"You'll have two squads aboard in an hour, sir."

Hakim silenced a nagging conscience suggesting the marines were less a protection against the loyalists and more a protection against the frigate's commander undoing his defection and returning the *Martadinata* to Indonesia with its rebel admiral aboard it.

Four hours later, Hakim watched Commander Basarah bring his frigate past Waigo Island's southern shore to show the new Papuan Morning Star flag to its populace. "Verify you're recording on all video and data feeds. We'll want footage to air publicly of this."

"I'm recording on all video and data feeds, sir. I also have half a dozen men topside recording as well."

"Excellent."

"Shall I increase speed, admiral?"

"No. Stay at eight knots to conserve fuel and to give our enemy plenty of time to react."

The comment raised Basarah's eyebrow.

"To give them no excuses for backing down and to show them we have no fear."

"Understood, sir. I'll maintain eight knots."

Forty minutes later, the *Martadinata* reached eight nautical miles from the nearest Papuan coast, marking four miles to the edge of the country's national waters.

The Indonesian navy had set the quarantine ten miles from rebel shores, declaring rights within the standard twelve-mile limit to undermine Papua's right to exist.

And where proximities of land masses made Papuan waters abut Indonesian waters, the quarantine tightened to single-digit miles at boundaries that appeared misshaped on nautical charts.

Difficult, at best, for commanding officers to navigate, geographically and politically.

For his demonstration, Hakim had ordered the *Martadinata*

on a course to reach Papua's twelve-mile limit where it touched an Indonesian twelve-mile limit.

He'd prove his freedom to operate to his nation's extent and also challenge those who challenged him by violating their waters as they violated his.

Standing by Basarah's side, he eyed a console's digital overview. "It looks like we'll have more company."

"Agreed, sir." The frigate's commander nodded towards the patrol boat which had paralleled them for three miles. "The *Lepu* isn't going away, and the frigate *Sudarso* will intercept us a mile and a half inside Indonesian waters."

"Perfect. We'll test their mettle." Hakim referred to the older approaching frigate's weaponry. "Has the *Sudarso* reduced its hostile posture?"

"No, sir. All its radar and fire control systems remain energized. We're being electrically painted by every weapon system it has."

"But we remain dark." It was a question and an order to continue acting in a disadvantaged posture.

"Yes, sir. We can't fight back without first bringing up weapon guidance systems, except for our Exocets, which are targeting the *Sudarso* and ready to launch."

Taking comfort in knowing a ripple launch of the *Martadinata's* eight anti-ship missiles would saturate the *Sudarso's* air defenses, Hakim counted upon deterrence. "They won't shoot."

"I doubt it, sir. There's not much they can do without starting a hot war they don't want."

The admiral looked out the starboard windows at the vessel which had posed the blockade's first challenge. Paralleling the Papuan combatant, a *Pari*-class patrol boat stayed five hundred yards off the *Martadinata's* starboard flank. "At least the *Lepu's* crew has stopped harassing us."

"Ah, no, sir. I just stopped piping the bridge-to-bridge radio over the loudspeakers. There's a team listening to them in CIC."

Hakim sniffed. "That's a pointless conversation, each crew

warning the other about being in their waters. Good idea to restrict it to a few participants."

From the *Martadinata's* Combat Information Center, loudspeakers carried the executive officer's voice into the compartment. "Bridge, CIC. The *Sudarso* has closed to ten nautical miles, and we're now within its cannon range. It's still closing at twenty-eight knots."

Basarah replied. "CIC, bridge. Aye."

Hakim marched to the nearest window on the port side, grabbed binoculars, and then pressed the optics to his eyes. What had been a gray spec on the blue horizon showed the harsh lines and crowded superstructure of an old frigate. "The main cannon is elevated and pointing at us."

Remaining steeled, the *Martadinata's* commander joined his boss, eyed the threat, and agreed. "Trying to scare us."

"Station armed marines along your superstructure."

The order caught Basarah off guard. "Marines, sir?"

"The *Sudarso* will approach close enough to see them, and I want them seen." The admiral doubled down. "And I want your crew interspersed beside them, also armed with rifles. We'll show a unified resolve across our service branches."

"I'll station my crew and marines topside with rifles, sir."

Hakim qualified his order. "Have them make no gestures, no matter how the Indonesians may provoke them. To appear frightened or angry is wrong. We need to appear confident, like we know that a free Papuan navy is our right."

"With pleasure, sir."

Half an hour later, an officer announced the *Martadinata's* exit from Papuan waters. "Passing the twelve-nautical-mile boundary! We crossed immediately into Indonesian waters, sir."

"Very well!" Basarah eyed his boss. "We've shown they don't have enough large combatants to stop our large combatants, sir. We've just strolled unchallenged from our waters into theirs."

"We've proven more than that." Hakim pointed to the small *Lepu* which still paralleled their starboard flank. "That ship couldn't stop us, and it won't stop an oil tanker either, especially if I station marines aboard with shoulder-launched rockets."

"Good point, sir." Basarah's tone was baiting. "We've technically run the blockade. I assume you wish to let this encounter play out with the *Sudarso*?"

Unsure if courage or ambition underpinned the commander's steadiness, Hakim answered bravado with bravado. "Exposing weakness in the quarantine is one thing. Penetrating their waters is another. But if we're to be taken seriously, it must be done."

Ten minutes later, the *Sudarso*, one hundred yards away, slowed to match the *Martadinata's* pace and course. The Indonesian frigate's cannon pointed at the Papuan combatant's main turret.

Unheeded threats forced the Indonesians to escalate, and the *Sudarso's* bow began its intended slip towards that of the *Martadinata*.

"Shall I allow the collision, admiral?"

Through binoculars, Hakim discerned the eye colors of sailors aboard his former nation's ship. From the port bridge wing, he could almost shake hands with his adversaries. "Slow speed... gentle angle. Yes."

"Aye, sir." Basarah yanked a mouthpiece from its cradle, lifted it, and sent his voice throughout his vessel. "Collision imminent. Brace for collision."

Though soft per maritime impacts, the thump and scraping sent shivers up Hakim's spine.

Standing beside the admiral, the *Martadinata's* commander shouted over his shoulder into the compartment. "Left ten-degrees, rudder! Hold ordered course!"

While the helmsman obeyed, the clashing bows separated, creating white swirls between the combatants of similar size.

Wisely, the *Martadinata's* commander eased off. "Rudder amidships! No course given."

After the helmsman acknowledged, Hakim nodded. "Good."

"How many more times shall I allow this, sir?"

"Two. Holding course during three collisions in their waters proves sufficient mettle."

"Aye, sir. I'll take us back to the ordered course."

Twice more, the aging relic nudged the Papuan flagship, and twice more, the frigates bumped, scraped, and separated.

Seeing indignance in the faces of Indonesian sailors, Hakim understood a psychological advantage.

Warriors of his former fleet felt betrayed. The indignance caking their visages burdened their hearts as a constant distraction.

The features also told stories of momentum.

With one of Indonesia's major fleets in Papua, the new country had confiscated a third of a major navy, had turned against its former master, and enjoyed the exuberance of radical rebirth.

Funded by regional allies who profited by destabilizing Indonesia, the reborn nation had inherited a civilian and military infrastructure with promises of ongoing fiscal support.

Excitement in the new nation's strong beginning gave Hakim's sailors upbeat carriages and bristling enthusiasm in contrast to the dour images of the betrayed Indonesians.

While the *Sudarso* steadied for a fourth run at the *Martadinata*, loudspeakers on the bridge carried the report of the Combat Information Center to the wing. "Bridge, CIC. Our airborne surveillance craft detected two attack aircraft taking off from Wattimena Air Base, Morotai."

The *Martadinata's* commander poked his head through the doorway and shouted. "CIC, bridge. Aye!" He faced his admiral. "That's an escalation, sir."

Hakim recognized his helplessness to fend off aircraft without energizing the *Martadinata's* combat systems and pressuring his adversary to incite hostilities. "We've made our point. Inform the Indonesians that we'll reverse course and leave their waters immediately. Then do so, and take us home at eight knots."

# CHAPTER 2

As the sun's morning light touched Tel Aviv, Terry Cahill hurled his fist at his wife's throat.

Rewarding his effort, Lieutenant Colonel Ariela Dahan sidestepped, grasped his hand and wrist, and redirected his punch. Continuing her motion, she wrenched his arm against itself until pain and momentum dropped him rolling to the mat.

Cahill grunted his protest. "Ow!"

Twisting his joints, she straddled and mounted him. "Did I hurt the big baby?"

He looked at her belly. "No, but take it easy on our baby."

She released him and stood. "It's his early Krav Maga training."

Living on a secure base with his Aman military intelligence wife, Cahill enjoyed learning a new language, a new culture, and a new martial art. Standing, he inquired. "It's a 'he'?"

"I think so. Just a feeling."

"Because he kicks hard? Women can kick hard, too, you know. It actually hurts when you forget that."

She squared her shoulders before him. "So, I let one little knee strike connect too hard. You were only on the ground for a minute. Technically, it's our baby's fault, and it happened weeks ago."

Cahill recalled stepping too close to his wife who'd been demonstrating the attack. Fate had laughed at the spouses when the unborn child kicked her mother's womb in synchronicity with her rising knee. The impact on his solar plexus had dropped him. "Me testicles came out me mouth."

She smirked. "I've seen worse. Come on. Your turn."

He checked the clock on the gymnasium's wall. Time had ended their morning workout, and the day's schedule required his strict punctuality. "Nah. I need to get going. Pierre's got a tight itinerary for me today."

Fifteen minutes later, a showered Cahill met his wife outside the ladies' locker room.

Its blouse untucked, her maternity uniform struck him as a paradox pairing the militaristic snuffing of life against the motherly privilege of growing it.

She lifted her purse. "Why are you staring at me?"

"I didn't know I was."

"Are you getting sentimental?"

Their pending separation saddened him. "Yeah. I guess so."

"Oh, you'll hardly miss me."

He knew she was wrong. Despite skipping the Nigerian mission, he felt compelled to dote over her while enduring an unfamiliar and unwanted aversion to his job. He lied. "You're probably right."

"You'll be back before you know it.

But he would miss events. Miss changes to her body. Miss his new family. "You'll be bigger."

"That's what every pregnant woman wants to hear. Thanks for reminding me."

"That's not what I meant."

"You're trying to say goodbye, and it's adorable. But you're worrying over nothing." She found her keys in her purse. "Let's go."

While his wife navigated the short drive across the urban military base, Cahill analyzed his bizarre life.

A pragmatist, he knew that in the world of spycraft and defense, love conquered nothing.

Aman had allowed him to marry one of its officers, invited him to live in Israel, and even provided him secure military travel to his workplace in exchange for limited information about his fleet.

The open agreement reduced marital tension, but it also

reduced how much Renard mentioned over the phone.

Her eyes red from the prior night's telephone intrusion, Ariela referred to the midnight call. "Did Pierre say if this would be a public mission?"

The question incited Cahill's despair. Lacking a clue about his mission's location, purpose, or duration, he only knew to report to Toulon, France for duty. But ignorance of Renard's plan was the historical routine, and he trusted his boss' judgment.

Bothering him, unlike any mission from his first as an eager junior officer on an Australian submarine, indifference weighed upon him.

Indifference.

A commander in the world's flashiest navy wasn't allowed to stop caring about his job.

Voices inside his head screamed about needing to appreciate his dream job. They also said he wasn't worthy. He'd been lucky, stumbling into the right place at the right time, and he was unqualified.

He wrestled with recent memories to expose the genesis of his indifference, and a whirlwind of forces presented themselves as reasons. Jealousy of Dmitry Volkov and Danielle Sutton, who dominated recent fleet achievements. Frustration with the near loss of Jake Slate, the fleet's beacon of invincibility. Doubt about starting a family and being capable of leading it.

Numb, he quipped. "We were on speakerphone, my forgetful angel. Or do you think he told me by telepathy?"

While slowing the vehicle for valet parking at the base hospital's main entrance, she snorted. "You have secret code phrases."

He snapped. "Hey, come on! If we were really that smart, do you think I'd be dumb enough to tell you?"

She smirked.

"Oh. You were joking."

"Got you! You're so easy to upset."

"Well if it's so easy, it doesn't prove anything. Why do it?"

She grinned. "It's fun! And you're so adorable when you

whine."

Baited again, he whined. "It's not whining." Self-realization struck, and he folded his arms. "Oh, put a sock in it, sheila."

Ten minutes later, Lieutenant Colonel Dahan's presence streamlined the final security check granting roof access to the awaiting helicopter.

The hospital's chief of security, an army major, escorted the spouses into the elevator. "To verify, Mister Cahill is flying by chopper to Palmachim Airbase for transfer to fixed wing transport to Toulon Navy Air Base."

Cahill grunted his agreement, waited while the car ascended without further talking, and then stepped into the helipad's foyer.

The major extended his badge to a reader and then pushed open the glass door behind which rotors spun. "Have a nice trip, Mister Cahill."

Standing beside the major, his wife toggled to her Aman officer persona and parroted the farewell with a loving grin. "Have a nice trip, Mister Cahill."

Feeling a strange loneliness, the *Goliath's* commander crouched and trotted to the aircraft that would carry him into uncertainty.

Five hours later, he deplaned onto the tarmac at Toulon Navy Air Base. At the bottom of the staircase, he stopped and extended his hand. "Pierre, you mongrel. What's this all about?"

Renard released the Australian's hand. "You don't sound too chuffed about our new mission. I thought after spending the Nigeria campaign on the sidelines, you'd be eager."

"Sorry, mate. Just grouchy. What's our mission?"

"I'll tell you in the helicopter."

"I thought we were driving to the docks."

"Slight change of plans. I'd like you to see Jake now."

Ninety minutes later, Cahill stepped into the climate-controlled antechamber giving access to Renard's helipad.

Surprising him, the Frenchman stopped before two people.

Cahill saw Danielle in a white dress. Beside her, Volkov wore a tuxedo. "What's going on?"

Renard explained the sensory overload. "Long story short, they're ready, and now's the best time."

Unsure how to react, Cahill hugged the bride and then the groom. "Congratulations. This is fantastic. First Jake wakes up, and now you two lovebirds are tying the knot." Despite his chipper words, he remained unfeeling.

Danielle clarified. "We kept it a secret until Jake recovered. And when we heard he was awake, we decided to do it immediately."

"That was quick."

"Yeah, real quick. We'll hold a recommitment ceremony later this year with our families and more friends, but Dmitry and I just knew we had to get married today."

"Well, I can't wait."

Renard clarified. "You won't have to wait long. You're the last guest to arrive. Follow me."

The chamber mimicked a hospital room with its adjustable bed, monitoring equipment, and a reclined man greeting him with a childlike smile. "Terry!"

Cahill folded himself over Jake and then released him. "I feared you were dead."

"I'm not sure I wasn't."

"How are you? Can you get out of bed?"

"I can barely feed myself, and I feel like garbage. But they're going to try putting me in a wheelchair tomorrow."

Cahill scanned the room. Wearing the same beige khaki and white collared shirt uniform he wore, Volkov's closest crewmen stood ready in witness. "That explains why they're getting married here."

"Yep. I got the best seat in the house."

Facing the other attendees, the Australian shared greetings with each ship's executive officer, Linda, Marie, Vasily, Sergei, and a gray-bearded man whose name he didn't know.

In a whirlwind, the guests sat in folding chairs facing the wall opposite Jake, where the betrothed stood on either side of a man with a funny puffy hat. A table looked to Cahill like someone had hurriedly decorated it into a makeshift altar.

With a French accent, the priest spoke. "I'm Father Thomas Leblanc from the Annunciation Orthodox Church. Please forgive my weak English. Also please excuse I do not know anyone. I must render some sacraments with little warning, but usually for the dying. What joy instead to be requested to witness loving people attending the wedding of their dear friends!"

The introduction corrected Cahill's belief that Renard and Volkov shared a religion. Having to find clergy unfamiliar to the Frenchman for the Russian's ceremony revealed the distinction. Unmotivated to consider the differences between their cults, he judged both belief systems in the realm of wishful fantasy.

Twenty minutes later, the short ceremony ended, the spouses kissed, and the audience applauded. Then came hugs and congratulatory remarks, followed by Volkov lifting his bride into his arms and whisking her from the room.

In the estate's sprawling kitchen, Marie and Linda finished cutting, chopping, and arranging a simple but elegant spread of vegetables, cheese, and meats.

With floor space for socializing, the eating area provided ample opportunity for Cahill to reconnect with comrades he'd missed. After each person shared with him their joy in the recent nuptials, a handshake and congratulations for his growing family followed.

The congratulations left him wishing he felt more alive.

After thirty minutes of chatting, Renard beckoned the warriors to the pending mission's briefing. "Attention! If I sign your paycheck, I need you in my study in ten minutes, please."

Cahill chided his friend. "Can we walk together so I don't get lost, or are we taking a taxi?"

"My home isn't quite that big, though I appreciate the sentiment." The Frenchman swept his arm towards a hallway. It's the fourth door on the left. Oh wait. Since only the adults are allowed to have the code, you'll have to walk with me."

"Bloody…" He stopped short of harsher vulgarities. "Is this Pick on Australians Day?

Fifteen minutes later, Cahill reclined into the shining leather of an easy chair facing the monstrous screen hanging in the posh man-cave-ish study.

In their easy chairs, his fleet's comrades also looked forward while Renard managed and narrated his presentation from his desk behind them. "Some of you don't know yet, but the mission is taking place in Indonesia, and we have the serendipitous surprise of a very generous client."

Warming to an assignment near his homeland, the Australian's cold indifference began to thaw. "That's me backyard! I did joint operations with those mongrels. Good sailors. Good navy." Then he tallied the month-long round trip and felt less engaged. "A damned good navy. Why do they need us?"

"There's an insurrection in Papua. They've lost a third of their navy and large portions of their other services. They want to retake their property–and their people–in salvageable conditions. Ergo, they requested our services to be rendered with railguns and slow-kills."

Cahill's interest grew. "Seriously? When did it happen?"

"It still is. Battle lines and equipment orders of battle are being written in pencil while stragglers decide which side to join."

The Australian's interest awoke. "Wow."

"Here we go." Renard invoked movement on the screen, zooming in on New Guinea's northwesternmost land mass. "We have distinct success criteria. We're supporting a troop landing. We don't know where yet, but the most likely target is Sorong, to retake Indonesia's Third Fleet headquarters, thereby cutting off the Papuan navy's head–its command and control center–and its major marine base, which is nearby."

Cahill sensed his day improving, but he noticed conspicuous absences. "Wait, Pierre. You can't start without our newlyweds. Shouldn't you wait for them to finish changing?"

Renard replied. "They're not coming. I briefed them last night."

"Then what are they doing?"

Renard's grin grew into chuckles, revealing the Australian's faux pas. "Oh, Terry. Don't you know? Or did you impregnate your wife by accident?"

The team laughed at him.

Blushing, Cahill retorted. "You mongrels can all kiss me bare hairy arse."

Henri, the man other than Renard to whom he felt closest, nudged his shoulder. "We kid because we love."

Still hurting from the day's chidings, Cahill pouted.

But then he enjoyed an epiphany.

Perhaps they did love him, and perhaps he'd been looking in the wrong places for his job satisfaction.

# CHAPTER 3

Her head spinning from travel, fatigue, and excitement, Danielle Volkova teased her Australian counterpart. "No wonder you'll be a day behind us."

Gazing into the dry dock basin which had swallowed the *Goliath*, its innards exposed where yard workers had cut and stripped hull plates from adjacent compartments, Cahill replied. "So much for replacing MESMA plant five."

She referred to his updated power sources. "But your new plants one and three are ready?"

"Plant one is. Plant three will be made ready underway. I'll be carrying maintenance techs to finish its post-installation testing."

Thoughts of military hardware performance penetrated the misty white veils of her romantically overwhelmed mind. "These upgrades will increase their output fifteen percent."

"Not today, they won't. Not until we get back from this mission, whenever the heck that is."

She ignored his dissatisfied tone. "Still, it'll be nice to get that extra knot of submerged speed."

"Right. But while I'm down a plant, I'm maxed out at eleven."

"At least you'll be safe against ten-knot torpedoes."

"Shut up." Cahill eyed her. "You're gloating, aren't you?"

"Maybe a little bit. My ship's buttoned up and seaworthy. Yours is in the middle of open-heart surgery."

"Bollocks!"

Behind her, Renard's shouting echoed off the dry dock's offices, off the covered worksite's far wall, and off the *Goliath* below her. "Commander Volkova!"

Disregarding the Frenchman, she retorted. "Don't be mad. I'll have the *Xerxes* in here soon enough for the same replacements."

Cahill looked over her shoulder. "Are you intentionally ignoring our boss?"

Renard yelled again. "Commander Danielle Volkova!"

"Oh, shit. That's me."

"It takes getting used to, I'm sure." Cahill became sarcastic. "But don't worry. I'm sure that won't confuse anyone else."

"Have a nice trip. See you in Socotra."

"See you in Socotra, Commander Volkova."

She marched to her boss and then followed him into Toulon's afternoon sun. "Sorry."

Ahead of her, Renard reached the utility van, stepped into the passenger seat and addressed the driver. "To the *Wraith*, please."

She stepped into the back seat where her husband chatted on his phone with Sergei. Hearing his full-speed Russian reminded her how much she had to learn.

With limited helicopter seats, Renard had flown the executive officers to the waterfront ahead of the commanders, allowing them to supervise ongoing deployment preparations.

Having earlier dropped off Cahill in the dry dock, the Frenchman now escorted his married commanders to their floating ships. "Did you enjoy your view of the *Goliath*?"

"Not really. It looks like a wounded animal, but now I know what to expect when it's my turn."

A five-minute drive brought the van to a metal brow giving access from the pier to the *Wraith*.

Hanging up with his executive officer, Volkov eyed his wife. "I kiss your hand and say goodbye?"

"Maybe. Pierre, is hand-kissing an acceptable public display for your married commanding officers?"

"No." Renard twisted towards the back seat. "But you're not in public yet. So, go ahead."

Volkov planted his lips on Danielle's hand, slipped out the door, and then spoke while sliding it shut. "I love you, Dani. I can't wait to see you again."

"I love you, too, Dmitry!"

As the driver took the van to the next pier with the *Xerxes*, Renard again twisted in his seat. "Are you okay?"

"With the separation? Yeah. It's my job."

"I'm sure you'll miss him, but you're strong enough to manage."

"Shall I prove to you again that I am charmed?"

He grinned. "Please."

Two hours later, she stood beside Taylor on the *Xerxes'* bridge. Through the window, she watched her husband's clumsy submarine float helplessly under the mercy of a mated tugboat.

Taylor smirked. "After working on this ship, I don't miss being on one of those."

"Don't think I don't love this, spinning out of this berthing on four outboards and dancing around without tugs."

Taylor eyed her. "Wow. Marriage has got you buzzing."

"I'm sure it'll wear off."

"I'm not." He focused his lovesick boss on her job. "Shall we get your husband?"

His comment centered her. She realized her entire crew, including herself, needed to refer to the *Wraith's* commander by name and never by his relation to her. "Yeah. Let's get Commander Volkov."

After submerging in the dredged harbor, she'd slid the *Xerxes* under the *Wraith* and then cradled it in her cargo bay.

By dinnertime, she carried the submarine in the Mediterranean Sea. After dinner, she let Taylor navigate towards Port Said, Egypt, while she enjoyed a video call in her stateroom.

Using translation software on her phone to gather her thoughts in Russian and using a speech-to-text application on her laptop for her husband's words, she watched his grin appear. "Hi, Dmitry!"

"Hi Dani."

She labored through her Russian. "We will be in Port Said in four days. Can you wait four days to see me?"

He spoke Russian into his phone, using it as she used hers for translation assistance. "No. But I will survive."

Eschewing further small talk, she jumped on a critical issue they'd discussed prior to their semi-elopement. "My ovulation cycle is optimum in four days."

"I assumed so. Very good. What shall we do?"

Having thought it through, she suggested a tryst. "We'll meet in my stateroom immediately after we dock. We'll need to be quick about it."

"I can do that!"

"Dmitry!"

"You will keep it a secret?"

She referred to her executive officer and a junior officer. "Mike and Kelly will have to know. He'll cover for me on the bridge, and she'll guard the door."

His face became ashen. "Guard the door? Not very private."

"Mike won't be able to intercept everyone who's looking for me."

"I don't like it."

"Do you want children or not?"

Lowering his gaze, he accepted the indiscretion. "*Da*."

After the tryst, which she prayed passed unnoticed, the stop in Port Said ended without surprises. Their ships refueled and their crews refreshed by a meal on solid concrete, the newlyweds deployed the *Wraith* and *Xerxes* towards the Suez Canal.

With Indonesian influence, the *Wraith-Xerxes* tandem took an uneventful day to pass the Suez Canal.

During her transit, Danielle called her younger sister. In her stateroom, she spoke into her laptop. "Hey sis."

The pixelated image replied. "Hey sis. Good to hear from you."

"Same here." Having focused her adulthood to advancing her career, Danielle felt distant to the once constant and beloved companion of her childhood. "How's it going?"

"Me? Same old same old." The sister referred to the husband

and children who'd enriched her life since her late twenties. "Jim's already putting in extra hours at work since he's up for a promotion. Colton's doing great on the piano, and Hazel is starting dance lessons."

"Nice."

"What about you? I'm still chuffed to bits about your marriage. I can't believe you eloped."

"Neither can I."

"Dmitry's moving in with you, right?"

"Yeah. He wasn't too upset about leaving Russia. His nephew was drafted for the Ukraine war, and his family hates it. They supported Dmitry coming to Britain."

"He seems like a good man."

"He is."

"I know, but I've only met him once when he visited. I wish I could have attended your wedding."

The sorrow of a marital ceremony without family weighed upon Danielle. "I know. I don't like it, but I'll try to make it up to everyone with a big celebration when there's time."

"Mom and Dad weren't too keen about it."

"I know, but I calmed them down when I said they could have grandkids now and a ceremony later, or they could let my biological clock tick away while I plan the perfect wedding."

"I bet that convinced Mom. She loves her grandkids."

"It did." Danielle wondered what might have happened had her parents rejected her last-minute nuptials. Grateful for her family's understanding and flexibility, she enjoyed a long conversation with her little sis.

Four more days brought the mercenary tandem to Socotra, where Danielle's world changed.

The day on the Yemeni island passed like a whirlwind, and as it ended, she navigated the *Wraith-Xerxes* tandem from its pier while recalling the activities.

Indonesian naval vessels had arrived the prior day to escort the mercenaries across the Indian Ocean.

With her husband and their executive officers, she'd met the Indonesian officers and had taken aboard an observing rider from her client's navy.

Then she'd been whisked away for photo opportunities with the Socotran governor, who'd reiterated her thanks for the fleet's prior Yemeni effort and who'd voiced appreciation for the refueling stop reminding her enemies of her ongoing relationship with the fleet-for-hire.

Other additions had included receiving crew members who'd delayed travel for personal reasons, and two translators per ship.

In the afternoon, the *Goliath* had appeared, hurried through its refueling, and then redeployed with the newly formed convoy.

With the sun behind her, Danielle stood on the *Xerxes'* bridge examining the convoy's formation. Unable to spare many large combatants, the Indonesians employed only three for the escort.

The light frigate, *Bung Tomo*, steamed off the mercenaries' starboard beams while the corvette, *Muda*, steamed off their port sides. Out front, the old corvette, *Nuku*, took the point position.

Lukewarm to her new companions, Danielle saw value in learning to work with the Indonesian task force. And she appreciated the constant presence of an anti-submarine helicopter searching ahead of the convoy.

Against the solitary Papuan submarine or those of the numerous nations Renard's navy had infuriated, the surface combatants relied on speed and a large ocean as their best defense against undersea threats. The helicopter added a safety margin.

As the three-day transit to Sri Lanka began, Taylor and their new Indonesian liaison rider joined Danielle on the bridge.

After touring the *Xerxes* with a junior officer guide, Commander Fadhlan Lestari expressed reverence. "Commander Volkova, I commend you on your ship. It's quite impressive."

She liked her new name. "Thank you. It's a special design

we built for ourselves. Nobody else needs to transport diesel submarines across the world. So, we're the only fleet using them."

"I wouldn't rule out the *Goliath* class for our navy. We're buying and building modern ships, and a vessel such as this could prove useful in our future."

"I imagine that's possible, especially while you're acquiring new submarines."

Lestari shared the grave sentiment which had oozed among his countrymen in the Socotran stop. "It's all speculation until we reverse this insurrection. We have to undo this."

She used a reverent tone. "Is there any good news?"

The Indonesian shrugged. "Militarily, it's pretty much unchanged. Most violence in the Papuan streets is between loyalists and rebels. Other than that, it's been saber rattling at the quarantine boundary while politicians negotiate a return to sanity."

"You think they will?"

"Maybe. Our best hope is to defeat the leadership and give concessions to the people in return for reunification. But if you want my opinion, I'm fine if every rebel burns."

Since she hadn't wanted his opinion. So, she ignored it and recalled a news report. "You lost a fighter aircraft, right?"

"It was a midair collision, but the pilot ejected safely. So far, there's been no exchange of heavy ordnance."

She folded her arms. "Let's hope we can keep it that way."

Four days later, she placed Sri Lanka to her stern and took the refueled *Wraith-Xerxes* tandem on its four-day leg to Jakarta.

Then, the bad weather arrived.

Really bad.

A tropical cyclone had formed off the Indian subcontinent's east coast in the Bay of Bengal, and its southern rainband created swells that tossed the convoy.

After eating half her dinner, she battled queasiness while walking to her stateroom. With the deck bobbing, rocking, and rolling, she sought a distraction by calling her husband.

But a glance at his face on video showed Volkov enduring nausea's misery. She bid him farewell to let him suffer in peace.

With her husband battling seasickness, she read a book to distract her from the harsh seas.

Taylor reported. "The Indonesians have secured flight ops. It's too nasty out there for landings."

"I'm not surprised, but I don't like it."

"I wouldn't worry too much, ma'am. Submarines can't hear us very well in bad storms."

Recalling how violently churning waters could hamper the propagation of sound, she relaxed.

Her stomach settled as it slowly digested her food, and she managed to drift to sleep.

From the ship wide speaker system, Taylor's voice woke her. "EMCON violation from the corvette, *Nuku*. Man battle stations."

In her sweatpants, Danielle placed her bare feet on the deck. Half-awake while the general alarm chimed, she jammed her toes into her slippers while wondering what had compelled the Indonesian corvette to broadcast a radio signal despite the restrictions of Emission Control.

Unwilling to waste time putting on her uniform, she marched to the control room with a coppery taste in her mouth and bad hair.

The midwatch supervisor reported over the continued chimes. "It's a global satellite phone frequency, ma'am. Iridium. We picked it up on ESM."

"Did the Indonesian ships report it, too?"

"Not verbally, ma'am. But it's on the short-range laser data link."

Sharing the violation over the tactical net allayed Danielle's fears of collusion between the Indonesian ships, but her life required constant and anxious vigil against clients betraying her for bounties, vengeance, or other nefarious motives.

She calmed herself for the seven seconds Taylor needed to repeat his ship wide report of the Emissions Control violation. The calming allowed her to think, and she bracketed the transgression's potential significance between two extremes.

One possibility was a distraught man calling home for innocuous personal reasons.

Another possibility was a traitor revealing information about the convoy to its enemies.

She had to account for the worst. "Make sure the *Goliath* knows about this, too."

"I will, ma'am."

"I'm heading up."

On the bridge, her executive officer updated her. "Ma'am, I just talked to the task force commander. Thankfully, he accepted my conversation without our translator, and his English is perfect."

"And?"

"And he's upset about this, but he has no more idea about what's going on than we do."

"Is he doing anything about it?"

Taylor steadied himself as a swell moved the *Xerxes*. "He's ordered the *Nuku's* captain to shake down the crew and find out who did it."

She nodded towards consoles showing the bridges of her fellow commanders' vessels. "Do they know?"

"Yes, ma'am. The *Wraith* is the senior ship, and we'll need orders from Dmitry if we want to maneuver."

Overhearing the conversation, the French watch officer in Toulon opined. "Until we know otherwise, we must assume the worst case. For all we know, it could be a signal to a squadron of bombers with coordinates for a saturation missile attack. You should submerge."

Seeking counsel, she faced her exec. "Mike?"

"It's the safe move."

She showed her undersea tactical knowledge. "Terry and I can take different headings and improve our listening, to see if there's a submarine around."

"How would we share data?"

"Communications buoys. We're already exposed with one satellite transmission. What's two more?"

"It's worth the risk, ma'am. I'll set it up with the *Goliath*."

"Concur. I'll brief Dmitry so he can assent to it, but don't wait for that. When you've defined it with the *Goliath*, come to our new course and speed, and make us heavy for submerging."

"Aye, ma'am."

She eyed Volkov's pixelated, ashen visage. "Dmitry?"

"*Da?*"

"You heard our discussion?"

"*Da.*"

"Do you agree with us submerging and taking a different heading than Terry?"

"I do. We go to one hundred meters. Terry goes to fifty."

While Taylor slowed and turned, the French watch officer added a final sentiment to all of Renard's commanders. "All ships, you should also guard your Indonesian riders. If this is a betrayal, they're possible agents working against us."

She picked up a sound-powered phone and whipped the dial.

A junior technician answered. "Control room."

"Control room, bridge. I need the supervisor."

Seconds later, her requested interlocutor spoke. "Supervisor."

"Is Commander Lestari in the control room?"

"Yes, ma'am. He got here a minute ago."

She formed her order carefully. "Assign two strong men as his permanent escorts while this gets sorted out. He's restricted from the control room and the engineering spaces until then."

# CHAPTER 4

Craving undersea tranquility, Dmitry Volkov lost his patience and spoke in English. "Can't you flood faster?"

His wife's digitized image replied. "You're too light. You'd rip off my hydraulic rams."

Volkov felt helpless while the angry sea rose through the grates of his ballast tanks, making his submarine heavy. But with his trim and drain tanks emptied to reduce mechanical stress on the *Xerxes*, the *Wraith* was a cork fighting the tandem's descent.

Seeking a positive thought, he admired the resourceful Pierre Renard for having convinced a linguist capable of English, Russian, and Malay to deploy on his warship.

Speaking in Russian, the unfamiliar interpreter tried to assist. "Shall I translate that?"

Eyeing the speech-to-text characters trickling across his screen, the *Wraith's* commander declined. "No. I understood her." He faced the console. "Tell me when my seawater intakes are holding below the waterline."

Danielle replied. "I will." She glanced offscreen. "Terry's submerged. We've lost his datalink."

Working two conversations in different languages, the translator repeated the Indonesian task force commander's request. "He asks you to stay surfaced and to stay in formation."

"Did he ask, or did you change his order into a request?"

"He asked."

"Good. An order would've infuriated me. Tell him we..." Volkov cringed as nausea interrupted him. "Tell him we appreciate his concern but must submerge per our fleet's protocol. We'll manage coordination through Toulon. Make sure he remains in communication with Toulon."

After the translator relayed the message, the Indonesian captain's curt response from a speaker revealed his reluctant acceptance.

The gray-bearded veteran at the ship's control station reported the *Wraith's* progress. "We've reached nominal seawater intake depth, but I recommend checking on the wave action."

"Very well." Volkov checked screens showing his vessel's sides from cameras mounted to the *Xerxes*. Lapping water intermittently exposed his hull's seawater valves. "Not yet."

"Aye, sir."

Fixated on the screens, the *Wraith's* commander watched the *Xerxes* drag down his cork-like submarine at the limits of strain of its rotating hydraulic rams. When the waves' troughs climbed over his valves, he sought concurrence. "Danielle. Can I use my intakes?"

"Yes! Flood your tanks!"

Volkov yelled to the gray-bearded mechanic. "Flood five thousand kilos to center trim tanks."

As the veteran obeyed, the *Wraith's* increasing weight pushed the mercenary tandem under the choppy seas.

Appreciating the depth's rocking gentleness, Volkov turned his attention to the Indonesians. "Anatoly, assign tubes one, two, and three to the *Bung Tomo*, *Muda*, and *Nuku*, respectively."

While the sonar guru coordinated the slow-kill weapon assignments, Sergei hung up a phone and reported. "Our Indonesian rider is under the escort of two guards and is restricted from tactical and engineering spaces."

"Very well." Volkov addressed his wife. "Is your towed array deployed?"

It just steadied. We don't hear any new contacts. Only Terry and the Indonesians."

Volkov eyed the screen showing sonar data coming over laser communications from the *Xerxes*. The line of hydrophones trailing the transport vessel let the mercenaries hear beyond their own ships' noises, but no undersea threats appeared. "That's good. I'll launch a communications buoy for Toulon stating that."

"Agreed."

After he sent the buoy upward, Volkov watched digitized characters trickle over the low-bandwidth feed. The news from Toulon confirmed receipt of the *Wraith's* 'all clear' report while revealing Cahill's empty sonar search.

With his fleet lacking evidence of a hostile submarine, Renard ordered his commanders shallow for a satellite link.

The *Wraith's* commander addressed his wife in English. "You see Pierre's note?"

"Yeah. He's taking this seriously."

From his sonar station, Anatoly yelled. "Torpedo in the water!"

Shocked, Volkov snapped. "Where?"

"Bearing zero-nine-one."

Sensing himself drifting through a haze of impulse and instinct, the *Wraith's* commander assessed the danger's scant evidence and decided to stay slow, quiet, and listening.

From his console, his wife disagreed. "Dmitry. We need to come to all-ahead flank, right?"

"No! We stay slow. We listen."

She looked uneasy but trusting. "Okay. But that bearing runs through the convoy. It's no accident."

Her comment spurred Volkov to share data with his endangered clients regardless of his suspicions and with Cahill, whose shallower operating waters placed the *Goliath* in loud surface turbulence. "Send a communication buoy to Toulon to warn Terry and the Indonesians."

"Will do!"

Several technicians seated at Subtics sonar consoles stirred and shared hushed comments. After they proved their skill at listening to the seas with one ear while digesting a neighbor's whisper with the other, Anatoly announced their findings. "We now hear two new torpedoes, for a total of three. All of them are on bearings near those of the convoy."

"Bearing rates?"

"Integrators still need data and time to calculate, but we hear them as small. Unlikely on intercept courses with us, although possibly intended to intercept us where we would've been if we'd continued with the convoy."

"Very well." Volkov hesitated while gathering his thoughts and then addressed his exec. "Sergei, give me evasion courses for the Indonesian combatants. You have one minute."

"One minute, aye, sir!"

Compounding the *Wraith* commander's stress, Toulon sent a message declaring a second EMCON violation from the *Nuku*, which the convoy's commander had shared.

After more animation among the technicians, the sonar guru gave an update. "We now have five total torpedoes."

Needing to spit orders quickly, Volkov tapped his translator's shoulder, nodded at the screen, and rattled off thoughts in Russian. "I need to go shallow to guide the Indonesian evasions. You'll need to send me updates on the torpedoes over the acoustic datalink."

She showed her tactical awareness. "I should also connect with Terry while I'm actively transmitting. He's close enough."

"Yes. Share data to improve your tracking of the torpedo. I'll send the solutions to the Indonesians."

"I'll get you the data. Should we release you when you're light enough?"

"Yes. Start making yourself heavy."

"I will."

Volkov raised his voice. "Attention in the control room. We'll undock from the *Xerxes* and drive to the surface while remaining rigged for submergence. When we lose the laser lock, we'll shift to the acoustic datalink and share our torpedo solutions with the Indonesians." He shifted his gaze to his gray-bearded veteran. "Pump five thousand kilos overboard."

"I'm pumping five thousand kilos overboard."

Volkov addressed his wife. "Release me when you can."

"You're still too heavy."

"Then give me speed while we wait. Eight knots."

"I'm coming to eight knots."

"I'll match your speed." The *Wraith's* commander shouted. "All-ahead two-thirds, make turns for eight knots."

From her console, Danielle reported. "You're light, Dmitry. The rams are holding you down. Prepare to undock."

"I'm ready."

"Undocking."

The gray-bearded mechanic shouted. "We're undocked!"

"Very well. Helmsman, drive us to the surface."

"Aye, sir! I'm driving us up!"

As the cyclone's fury tossed his rising ship, Volkov tapped icons and announced his intent. "Raising the periscope." After the quick ascent transformed his surfaced vessel into a bobbing metallic cork, he enjoyed high-speed communications.

Two people stared back at him, the Toulon watch officer and the fleet's handsome but hastily awoken and disheveled owner.

Renard spoke first. "Dmitry! What news?"

Volkov used his translator. "I surfaced to communicate. There are five torpedoes aimed at the convoy!"

Renard replied. "My watch officer told them about the first three, and all ships have reversed course and accelerated to flank speeds. I judged this suboptimal evasion acceptable while awaiting targeting solutions."

A swell tossed Volkov's back into his seat. "I have an acoustic link with Danielle, and she'll link to Terry. I'll send my link to you over satellite. I'll also broadcast to the Indonesians. They need to change courses to slide out of seeker acquisition cones."

"Agreed."

The translator took a call from the surface combatants and then relayed the message. "The task force commander welcomes your review of the new evasion courses as they're updated over the link."

Checking a chart, Volkov saw adjustments to the torpedoes' positions using parallax from the *Goliath's* hydrophones.

Encouraged he could improve one ship's fleeing, he recognized the *Muda's* need to straighten its run. "Bring the *Muda* fifteen degrees to the right. It's running too perpendicular to its pursuing weapon."

"*Muda* fifteen degrees to the right." The translator relayed the correction. "The *Muda* will comply."

After verifying the *Muda's* compliance, Volkov noticed the speed leader of one torpedo's icon intercepting the foremost corvette before the threatened vessel could slide from the seeker's acquisition cone. His lungs froze, and he bit back a sensation of doom. "Is the task force commander on an open microphone?"

"I believe so."

"Ask him to take my next report in private."

"Okay." Through a headset, the interpreter held a rapid exchange. "He's alone."

"We see one weapon closing on the *Nuku*. Unless these shots were taken from far away and the fuel runs out, it will detonate underneath the *Nuku* before it can escape."

His face pale, the translator relayed the message. "He asks if you're certain."

Volkov raised his voice. "Sergei, am I certain?"

"I was double checking when I overheard you. You're certain."

"I'm certain."

"I'll tell him." After the exchange, the interpreter's tone was tense. "He asks how much time they have?"

"Two minutes."

The exchange was quick. "He says he's giving the *Nuku's* commander permission to abandon ship."

"Tell him I concur. They'll have to use life rafts in the cyclone."

"I'll tell him."

Two agonizing minutes dripped away in a heavy silence interrupted only by whirring fans and whispered exchanges. In retrospect, Volkov thought the time had passed in a blink.

Coldly, Anatoly announced the pending destruction. "Terminal homing on the *Nuku*."

Volkov sighed. "Very well."

Seconds later, the distant explosion rumbled through the *Wraith's* hull, and the sonar guru affirmed the obvious. "The *Nuku's* gone."

Volkov cleared his throat. "Very well." To lift the somber mood, he asked a question to which he knew the answer. "Will the *Bung Tomo* and *Muda* escape?"

"If they maintain course and speed, yes."

"Keep watching the remaining torpedoes to make sure they do."

"Aye, sir. Two weapons have passed the *Bung Tomo* and *Muda* and are heading where we and the *Goliath* would've been had we stayed surfaced on our original course."

Volkov knew the mercenary combatants were safe, but he appreciated Anatoly's uplifting report. "Very well."

Interjecting his own silver lining, Renard quipped. "The *Nuku's* tragic loss wasn't in vain. It gives us valuable information."

Regaining his seated balance after a large wave rocked the *Wraith*, Volkov faced his console. "How so?"

"We know the *Nuku's* EMCON violation couldn't have been a betrayal of the Indonesians against us, but it may have been a suicidal betrayal of a crewmember against his own colleagues."

The *Wraith's* commander had subconsciously grasped the Frenchman's meaning, and hearing it elucidated brought him solace. "Good point, Pierre."

"We'll make sense of this. I'm sure I'll get insights from President Widodo's staff about such a traitor. If not, I can't see continuing on this mission."

The Russian tested his boss with a risky proposal. "The hostile torpedoes' launch platform is either the Papuan submarine, or it's an ally of theirs. I need to go after it."

"No. It's too far away, its crew knows more about your location than you know of theirs, and the four remaining warships around you have no way of distinguishing you from them."

Volkov was an instinctual man of action. "But–"

49

"No, Dmitry. The priority is rescuing the men on life rafts, and that will require a fully coordinated anti-submarine defense with helicopters after the weather clears. I'm sorry, but you can't chase that submarine."

"I don't like it, Pierre." The *Wraith's* commander slumped his shoulders. "But I understand."

# CHAPTER 5

Rear Admiral Hakim's laugh was haughty. "What a courageous and noble victory!"

The cowardly, pudgy naval captain beamed. "The *Nagapasa* has brought us glory, sir. It's the first Papuan naval combatant to sink an enemy warship."

Hakim recognized a need to placate his underling's ego to prevent unacceptable ambitions. "Captain Moeljadi, I commend you for sending a submarine on a dangerous long-range ambush. And this after I forced you to accept the *Nagapasa* as an outlier in your squadron of surface ships. Well done!"

The man nodded. "It was my pleasure, sir."

"You'll have to prepare a commendation for its crew."

"I will sir. I also wish to honor the quartermaster on the *Nuku* who sacrificed himself to send us the convoy's position."

Hakim wondered how a man could sacrifice his life as a pawn for a cause. "He's a hero."

"His family is being well compensated. He was unmarried, but his siblings and parents will appreciate the gesture."

"He deserves a posthumous award. Our greatest." But Hakim's new navy had no awards to give. Indonesian medals had been abandoned, leaving white uniforms empty above their breast pockets. "I want you to draft qualification criteria for medals for the *Nuku's* quartermaster and the *Nagapasa's* crew. Oh, and a special one for the captain."

"It will be my honor, sir."

"Where's the *Nagapasa* now?"

"Returning to base, sir. It slipped by the quarantine's weak undersea defenses once and will do so again."

"What about fuel?"

The captain smirked. "It's rendezvousing with a Chinese naval tanker for underway replenishment."

Hakim disliked his dependency on the Chinese Communist Party, but it provided the lion's share of money for the insurgency, spies in key locations, and maritime assistance beyond the quarantine. "When they get home, we'll need an awards ceremony."

"I'll prepare that, too, sir."

"Schedule it as a private affair, at least until I see how Jakarta responds. They may try to hide their defeat by claiming an accident of some sort."

"I'll keep it private but worthy of their honor, sir."

Although encouraged by the *Nagapasa's* sinking of the Indonesian corvette, Hakim hid his disappointment in the mercenaries' survival. They'd been the primary targets, and he understated his concern. "Unfortunately, all three mercenary ships escaped. The Indonesians were screening them in their formation's center. We'll have to deal with them when they get here, but we know the appropriate tactics."

The fat captain boasted. "Jamming their guidance, placing sandbags over key propulsion and weapon systems, liberally using our close-in weapon systems, and assuring that our damage control teams are well trained in shoring small holes."

"Correct. You've stated the tactics thoroughly."

"Yes, sir. The railguns and limpet torpedoes are unique naval threats, but like every threat, they have countermeasures."

"Of course. And I've had a training manual drafted for countering these hirelings. Have copies sent to all ships, and I'll personally inspect each major warship for readiness in five days."

"I'll take care of it, sir." For the second time in two weeks, the portly officer publicly challenged the admiral. "Sir, jamming becomes ineffective against railguns at close range. When the mercenaries arrive we'll need speed and maneuvering."

Hakim assessed the comment as vain for its challenge but true for its reference to the nation's dwindling petroleum supplies.

He made a mental note to watch the hefty officer for future signs of ambition. "Then perhaps now, before they arrive, is the perfect time to schedule the tanker quarantine run we've been anticipating."

Looking proud for having influenced his boss, Captain Moeljadi boasted. "I've updated the plan for recent Indonesian ship and aircraft patrol patterns."

Hakim shared knowledge from General Purnomo's inner circle that he'd kept secret. "I can call upon Chinese tankers carrying diesel fuel to run the quarantine with less than one week's notice."

The comment unsettled the coward. "The Chinese are willing to run the blockade?"

Hakim enjoyed his underling's unbalance. "Remember that Jakarta still won't declare it a blockade. That would be an act of war, and a war requires recognizing your enemy's sovereignty."

"Sorry, sir. The quarantine."

"Yes. The Chinese are willing to risk the tankers, but they won't be flagged to China. They'll be flagged to whichever puppet nation the carrier company uses. And the funding for the operation will come from holding companies untraceable to the party itself."

"I see, sir."

"In three days, present me a plan to run the quarantine."

"Of course, sir."

Expecting a courageous plan from a man incapable of leading it, Hakim allayed the craven's fear. "I'll be aboard the *Yani* for this. Therefore, I'll need you here coordinating the fleet."

"I'll take care of it, sir."

Six days later, Hakim stood on a commercial waterfront of his fledgling nation's capital, Jayapura. With the city at his country's northeastern extreme, the frigate, *Yani*, and its smaller escorts were anchored in the harbor as his fleet's most distant outpost.

He boarded a waiting skiff for an uneventful ferry ride to his major warship.

After touring the combatant for readiness and then giving a brief to key crew members and those of the two escorts that would join the tanker mission, he watched the sun rise from the *Yani's* bridge.

He tugged his ball cap to his nose when the tethered bow swung towards the sun. "Are the other ships ready to get underway?"

The vessel's commander, a notorious tyrant among his crew, referred to a Soviet-era refurbished anti-submarine corvette and then a modern missile boat with four Exocet anti-ship missiles. "Sir, the *Umar* is underway. The *Tombak* is weighing anchor."

Disliking the man's authoritarian tone, Hakim reminded himself to preclude the potential rival by stopping his career rise below the first star of admiral rank. "Very well. Station me as the tanker escort task force commander. Weigh anchor and get us underway."

Twenty minutes later, the *Yani's* commander reported. "The task force is in formation and underway at the ordered speed of twelve knots and on the ordered course of one-zero-eight."

"Very well." Hakim lowered his gaze to a table's digital chart. With his underling as his captive audience, he bragged of his plan. "We have four undersea drones operating on this side of the island. That mitigates the submarine threat."

Referring to Chinese weapons procurement support, the *Yani's* commander seemed to enjoy the shared bravado. "It's good to have generous benefactors, sir."

Hakim then eyed the icons of the incoming diesel carriers. The six tankers had passed the Strait of Malacca, had veered around New Guinea's eastern edge to steam off its northern coast, and were driving towards the shipping route's terminus of Wewak.

But instead of making their scheduled landfall, they continued past Papua New Guinea's port and began their two-hundred-mile renegade trek to the new nation's waters and its capital of Jayapura.

The admiral commented. "Our airborne surveillance shows

the tankers diverting from their planned terminus."

"I just spoke with our radio room, sir. Wewak port authority is already screaming obscenities over the net."

Hakim smirked. "And New Guinea's navy?"

The *Yani's* commander finished the joke. "Who, sir?"

"Exactly." Hakim enjoyed frivolous chuckles. "Slow, impotent patrol boats. I doubt they could even catch them if they tried."

"And no air force to speak of, sir. The only thing that can stop us is Jakarta's combatants."

Hakim shifted his gaze to icons representing vessels of the Indonesian quarantine. Among the twelve corvette-sized or larger combatants forming his maritime pen, the loyalist navy stationed two frigates and four corvettes one hundred nautical miles apart, stretching the de facto blockade's thin net.

Twelve missile boats patrolled halfway between each major combatant around the quarantine's full perimeter. With at least four anti-ship missiles and cannons of forty-millimeter bore, these smaller vessels joined the corvettes and frigates as missile shooters of credible firepower. Six of them operated in the island's northern waters in the open Pacific Ocean.

Plugging the fifty-mile gaps between the Pacific Ocean's twelve missile shooters, Indonesia placed enough of its two-hundred-ship patrol fleet to put human eyeballs on every mile of its perimeter.

With airborne and seaborne sensors monitoring the waters, nothing entered or exited the shores of Hakim's new nation in secrecy, except the submarine which had escaped to attack the mercenary sell swords and their escorts.

As Hakim stepped to the *Yani's* bridgewing, he inhaled the sea air and contemplated his navy's posture.

Among his ten major combatants, four corvettes lacked anti-air missiles, leaving him six sky fighters anchored, to conserve fuel, around his country's major landfalls. The anchored ships helped airborne assets monitor the heavens and extended the army's coastal anti-air defenses seaward at Sorong, at the army's main base at Arfai, and at the nation's four largest seaports.

One seaport included the nation's capital, the seat of the former Province of Papua, at Jayapura, which grew smaller as viewed over the *Yani's* stern from the bridgewing.

The frigate's commander joined him outside the air-conditioned compartment. "Sir, we've got a shadow."

"Which one?"

"The *Mangkurat*. It's making twenty-four knots to catch us."

Hakim recognized the Indonesian vessel as a mediocre anti-submarine corvette of the same class as his task force's *Umar* and the sunken *Nuku*. "I had expected a greater response from Jakarta."

The *Yani's* commander was smug. "They're going out of their way to avoid operating in Papua New Guinea's waters. They fear a hot war, and they fear getting another nation involved."

"Agreed." Since Indonesia's proper fleet had developed a habit of shadowing Papuan combatants on the rare occasions when they burned precious fuel, Hakim clarified the advantage. "A shadow was all but certain. But Jakarta's showing its hesitancy to escalate tensions at sea."

"There's still the submarine threat, sir. They want revenge for the *Nuku*."

The admiral eyed the anti-submarine helicopter pinging the water ahead and seaward of his ships. With his adversary's scarcity of submarines, the shallow water ahead, the coastline's protection, and his mission's theater in third-party waters, Hakim expected a single deployed helicopter to keep undersea threats at bay. "This is a weak response from Jakarta."

"Indeed, it is, sir."

Hakim showed the decisiveness he thought a nation's military leader must show. "We don't need the *Umar* or the *Tombak*. Dissolve the task force and send them back to Jayapura, but keep the *Umar's* helicopter to provide a two-aircraft rotation. We'll perform this mission with just your ship."

Appearing eager to retain full credit to himself, the arrogant commander grinned. "With pleasure, sir."

After the officer returned into the bridge compartment,

Hakim scanned the seas north of the shrinking capital city.

Behaving as seaborne contraband inspectors, the distant Indonesian combatants hosted teams who boarded incoming commercial shipping via small boats. Certain the bulk of the inspections were paperwork checks of cargo manifests, the admiral deduced he could sneak in weaponry if needed.

Closer, the aging adversarial corvette, *Mangkurat*, sent a white wake over its bow. But it didn't chase down the *Yani*. Instead, it stayed further seaward to keep itself outside the twelve-mile zone of the fledgling nation's island neighbor.

The frigate's commander appeared in the bridgewing's doorway. "Sir, we've exited our national waters and have entered the waters of Papua New Guinea."

Hakim acknowledged the violation of international law. "Very well. How long until we reach the tankers?"

"Five hours, fifty minutes, sir. And after we reverse course and escort them at seventeen knots, we'll have another four hours and ten minutes to bring them back to our waters."

"Ten hours until they're in our waters."

"Right, sir."

"Thank you, commander. That answers all my immediate questions." Hakim's tone implied his desire for solitude, save for the young sailor standing watch as a lookout, upwind.

The frigate's commander obeyed and pivoted towards the bridge's innards. "Of course, sir."

Believing his voice was beyond the lookout's earshot, the admiral lifted his phone and called Major General Djoko Purnomo.

The junta's leader replied. "Admiral Hakim."

"Good morning, general. How are you, sir?"

"Very well. More importantly, how are you?"

Hakim boasted. "I'm in the waters of Papua New Guinea, unchallenged by our neighboring nation's vapid navy and being mirrored by one of Jakarta's weakest corvettes whose captain is afraid to leave international waters."

The general remained reserved. "That's a good start."

Hakim wanted to garner his boss' favor by highlighting solutions he offered to his supply chain crisis. "I trust that six tankers worth of diesel fuel will improve the situation at public refueling stations, even after I keep some fuel for my fleet."

The general sounded more like the statesman he was becoming and less like a warrior. "It will certainly help, as will the publicity. My administration is gaining favor with the people, and your efforts are appreciated."

"I am honored to help, general. I can penetrate this quarantine when needed, and I expect to prove it today unchallenged."

"Excellent. Your efforts will strengthen support for my offensive into the treasonous provinces, which I'll have in my control within two weeks. With such a groundswell of civil support from people grateful for their liberation, it's time to take the offensive."

For a moment, Hakim wondered if Purnomo spoke as a nation's leader should, stating vapid declarations of confidence, or if he'd become something different, something lesser than the warrior who'd promised new beginnings.

# CHAPTER 6

In the *Xerxes'* control room, Danielle questioned her rider's visible angst against the Papuan junta. "The media says the Papuans are embracing their new government."

Beside her at the plotting table, the agitated Commander Fadhlan Lestari answered, scowling and flailing his hands in hard gestures. "The media's lying. Support for the new government is weakening under the austerity measures and the policing. Riots and protests are happening in all six provinces. We estimate the death toll's at least ten times what's being reported. It's terrible. Just terrible."

She recalled an adage stating that one death was a tragedy, a thousand were a statistic. "Shit."

"The only ones benefiting are those in power and those with ambition for it. We estimate that sixty-five to seventy percent of the populace are against the insurgency."

"It's really that bad?"

"And it's getting worse. The junta's military will only increase its abuses as the people resist."

"This puts pressure on us to act."

The Indonesian naval officer nodded. "It's going to compress the timeline of our landing operation, but we still have time for our exercises today. We still need a week to amass our troops."

On the table's adjacent side, Taylor tapped an icon to bring up a training schedule. "Shall we review the agenda?"

Danielle appreciated the segue. "Go ahead."

Taylor's scalp reflected the lighting as he eyed the chart. "We'll take sound cuts both ways, with the Indonesian ships tracking us and vice versa, as a *Wraith-Xerxes* tandem, and then we'll repeat the exercise with just the *Wraith*. This includes the submarine *Alugoro*, so we'll know what to expect when approaching the *Nagapasa*."

Hearing about the rebel submarine that had sunk the corvette *Nuku*, Danielle cleared her throat. Thinking of her new bridegroom facing the *Nagapasa* in combat worried her. "Good. Keep going."

"After sound cuts, the *Wraith* will shoot limpets at the Indonesians for analysis of the limpet pattern, which will be proxies for slow-kill bomblet patterns. This will guide the *Wraith's* warhead settings for each class of rebel combatant."

Commander Lestari opined. "This should optimize the crippling of the rebel ships with minimal damage. We'll analyze the expected flood rates of slow-kill bomblets based upon the number of limpets which attach to each hull."

Danielle eyed the table's system clock. "We need to dive if we're going to keep our schedule."

Lestari replied. "Our ships are ready. We're awaiting Commander Volkov's word."

She faced her husband's image in a window on the charting table. "Are we ready to dive, Commander Volkov?"

"Yes. I'll inform the task force commander."

As she pushed away from the table, she noticed a soreness in her chest she attributed to pushups from the prior day's workout. Blocking the discomfort from her mind, she led Taylor and their rider up the stairs to the bridge.

When she reached her command console, her husband's pixelated visage spoke. "Are you ready to submerge the *Wraith-Xerxes* tandem?"

"I'm ready to submerge the *Wraith-Xerxes* tandem."

"Hold our present speed of five knots and submerge the *Wraith-Xerxes* tandem."

She acknowledged, obeyed, and watched the Indian Ocean south of Java rise up the dome.

Settling her keels at fifty meters, she asked her rider to test the wire floating from the *Wraith* to the aging corvette above. "Commander Lestari, test communications with the *Pattimura*."

The rider obliged by casting his voice upwards to overhead microphones. His Malay was indecipherable, but the tone of the response from the corvette implied a reliable connection.

"The communications check is satisfactory. He orders you to hold course, speed, and depth while our ships maneuver around you during sound cuts."

Danielle folded her arms. "Easy enough. We'll hold course and speed." Then she raised her voice. "Control room, bridge. Are you ready to record sound cuts?"

Over the loudspeakers, the supervisor replied. "Bridge, control room. We're ready to record sound cuts."

During a slow three hours, Indonesian ships, including the submerged *Alugoro*, maneuvered around the *Wraith-Xerxes* tandem, giving Danielle and her husband sonic information about the classes of combatants they'd encounter against Papua.

As the ships varied speed from five to eleven knots and presented different angles of approach, Danielle drifted into the refuge of her thoughts.

Upon candid reflection, she noticed an uneasiness consuming her. Although she recognized herself as herself, she felt unfamiliar in her own skin.

Her whirlwind marriage had affected her in ways she was only beginning to understand.

Raised in the Cold War's final years, she'd never dreamed of marrying a Russian man.

She'd never dreamt of being 'Volkova'.

The rapid onslaught of intimacy had transformed her husband from a flirtatious colleague into something different. Something closer to her than any soul had been. Something closer than she'd previously conceived.

Something frightening.

The loudspeakers brought her back to the *Xerxes*. "Bridge, control room. Sound cuts are complete."

Although she'd half-listened to reports of the knowledge gained during the exercise, she sought a summary. "Control room, bridge. What stands out as highlights?"

"Bridge, control room. I'd say the *Alugoro*, ma'am. It's quieter than we'd expected."

She'd expected the loud *Wraith-Xerxes* tandem to suffer an acoustic disadvantage against the South Korean export submarine. "Very well, control room." She faced her husband's digitized profile. "Dmitry!"

His image eyed her. "*Da.*"

"The *Alugoro*?"

With his seated translator's shoulder visible on the screen, Volkov shook his head. "Quiet. Very quiet."

"You'll do better when you're free of the *Xerxes*."

"I know. But it still may be at acoustic parity. I may even be at a disadvantage at some speeds."

"You'll find out after our next sound cuts. I'll be maneuvering us as a tandem. Are you ready?"

After verifying his understanding with his translator, Volkov replied. "Yes. Go ahead."

Danielle addressed her rider. "Have your ships stay on course and speed, and we'll vary our speed and angles."

"Of course, commander."

During her stint at meandering amidst the listening ships, she spent less time within her head and more time watching her ship and the *Wraith* accelerate and turn.

But a voice whispered within her that her world had irreversibly changed. And as she tried to pinpoint concrete reasons for the voice, her thoughts kept returning to her vessel's next maneuver.

After the task force finished with the mercenary tandem, Danielle released her husband's ship to redo sound cuts by itself with the Indonesian combatants.

With hours to waste in waiting, she surfaced and left Taylor on the bridge.

In her stateroom, she sought her boss' counsel and camaraderie through her laptop. "Hey, Pierre."

"Good evening, Commander Volkova."

Hearing her new name unsettled her, and she deflected her

darkening thoughts to lightheartedness with a forced smile. "Sometimes I think you like saying that more than I do."

Renard shrugged. "I do take a modicum of pride in having played matchmaker with two of my charmed commanders."

She appreciated his calm confidence and the joy he showed in simple chitchat. While climbing the ranks in the Royal Navy, she'd thought she'd enjoyed a similar sentiment, but she now wondered if she'd been fooling herself.

After committing her life to another person–but lacking comfort or joy in their union, she doubted a lifetime of self-perspectives. "You're always so chipper."

"I've always considered myself even keel. Perhaps you see things my other colleagues don't."

"Perhaps." She let her observation die. "What are you seeing from far away? Commander Lestari said Papua is becoming a volcano and that we need to act sooner rather than later."

"All generalities, but I confirm his report. Underneath the storylines of international news, the rebel provinces are becoming more violent and not less so."

Six million people suffering under austerity measures, tyranny, and the threat of war saddened her. "What's it mean for us?"

"Pragmatically, it means we're facing a deadline."

"How so?"

"The civil populace in Papua is fighting between independence and loyalty, and those siding with Jakarta are gaining ground, especially in the loyal provinces. If we don't defeat this insurrection soon, the junta will escalate to atrocities en masse to assert itself."

"We need to conduct the landing soon and with little time to soften the defenses."

"Terry will soon contribute to that."

Recalling Cahill's escorted sprint around Papua's eastern edge to stop the Chinese tankers on the north side, she rejected her boss' attempt to placate her. "He'll cripple one combatant at best, Pierre. You know what I meant."

After a deep, contrite sigh, the Frenchman admitted his doubts. "Fair enough. Indonesian leadership is debating where to land, how much softening of the defenses can be achieved, and what losses on both sides are acceptable. The choices aren't obvious."

Danielle considered the strain of deciding the fates of thousands. "I don't envy the decision makers."

"I fear I'm among them. The more chaos reigns, the more they seek my counsel."

"Then I don't envy you."

"Neither do I." He glanced offscreen to gather new thoughts. "How's Dmitry doing?"

She recalled her latest mundane update. "He plunked inert limpets from one weapon onto an old corvette. Divers are over the side marking their locations and prying them off."

"Just one weapon so far? I'm sorry, the data link doesn't track the status of friendly limpets."

"Just the one. They want to make sure they can be mapped and come off easily before they let him shoot the other ships."

"Understandable."

She grew curious. "In fact, let me check." She hailed the bridge.

Taylor's voice filled her stateroom. "Bridge."

"Mike, it's me. Any word on the first limpet weapon's outcome?"

"Nothing in the last twenty minutes, ma'am. But the initial report was that Dmitry's team thought they counted twenty-one limpets attached out of twenty-four, though you know it's hard to count from just listening."

"I know. How about from the Indonesian side?"

"They say the divers have good visibility and will likely find and map them all. We should get good data."

"Whatever that is. I guess we're trusting Indonesian engineers to figure out the right amount of damage to send a ship back to port in repairable condition."

"Be happy you're not an Indonesian engineer, ma'am."

The comment sent her emotions into a new direction.

Realizing this was her so-called honeymoon, she found herself jealous of someone sitting at a desk in a comfortable building analyzing equations and physics.

They would go home safely to their loved ones.

But she felt alone, distant from her colleagues and her husband. Unexpected doubt bothered her and taunted her with suspicions that she'd married a stranger.

Instead of a partner she'd come to know via a relationship, she wondered if she'd married a heroic caricature.

Was it her fault?

Was she too wounded to love and be loved?

She felt trapped.

A desire to run away overcame her.

She wanted freedom.

She wanted out of this mission. She wanted out of this fleet. She wanted out of this marriage.

"Thanks, Mike." She silenced the circuit.

From her laptop, Renard probed. "I overheard that. It's slow and requires patience, but we have time while the landing's planning solidifies and the pieces move about the chessboard."

Agreeing, she feared the boring hours ahead, the kind that fill warriors' thoughts with anything but comfort.

# CHAPTER 7

Terry Cahill sensed uneasiness rising within him.

Ariella's pregnancy, Jake's recovery, and the Volkov wedding overloaded his emotional awareness, but he also detected winds of change blowing through Renard's fleet.

Ill winds.

He shook off what discomfort he could, and he stuffed the rest inside himself to focus on stopping six Chinese tankers from refueling the Papuan separatist machine.

Standing under the *Goliath's* dome, he glared through the glass at a trawler. "Another crazed fishing craft. Are they tempting us to cut them in half?"

Beside him, Liam Walker raised his eyebrows. "Good question, sir." The executive officer gave a sideways glance to their Indonesian rider. "Commander Pasaribu?"

With a thin Malay accent, the tall officer replied. "I've never operated in these waters, but I've heard of such stubbornness from my colleagues who patrol here. They dare our ships to collide with them."

Shielding his eyes from the setting sun, Cahill recalled the hard faces he'd seen on commercial and fishing traffic north of the island's eastern half. "The merchant fleet of Papua New Guinea is hardly welcoming."

Pasaribu replied. "Our relations with PNG have been strained since the 2019 uprising. And now it's only getting worse."

"No kidding." Cahill watched the lead ship of the small group come right to avoid the obstinate trawler. "Liam, guide us around that arse ache and keep us in the *Basri's* wake."

Keeping the *Goliath* far from the fishing craft's extended gear, the executive officer obeyed. "I'm keeping us in the *Basri's* wake, sir. No course given."

Cahill watched the old corvette navigate an educated guess at avoiding nets of unknown length and depth. "Another detour. Another five minutes wasted."

Walker tried to sound chipper. "We'll get there, sir."

As his ship veered from its most efficient path, the *Goliath's* commander checked his estimated arrival time–more precisely, the estimated moment when his railgun rounds could reach the closest Chinese tanker–slip further into the future. "We'll have at best twenty-five minutes of margin before they reach port. And that's if we don't have any more detours."

Again, Walker tried to lift the mood. "The helo doesn't show any vessels in our way."

"Yeah, I know. But they find ways to reposition themselves in time to screw us." Cahill looked at his Indonesian rider. "You're sure I can't just punch holes in the tankers if they reach port?"

"If it were up to me, I'd allow it. But the orders came from Jokowi himself. We're not creating an oil spill in Papua. We could do it with our own cannons if we wanted to."

The *Goliath's* commander further lamented Indonesia's constraints on stopping the fuel-carrying vessels. "And strafing runs might not penetrate the propulsion casings."

"Maybe. Maybe not." The rider shrugged. "But our pilots would risk the *Yani* shooting them down if they tried."

"Right. I was just complaining for the sake of complaining." To distract himself from his dwindling margin for crippling his targets, Cahill aimed his voice at his boss' image. "Pierre?"

From a screen, the Frenchman replied. "I'm listening."

"Any luck on those tanker schematics?"

"Plenty! The ones I've already sent you are quite detailed."

"I mean verifying them. Any mongrel can post whatever he wants on the internet."

"I'm awaiting a call back from STX Shipbuilding, but I can't promise you they'll help me disable their own products. Keep your shots targeted on the engineering spaces, and with enough rounds, you'll succeed."

Thoughts of the wounded behemoth vessels coasting into the renegade piers of Jayapura despite his best efforts mocked the Australian. "The forty-five-degree arrival angles should help me avoid the fuel holds. But I've got twelve propulsion plants to disable on six monstrous ships, and I'm racing the clock."

"Do your best. That's all I can ask, but I believe the odds favor you making an impact on that fuel delivery."

Cahill wanted to silence Renard's optimism, but the Frenchman's visage remained plastered to the screen. And sensing himself being pessimistic for no apparent reason, he steeled himself. "You can count on me, Pierre."

An hour later, Cahill judged his success possible while studying a chart. "We're twenty minutes from shooting."

Walker echoed the hope. "And ten minutes later, we could be done with crippling six tankers."

From the console, Renard sounded tentative. "Uh… gentlemen. If you'll forgive me, I'm adding to your target priorities."

Cahill quipped. "You want the frigate crippled, too?"

"Correct. A spy has informed Jakarta of the Purnomo's updated invasion timing against the loyal provinces, which is in five days. So, our landing will be accelerated to six days, which sounds a day late but actually forces the rebel group to fight on two fronts, counting the entrenched militias."

"The provinces' loyal resistance in front of them and Jakarta's landing forces behind them."

"Right. And it may seem slow, but they're calling up reserves, merging troops from different commands, and moving assets across four time zones. As I watch them plan, I applaud the Indonesian planners for remaining patient and carving out their advantages, as opposed to succumbing to their urges to react immediately."

Cahill saw the subtle shift in priorities. "So, you'd like a real-world answer on what two railguns can do to a lone frigate?"

"Indeed."

Cahill recalled the tactic his fleet would employ by pairing the *Xerxes* and *Goliath* together to overwhelm single combatants with four-railgun salvos. "By meself?"

"I understand the challenge, but I hope you can prove to me once again that you are charmed. Test their defenses."

After moments of rumination, Cahill shared an idea. "You don't care if I bait the frigate into showing its broadsides by attacking the tankers first?"

Renard glanced away in thought and then answered. "Sure."

"Alright then. I'll do what I can."

Fifteen minutes later, a message flashed on Cahill's console informing him of a Chinese tanker's entrance into his railguns' reach. "We're in range."

Walker replied. "Do you want to shoot dark?"

After mentally translating the code phrase, the *Goliath's* commander answered. "Yes. Make a final adjustment for the wind down range, and we'll keep our radar dark until the last seconds–or until the *Yani* reacts."

"Aye, sir." Walker tapped keys. "I'm committing the latest wind data to our solution. All tankers and the escort frigate *Yani* will be in range within four minutes."

"Prepare twelve splintering rounds for simultaneous arrival on the tankers, assuming they maintain course and speed."

After acknowledging the order, Walker tapped keys. "What about the frigate, sir?"

"Prepare rounds thirteen through sixteen aimed at its close-in-weapon system."

Curious about the order, the exec raised his eyebrows.

The *Goliath's* commander answered the unasked question. "If these mongrels have studied our tactics, they'll have sandbags over their reduction gears. And if they have any guts, they'll try to shoot down our rounds. Let's face that head on."

"Right, sir." Walker tapped more keys. "Twenty splintering rounds are readied."

"Very well."

After placing all enemy ships within reach, Cahill cast his voice upward. "Port and starboard weapons bays, raise your railguns."

Icons showed the primed weapons as speakers carried the gunner's voices. "Port railgun is raised and ready... Starboard railgun is raised and ready."

Wanting computer-controlled barrel angles launching the rounds on differing ballistic arcs, Cahill studied the graphical prediction of their flights showing simultaneous impacts. "Looks good, Liam."

"Aye, sir. We're ready. Shall I, on automated control?"

"Launch twenty splintering rounds on automated control."

Walker obeyed, and dual hypersonic cracks thumped the bridge's strong windows.

With a helicopter's radar painting the convoy, Cahill watched the Chinese tankers hold their course and sprinting speed. "Either they don't detect our rounds yet, or they don't plan on dodging them."

"Agreed, sir. The frigate will probably attempt jamming."

More hypersonic rounds cracked.

While listening on a headset, Commander Pasaribu became animated and then reported. "The *Basri* sees a fishing vessel coming towards us on an intercept course."

"Us? The *Goliath*?"

"Yes, sir."

"That's bad. What are they doing about it?"

"The *Basri* is hailing the fisher and sprinting towards it, but no response yet."

"Where'd it come from?"

The nineteenth and twentieth rounds cracked, ending the volley.

"It was drifting deeper inland, well inside PNG waters, when the crew of the *Basri* noticed it accelerating."

Cahill glanced at icons predicting his ship's and the fishing vessel's motions. "Keep it out of the way! It's going to interfere with our chance for another volley."

The Indonesian nodded. "I've given the *Basri* permission to send warning shots across the bow."

"Very well."

"They'll take care of it, sir."

Walker announced a change in status. "Sir, the *Yani* has reversed course. It's doubling back toward its tankers."

"Alright. They've detected our shots. Let's commence active guidance." Cahill reached for an icon. "Energizing the phased array radar." Bringing the tiny electrical innards of each round to transmitting life, he saw their positions adjust on his screen. "Looking good. All rounds are on target."

Walker agreed. "The tankers are holding course and speed as if they don't care."

"Or they're too big to maneuver in time to matter. They're trusting the *Yani's* jamming."

"No sign of jamming yet, sir."

"It'll come."

While waiting for signs of an electronic war between his radar and that of the rebel frigate, Cahill heard a whump.

His Indonesian rider announced the noise. "The *Basri* just sent a shot from its main cannon across the fisherman's bow."

"Very well." The news annoyed the *Goliath's* commander. "Liam, keep an eye on that fishing vessel. I'll watch our rounds."

Walker lifted binoculars towards his face. "Aye, sir."

Curious, the Indonesian rider inquired from Cahill's shoulder. "Those numbers are times to impact for each round?"

"Right. We'll know the outcome in less than a minute. Hopefully we won't even need–"

Gasping, the Indonesian rider listened to his headset and then barked. "Torpedo in the water!"

Cahill gasped. "What?"

"From the fishing boat. The *Basri's* captain saw the splash! It's got a torpedo nest bolted on its deck!"

Cahill concluded the fisherman had launched at him, eyed his screen, and selected his evasion course. "Right ten-degrees rudder. Steadying on course zero-eight-four." He tapped keys, and the twin bows pointed towards the Pacific Ocean's vastness.

Walker confirmed the threat. "Bloody hell. It's got a triple-tube launcher." He lowered his binoculars. "It just launched a second torpedo."

The *Basri's* cannon spat five rounds into the hostile vessel, engulfing its forecastle and the triple-launcher's unused third weapon in flames.

His wavering voice betraying mortal fear, Commander Pasaribu announced his fleet's assistance. "The *Basri* is slowing to listen for the torpedoes. Its raw data is being shared over the link."

Cahill watched his screen in confirmation, and he dared not slow the *Goliath* to listen. "It's good information."

Also examining icons, Walker spoke dryly. "We're not going to evade, sir."

The *Goliath's* commander grunted his agreement.

Over the loudspeakers, the control room's supervisor's tone carried fear. "Bridge, Control Room. We have two Chinese Yu-7 lightweight torpedoes in the water. They're accurate shots, sir, coming at us!"

"Control Room, Bridge, aye."

Walker prodded. "Shall I prepare to abandon ship?"

The rider interrupted. "The *Bung Tomo's* commander has offered to sacrifice his ship in your stead."

Cahill addressed each man's concern in order. "Yes, Liam, prepare to abandon ship."

"Aye, sir."

Undaunted, the rider chirped. "The *Bung Tomo*, sir? I know its captain. He's serious about the sacrifice."

"Commander Pasaribu, why the hell does the *Bung Tomo's* captain..." In mid-sentence, Cahill's world became a frigid bath of bristling darkness.

Walker's voice tapered away. "Sir, are you..."

Cahill's world became horrors engulfing the *Goliath*.

While in a seeming trance, he groped through terror for understanding. Muted sounds and blurred visions enveloped his increasingly cold frame.

Time alternately froze and lurched forward in discrete slices.

The *Bung Tomo's* heroic sprint to intercept the incoming death in sacrifice fell short, and the torpedoes continued.

Walker seemed a mile away. "Sir, we need to abandon ship."

Unsure if he answered his executive officer, Cahill scanned his vessel's weather decks. Mustering on each hull, crewmen appeared as obscure humanoid shapes.

Fear spurred the abandonment regardless of an order.

The Indonesian rider murmured something unintelligible as he disappeared down the stairs.

Walker's hand was a frigid icepick on his boss' shoulder. "Forty seconds. Let's go!"

Wondering if his mouth spoke his thoughts, Cahill issued his sentiment from his heart. *A captain goes down with his ship.*

His throaty yell landing as a muffled drone, Walker yanked his boss towards the stairs and screamed. "Come on, Terry!"

They'd waited too long.

Reaching the starboard hull, the first weapon's warhead detonated and shook the deck below Cahill's feet.

With the rider passing through the watertight door, sounds echoed from the control room.

Ripping metal.

Roaring water.

Screaming men.

The second torpedo erupted underneath the far hull, transforming the *Goliath* into a tomb for all who remained trapped inside.

Dreadful thoughts pounded Cahill.

*I'm a failure.*

*I'm going to die.*

*My life has been meaningless.*

*Existence is hopeless.*

*Was my every struggle vanity?*

As he fell, he sensed his heart–not the organ, but his deepest inner self–passing through his stomach, his intestines, his loins, and finally into the desolate depths of infinity.

Instead of the spitting rage he'd expected upon dying, a sorrow of limitless weight crushed him. His flesh felt like putty pulled into eternity as his body flattened to the thinness of atoms.

Beside him, Walker struggled from his belly to his knees and exposed his face.

Seeing twisted and distorted agony contorting the bones and flesh above his companion's neck, Cahill stopped breathing while ogling the visage replacing his executive officer's human features.

Instead of irises and pupils, pools of black filled the eye sockets of the Walker-thing.

Morphing in Cahill's eyes into a disgusting demon, his companion became an image of torment. Its face became a twisted aberration of sagging and torn skins. Fangs protruded from the slimy mouth, and the long, crooked nose hinted of a devil. The Walker-beast had a body of scarred and blighted leather, and it showed horns, a pointed tail, and cloven hooves.

Trying to howl in anguish, Cahill found his throat unresponsive.

The Walker-demon raised its arm, from which extended a gnarled talon. Lowering its appendage, the beast swiped through its victim's shirt and carved bleeding lines across soft abdominal flesh.

Writhing, Cahill tried to kick and scream, but his bleeding body was unmoving. Then, a brilliant orb of white appeared through the dome, and soothing warmth billowed through him.

The Walker-animal receded.

Ecstasy enveloped Cahill.

Something or someone seemed to be rescuing him.

Then darkness.

Then reality.

His executive officer shook him. "Terry? Terry?"

Escaping from his waking nightmare, the *Goliath's* commander replied. "Yeah?"

We've got some tough decisions, sir." Walker seemed calm relative to the dangers. "You've got some tough decisions."

Despite his vision's palpable substantiality, it vanished, and Cahill again stood on the racing and seaworthy *Goliath.*

The *Goliath* still evaded, and its Indonesian rider remained on the bridge. "Commander Cahill. I need your answer."

"Yeah, mate?"

"I said that he's willing to sacrifice his ship for us."

The *Goliath's* commander was regaining his grip on actuality. "The *Bung Tomo's* captain?"

"Yes, Commander Cahill."

The *Goliath's* commander realized his visionary ordeal had lasted only moments, and he wondered if it had been anything beyond a hallucination.

But then he caught himself possessing an idea, an idea which had formed during his silent exchange with an unknown entity who'd intervened during his death-vision's final moments. "Tell him to slow and listen for the torpedoes."

Commander Pasaribu canted his head. "Sir?"

"He doesn't have to sacrifice himself." Stunned by his own calmness, Cahill uttered. "I've got a better idea."

A minute later, Cahill glanced at iconic data. The *Basri* and the *Bung Tomo* moved at speeds allowing their sonar systems to pinpoint the hostile weapons, which closed upon him with detonation times of two and two and a quarter minutes.

The coastal water constrained the incoming warheads to shallow depths, and the odd luxury of two friendly sonar systems tracking them allowed for precision and accuracy.

The metaphor of shooting bullets with bullets ran through Cahill's mind as he slowed the *Goliath* to twenty knots to lower the strain on his torpedoes' guidance wires.

Walker announced the readiness of his boss' plan. "Sir, tube one is ready."

"Shoot on generated bearing."

As his weapon swam and turned behind his vessel, Cahill

checked the fruits of his railgun strike. Five tankers continued at full speed under the rebel frigate's escort, after the *Yani* had intercepted the rest of the *Goliath's* projectiles with its close-in weapon system.

But one round had damaged an engine room of a solitary Chinese ship, prompting Walker, who also glanced at a screen, to opine. "The rest have gotten away, but we should halt that crippled tanker, sir."

"Stay focused on our torpedo defense. Let the gunners handle it. They have my permission to send up to four splintering rounds into the crippled tanker's viable engine room."

"Up to four rounds, sir. I'll coordinate with the gunners."

Pasaribu risked optimism. "We'll catch that tanker even if your next rounds miss."

Although the conversation was a distraction from the mortal dangers pursuing his warship, Cahill appreciated talking about something other than being blown up. "You don't have the speed. Not from here."

"But we've got helicopters and enough machine guns to influence the crew and to board them, if they're foolish enough to force it."

Walker addressed the *Goliath's* defense. "Our weapon is thirty seconds from intercepting the first torpedo, sir."

"Very well."

Thirty seconds later, Cahill ordered the detonation. With the gnat's-ass accuracy on the hostile torpedoes, he evaporated the first and disabled the second with his single heavyweight warhead.

As the fog of combat lifted, the *Goliath's* commander found himself numb, vapid, and wondering what hell had triggered his waking nightmare.

A waking nightmare and its salvific anti-torpedo epiphany.

# CHAPTER 8

His vessel cradled atop the cargo bed of his bride's vessel, Dmitry Volkov devoured the news. "That escape was brilliant."

In the split screen, Terry Cahill seemed laconic and uninterested in his own existence. "It was a shock."

The *Wraith's* commander read the Russian speech-to-text translation before replying. "I'm happy you survived."

"Sure, mate."

Volkov spoke Russian into his phone and then English towards his laptop. "You borrowed the anti-torpedo tactic Dani and I discovered in the Niger."

"Yeah."

Wondering about his colleague's terseness, the *Wraith's* commander prodded the Australian for signs of life. "That's not supposed to work in open water, my friend."

Cahill remained distant.

Volkov tried harder. "True, you had two Indonesian sonar systems tracking the torpedoes for you, but what made you think of trying such a radical defense?"

"Dumb luck."

Thoughts of shell-shocked wartime trauma danced in Volkov's head, and he wondered if his Australian friend suffered from the naval equivalent of the empty 'thousand-yard-stare".

His twisting features betraying his inability to bear the silence, the fleet's French boss intervened. "Terry did what any of you would have done. He remained calm, considered his options, and carried out a brilliant plan to perfection."

Doubting Renard's assessment, Volkov quipped. "He looks calm now. I bet he wasn't with two torpedoes chasing him."

"He merely proved again that he was charmed."

Cahill corrected his boss. "I was afraid."

"I'm sure you were as calm as anyone could've been." Renard segued to tactics. "And you gathered valuable information in the process. Our new situation is challenging, given that we can no longer distinguish neutral shipping from hostile."

The fourth interlocutor, his wife, added her concerns. "And we verified that two railguns aren't going to punch through any combatant's close-in weapon system and jamming. Terry and I will need to consolidate our attacks."

"I've already told the Indonesians, and they're planning the landing accordingly."

Scraps of information about the landing operation had reached the *Wraith's* commander, and he disliked what he knew. "You've shared only small pieces of the plan, but it ignores the submarine."

"The *Nagapasa* is one reason I've rejected each iteration of the plan I've seen."

Danielle raised an eyebrow. "You have a veto?"

"Of sorts. It may be all for show, but I will earnestly share my concerns with the planners, especially about the *Nagapasa*."

Volkov felt the world's weight shift to his shoulders. "I must defeat it before it can interfere."

"Indeed, my friend, you must. And well before the landing. You'll also need time to soften the rebel surface fleet with your slow-kill weapons as well."

"*Blyad*! There's no time."

"The clock is indeed ticking. Danielle and Terry can help from a distance as well."

"This can't be rushed."

Renard's eyes flitted from the screen to gather his thoughts and then looked to his camera. "The date is still malleable, as is the landing's location. Jakarta's keeping the truth quiet to avoid tipping off spies. There may be an opportunity to adjust the timing based upon your efficiency in dispatching the *Nagapasa*."

Disliking his boss' rampant optimism after Cahill's flirtation with death, the *Wraith's* commander shared his frustration. "We don't even know where it is."

"Ah, but we have a good idea, and the Indonesians are searching furiously for it. They know it must be stopped to avoid making the troop carriers easy targets for it."

Danielle interjected her idea. "Why don't we do the landing now, while the *Nagapasa* is still too far away to matter?"

The Frenchman shook his head. "The ground forces are dispersed among a multiplicity of islands, and concentrating them requires a good deal of time to coordinate sealift and airlift operations. Most forces are coming from Jakarta, and that's nearly two thousand miles away, or a six-day journey for most transport vessels."

She shrugged. "I figured as much, but I had to ask."

"Nevertheless, the clock continues to tick, and Jakarta needs us to clear the way."

With the mounting time pressure, Volkov felt an invisible weight upon his chest, but he refused to complain about his own challenges and instead referred to those of his client. "What about the arming of civilian vessels? How can the loyalists account for all of them?"

"They have enough small boats to keep civilian shipping away."

Sensing his fleet's mission slipping from possibility's grasp, Volkov vented his doubt. "Really?"

Renard was adamant. "Need I remind you our client is a nation of islands and has wisely armed itself with hundreds of small naval vessels?"

Surprising himself with his own defiance, the *Wraith's* commander flicked his fingers. "Bah!"

The Frenchman segued. "Very well." As a creaking door and murmurs distracted him, he looked away. "Ah, he's here." He faced the screen. "I brought a surprise to lift your spirits."

Henri Lanier's familiar voice added. "No, I brought him, and it took more patience than you'll ever have."

Renard smirked at his off-camera assistant. "I should terminate your employment for insubordination."

"You'd die without me."

Renard blushed. "True." He slid aside to make room for Henri's lumbering companion. "Here he is."

With a weak smile and pale skin, Jake Slate stooped before the computer. "Hey guys."

A chorus of greetings rose from the commanders.

In a fit of candor, Volkov appended his salutation with a critique. "You look like a moist turd."

His bride scolded him. "That's not nice, Dmitry! You shouldn't say that."

With droopy eyes, Jake replied. "It's okay, Danielle. He's right. I feel like a moist turd. In fact, I need to lay down again. I just wanted to say hello and wish you guys luck."

The *Wraith's* commander softened his assessment. "It's good to see you on your feet."

"Thanks, Dmitry. Don't get killed out there."

Henri exchanged words in French with Renard that escaped Volkov's understanding, and then he escorted Jake away.

Alone, Renard speculated. "We could bait the *Nagapasa* into exposing itself if Terry and Danielle combine their firepower to harass and hopefully disable rebel surface combatants."

While speaking Russian into his phone's translation program, the *Wraith's* commander sought softer synonyms for the words 'chaos' and 'guessing' but failed. "Forgive my cynicism, but it looks like we are guessing and reacting more than planning. It appears to me too much like chaos."

"You see much, my friend, and I shan't deceive you. We are reacting within a loose planning structure, but we've been through this before together many times."

Something numinous billowed throughout Volkov's flesh, and goosebumps rose on his forearms. But he was unwilling–even unable–to understand the sensation. So, he remained compliant with his boss' opinion. "I concede that point, Pierre."

"Alright, then. If you're all ready to pay attention, I'll share my idea to bring Terry and Danielle's firepower together to disable rebel combatants which I believe are vulnerable."

In concert with his fellow commanders, Volkov nodded his agreement and paid attention while ingesting his boss' ideas.

That evening, his submarine bobbed atop his wife's ship in the rising swells of the eastern Banda Sea.

During a laser-lock video call with Danielle, he sensed her mental fog–her lethargy in digesting the tactics they'd consumed earlier that day from Renard. "Dani?"

"What?"

"You're distant. You're not your usual self."

"Maybe Terry's close call is bothering me. Maybe so is seeing Jake with one foot still in the grave. I don't know."

"But you agree there's something wrong?"

She reflected before answering. "Yeah, but we agreed not to talk about our marriage while on this mission."

The tacit admission scrunched his stomach. "Our marriage is bothering you?"

She shrugged.

"Worse than Terry or Jake's issues?"

"I don't know." Her eyes locked with his and weakened him. "Did we move too fast, Dmitry?"

"Getting married?"

"Yeah."

"No." He reassured her. "Absolutely not! We were destined to be together from the moment I saw you."

She nodded. "I know. I believe it, too. But I'm not feeling it."

"Feelings can run wild, independent of what we know. We can get through this. Maybe you'll feel better when I can give you a proper honeymoon."

Her smile was feeble. "Okay. Sounds good."

"Good."

"We've reviewed Pierre's ideas enough. I'm tired."

He took the hint. "Yeah. Agreed. Good night, my love."

"Good night, Dmitry."

Two hours later, Volkov verified his submarine's location

atop the *Xerxes* cutting circles in the Banda Sea south of Main Naval Base Ambon, which had lost its surface combatants to the rebellion but which had retained its shore-based assets and personnel.

Surrounded by dozens of Indonesian capital warships and smaller combat craft, he felt safe–for the moment–and his mind wandered to dangerous places.

It wandered into uncertainty.

*I have a wife now. I can't risk my life like this.*
*I'm too old for mortal combat. I should make a home with Dani.*
*There's darkness over my normally illuminated team.*

To escape his doubts, he sought the solace of sleep.

While reclined in his rack, he slowed his thoughts and awaited slumber's soporific escape.

Then his laptop's hailing chime filled his stateroom.

"*Blyad*. That woman is needy." He slid from his sheets, stooped over his laptop, and opened it.

Surprising him, the caller wasn't his wife but his best friend. "Vasily? What's going on?"

Southern France's midday sun bathed the dolphin trainer's tanned skin. "She's perfect, Dmitry! She's the one! She's the one!"

The *Wraith's* commander chuckled. "Who's the what?"

"The French dolphin trainer. She's perfect!"

"There's a French dolphin trainer?"

Vasily deadpanned. "Who do you think has been training the Iranian dolphins?"

Volkov recalled having captured the Persian cetaceans five years earlier. "Apparently a comely French woman."

"She's beautiful! She's perfect!"

"And apparently, she's perfect. I imagine she's good with dolphins?"

The enamored trainer beamed. "She practically is a dolphin. She's so beautiful when she swims, and she's made her Iranian girls almost as smart as my babies."

"How are your babies?"

"Mikhail is bored, and Andrei is back to about eighty percent healthy. He'll be ready for work in another month or two."

"Good. I could have used them now, but oh well."

"I know. But they're getting good training."

"How so?"

"We're going to try parallel training with the Iranian dolphins. We're teaching all four dolphins to obey commands with new calls so they can work in the same water. Brilliant, huh?"

"Yeah. That's smart."

"It was her idea. I didn't think my babies would adapt so quickly, but for her they are. I think they love her, too!"

"So, you're serious about her."

Again, the infatuated man deadpanned. "Would I be this emotional for just any woman?"

"Hah! You get emotional about everything, my friend."

Vasily scowled. "No! This is different." He relaxed his features and assumed a regal tone. "We'll be married, and you'll be my best man, if you would agree, of course."

Warmth billowed in Volkov's chest. "I'd be honored."

"Wonderful!"

"How well do you know her?"

"Three dates already!"

"And…you're sure?"

"Of course!"

"What's her name?"

The trainer blushed. "I…uh."

"You know her name, don't you?"

Vasily scowled. "*Blyad*, Dmitry! Of course, I know her name."

"Well then?"

"I can't pronounce it. She laughs when I try."

Volkov released the first honest laugh since leaving France. Among all his comrades, only his distant friend glimmered with enthusiasm. "Try it. I won't laugh. I promise."

Vasily furrowed his brow and scrunched his mouth while trying his best French. "Moo…ree…el."

"Murielle?"

"That's what I said. I think. But you say it better than me."

"Maybe. But if this is serious, I'll learn it well enough to–"

Sergei's voice boomed from the *Wraith's* annunciation circuit. "Captain to the control room, please."

"Got to go, Vasily." Volkov shut his laptop and darted towards the control center.

Sergei radiated excitement. "They found the *Nagapasa*!"

Thrilled, Volkov barked. "Where?"

"A reconnaissance aircraft found it, just after sundown, refueling from its trip in the Indian Ocean."

The *Wraith's* commander recalled the sunken *Nuku*. "I remember tangling with it in the Indian Ocean. This is personal. But you say it's refueling in open water?"

The executive officer nodded. "Underway replenishment with a tanker owned by–you could have guessed it–a Chinese company."

"Of course, China. Do we have tasking yet?"

"Commander Volkova already has us accelerating with escorts while Jakarta declares and forms an official task force for this."

Volkov realized he'd ignored the increased rolling from the *Xerxes* accelerating underneath him. "Good."

"We caught a break, Dmitry."

"We needed it." Volkov sat in his captain's chair and raised his voice to a compartment that had attracted curious crewmen. "Let's go hunt a submarine."

# CHAPTER 9

The next morning, Rear Admiral Hakim gathered his thoughts. Once convinced of his appropriate retort, he spoke into his phone. "Like you, general, I regret the loss of the tanker, but in protecting the other five, I secured desperately needed fuel."

"Desperately needed, yes. But the populace is growing more hostile in their protests. I must appease the angry sheep with petrol."

Hakim disliked the junta commander's tone and worried about his boss' next comment. "And so they're getting my reserve fuel?"

"It was never yours, admiral, especially after losing the sixth tanker. I only promised you the overage, of which there is none. Anything my forces can spare will go to the cities where the civilians have wisely allied with us."

"I had planned to put combat jets on patrol to support your ground campaign, sir."

"And what's stopping you? You'll know when it's time."

Hakim noticed the withheld details about the pending attacks against the loyalist provinces–and against the increasing riots within the rebel states. He hoped the withholding had arrived from a security concern for a tapped phone and not from intentional exclusion. "Understood, sir."

Purnomo was gruff. "Anything else?"

Despite its dismissiveness, the opening compelled Hakim to express his concern about joint operations. "I had intended to start the air patrols immediately, sir, to practice coordination with your troops and to see Jakarta's reaction."

"I'm not concerned about Jakarta's reaction. I have plenty of surface-to-air missiles, as do you. I'll tell you when to put your jets in the sky." Before continuing, the general inhaled a loud sniff. "Or do you not trust my judgment?"

Accused, Hakim saw only appeasement as a defense. "Of course, I do, sir." Unwilling to remain off balance, he argued his success. "Just as you can trust mine. In fact, despite the tanker's loss, I gained valuable knowledge of the enemy's tactics."

The general sounded unimpressed. "Go on."

"It's the jamming, sir. Hypersonic bullets require accuracy, and we can overpower their guidance with our own radar systems."

"The mercenaries don't know how to counter that?"

"No, sir. The laws of physics favor us. The closer the rounds get to our radars, the more our radars overpower theirs. We flood the full spectrum of guidance frequencies, including cellular if they try it, and the rounds become deaf, so to speak."

The general's tone was accusatory. "And you'll guarantee the railguns' inaccuracy?"

Hakim boasted in terms the soldier would grasp. "The railgun rounds may as well be sniper shots from across the island. You have nothing to worry about, sir."

Purnomo grunted. "Good. The location or locations where Jakarta attempts to land is still a matter of debate, especially as I keep my intended troop movements against our protestors secret. Make sure your forces are ready to react."

"Always, general."

"I'll contact you when I need you."

Silence overtook Hakim's phone, which he pocketed. He sighed and grumbled. "I sent the *Goliath* fleeing with a fishing vessel, and he's complaining about losing one tanker of six."

Alone in the plush office which had served as the Indonesian Third Fleets' headquarters, he sensed the isolation of his new nation, dangling on the precarious edge of a ring of islands and the Pacific Ocean's vastness.

Images of himself as an exuberant child receiving his father figure's chastisement while seeking approval filled his head, and he realized he'd let Purnomo's withholding of praise for the encounter against the *Goliath* unsettle him. To soothe the wound, he hardened his soul as he passed through his door into the command center.

Bigger problems than a tyrant's disdain required his immediate attention.

He reached the table around which stood his waiting underlings. For inspiration, he glanced at the wall behind his staff at the Morning Star flag, the fledgling Papua's new standard.

His chest swelled as he convinced himself of self-serving untruths, pasted a smirk on his face, and lied. "The general is quite pleased with our success in bringing the tankers to our country."

Multiple pairs of inward-looking, glossy eyes stared back at him atop smug smiles.

Hakim tested his marine corps leader. "Colonel Pardi, tell me about the land war. What do we know about Jakarta's intentions to conduct a landing?"

The lean officer shook his head. "No, sir. And my marines are still operating side by side with the army. If there were any talk of it, I'd know."

The response confirmed a lingering fear. Despite his oozing confidence, General Purnomo had no idea where or when the enemy would strike, and doubt disturbed Hakim's thinking.

Everything within the revolution depended upon Purnomo's invincibility. The slightest sign of weakness would pierce the new nation's paper-thin armor.

Hakim noticed an infinite chasm separating him from blissful memories of sipping single malt scotch, smoking Cuban cigars, and dreaming out loud with the general and his would-be junta's other confidants about how they could build a better world.

A wave of honest self-reflection consumed him, and he questioned if he and other revolutionary leaders lied to the people and to themselves about fighting for a utopia.

Did they act instead for simple personal gain?

Was he a selfish dreamer?

He blinked away the defeating thoughts. "Colonel Pardi, what's the status of securing the streets?"

"We're no longer on schedule to end martial law in the free provinces, sir. The situation has escalated with urban resistance, which is why General Purnomo has called for a military policing action of the freed provinces."

"Has he shared anything about the details of his policing?"

"No, sir. And I'm sure my marines would've heard."

"But you believe the army can handle it, with the assistance of your marines?"

"Yes, sir." Pardi clarified. "I'm willing to assist if the general needs support. The resistance has grown stronger than originally seen. They've organized and are well armed, and they seem to be operating under competent leadership."

The update disagreed with the confidence General Purnomo had portrayed during Hakim's recent call. "Really? Where are they getting their weapons?"

"Partially by smuggling from loyalist provinces, partially by capturing stocks from the army and the police."

Hakim's cocked head and raised eyebrow posed a silent question.

"That's correct, sir. The resistance overran a police station, procured its weapons, and used them to defeat an army platoon."

"But not your marines?"

"No, sir. But even my marines would've fallen under the same attack. The resisting civilians know their streets, and they're willing to die for victory. It was a well-executed ambush."

"Thank you, colonel." After digesting the juxtaposition of increased venom from a people he intended to rule in peace, Hakim continued. "With the rising operational tempo of the general's land forces, he'll need all the fuel for his land campaign."

The air commander winced. "Does this disrupt our timing for establishing a constant jet fighter presence?"

The admiral eyed a short Air Force colonel. "Yes. You'll have to wait until the attack begins to launch your combat air patrols. Is that a problem?"

As his role in the rebellion shrank, the air boss frowned. "No, sir."

"Good. We'll take reserves from the loyalist provinces, once they're in our control. I may then allow you a greater air presence."

"Understood, sir."

Hakim cast his voice around the table. "But my success with the tankers has shown vulnerabilities in the long-range railgun attacks. We can negate them."

The pudgy naval officer smirked. "And then we'll hold the advantage as defenders do against equally matched attackers."

"You're correct, Captain Moeljadi. Jamming makes the railguns useless at long range."

"And we know our close-in weapon systems can take down accurate shots, as you proved on the *Yani*."

Hakim restrained a wince as the underling's obsequiousness sickened him. "Again, you are correct, captain. I'll trust you to organize our surface combatants to optimize our defenses."

"Of course, sir."

Reminding himself that the man's submissiveness served his power structure, Hakim cleared his throat and segued. "On to more immediate matters. Where's the *Nagapasa*?"

Micro-expressions of doubt broke through the cowardly officer's fleshy features. "There is a concern, sir. Its captain is wary about having been detected while fueling."

"Don't give me any concerns! Was he detected or not?"

"We should assume that he was, sir."

"Are the Jakartans reacting?"

"Yes, sir. A small force is racing to intercept the *Nagapasa* on its direct route home."

"And what are you doing about it?"

"I've ordered the *Nagapasa* home on a longer route that will be less obvious and a greater distance from Jakarta's task force."

"A longer distance, but still within their reach?"

"Yes, sir. It can't be avoided. But I've also ordered a dozen ships with sonar systems to intervene."

"Intervene?"

"To listen for Jakarta's submarines."

Remembering his edict to conscript civilian maritime assets when useful, Hakim became hopeful. "Civilian ships?"

Relieved by his boss' optimism, the captain became chipper. "Yes, sir! Most are fishermen, although I also included a recreational diver and an oceanic research vessel."

The admiral offered a rare complement. "That's smart. It spreads suspicion across multiple types of civilian shipping."

Moeljadi's cheeks flushed. "Thank you, sir."

"And you had them all equipped with manual dipping sonar systems?"

"Yes, sir! I've been equipping civilians for three days. Most of them will earn stipends for simply carrying the sonar equipment, and the lucky ones will earn bonuses for acting, and even larger bonuses for detecting the enemy."

"And they're all loyal to our nation?"

"Patriots, indeed, but also well compensated, sir."

"What about our undersea drones? Can you redirect one of them towards the *Nagapasa* to help?"

"I've already redirected two of them, sir. With the six extra that arrived from China two days ago, we have sufficient coverage around our island."

Hakim was stoic. "Well done."

"Thanks again, sir."

Wary of the craven's newfound initiative, Hakim tested him further. "Have you considered arming civilians, as I did for the tanker run on the north shore?"

"I've considered it, sir, and I have options available. But I wouldn't dare without your permission."

Thoughts raced through the admiral's mind, and the one surfacing above the others was his being overwhelmed.

Events unfolded rapidly, and he sensed the maritime

elements–his responsibilities–taking on lives of their own, morphing into a beast bred to destroy him. He was a man sprinting from a ravenous animal, looking over his shoulder only to find his hunter gaining speed as he grew fatigued.

Every decision, every step, and every moment compounded the pressure and fear–fear of failure's shame, condemnation, and punishment along with fear of success' unintended consequences.

A pang of terror struck him but then released him as the thoughts billowed throughout his frame before evaporating.

When his head cleared, he shared confidential information. "Captain Moeljadi, Twenty triple-launchers of Chinese Yu-7 lightweight torpedoes arrived two hours ago at Osok Airport. They're in a hangar under guard."

The chubby officer raised an eyebrow.

Hakim continued. "They're yours now. Get them and place them on the twenty most trusted civilian ships you can find."

# CHAPTER 10

The next morning, after an escorted race northward atop his wife's transport vessel, Volkov desired the pending solitude of a one-on-one hunt.

Sensing a pallor over the fleet–a sensation he could define no better than 'bad vibes'–he wanted to distance himself from the others and enter into his prime element of chasing an equally matched submarine.

He doubted he'd even miss video chats with his new bride, who appeared troubled on his laptop screen. "Dmitry?"

He snapped back. "Don't."

"Don't what?"

"Don't make this difficult."

"It's already difficult. It was difficult before we were married. Now, it's only worse."

"That's why I said 'don't'."

"I want you to come back safely."

He considered reinforcing his edict of 'don't' but acquiesced to her emotions. "I'll do everything I can to see you again."

"I know."

"May I go now?"

"Okay."

He chuckled. "You should head to the bridge if you want to get rid of me."

"I don't ever want to get rid of you." Her image in his laptop shifted from a sorrowful wife to a warship's commander. "But I'll have you off my back as soon as I can."

Twenty minutes later, Volkov stooped beside his Indonesian rider and pointed at a canted rectangle drawn upon the charting table. "Is this our confirmed water?"

Gazing upon the passage between Sulawesi Island and the southern edge of the Philippines, the commander replied in Russian. "Confirmed. We've got aircraft dropping sonobuoys from the northern tip of Sulawesi to Tahuna. The Philippine Navy has agreed to patrol its waters south of Sarangani, leaving you one hundred and fifty kilometers to guard here." He pointed to the eastern edge of the Celebes Sea.

"Which explains the sinking feeling in my gut. That's a lot of water to cover."

The Indonesian officer shrugged. "That's why we expect the *Nagapasa* to take that route. It's the widest passage."

Volkov broached a subject he'd been pondering. "The *Nagapasa's* commander. What can you tell me about him?"

"I know him, mostly by reputation."

The *Wraith's* commander eyed the submarine pin on his rider's uniform. "You've trained with him."

"With him and against him. Our submarine community is small enough that the officers know each other. He was the exec of the *Alugoro* when I commanded the *Ardadedali*. I had many opportunities to watch him in our training simulators."

"And?"

The rider folded his arms and sighed. "He's a brilliant tactician. Maybe our best."

Having read his adversary's dossier, Volkov was unsurprised, but hearing about his enemy's prowess caused anxiety. He slumped his head between his shoulder blades and sought a silver lining. "What are his weaknesses?"

"Tactically, nothing."

"How about not tactically? He's not a robot."

"Good point." The rider folded his arms and grunted. "He's a loner. He has no friends and seems to prefer it that way."

"That may explain why he's sided with the rebels. No future in his true navy since he hasn't built a personal network."

"Come to think of it, yes. I could never picture him getting promoted beyond commander. He's kind of an ass."

"An ass who sunk the *Nuku*." Sensing an even battle ahead, Volkov sought his adversary's mindset for an advantage. "Is he quiet or vocal?"

"I'd call him a quiet outcast, except..." The rider probed his memory. "Except I noticed him expressing himself more angrily as he grew in rank."

"As he gained more positional authority, with fewer people to tell him to shut up?"

"Yeah."

"So, he may be easily angered."

"Yes. And impatient."

"If he gets flustered, he may become irrational."

"I saw it happen only once, but yes, I remember it well because it was so unusual. So, it's possible."

"Perhaps I can bait him to shoot early–or to simply shoot at all if he doesn't need to."

"What's that mean?"

"He has no need to defeat me. He only needs to get by me. But if he's got something to prove, I'm a prized target."

"Then I pray you can force an error, Commander Volkov." The rider stood straight. "Because he's damned brilliant."

An hour later, the *Wraith's* commander sat in his captain's chair watching his executive officer oversee the tacticians.

After a verbal exchange with the sonar guru, Sergei looked to his boss. "Both drones are deployed ten miles away, sixty degrees to our left and right, matching our speed and course."

"Very well."

Seeing an opportunity for a hushed conversation, Sergei stepped to the captain's chair. "I wish we had Vasily's babies."

"So do I." Volkov snorted. "But don't mention it again."

"I won't, sir." The *Wraith's* executive officer turned.

Feeling he owed Sergei an explanation, Volkov tapped his arm. "I mean not to mention it because I suspect the crew's morale is thin."

Sergei glanced around the control room, as if verifying his

reply. "I agree, sir. There's something rotten in these waters, and it's bothering everyone."

"Yeah. Something."

"I wouldn't dwell on it, sir." Sergei stepped away.

"No. No, of course not." Despite their spoken agreement, Volkov noticed his executive officer's body language, with traces of anxiety in his voice and stiffness in his movements, betraying his dwelling upon both thinning morale and thinning courage.

Seated at his sonar console, Anatoly inquired. "Do you want the drones on a secure active search?"

Volkov wanted his tethered robotic hunters using tight clicks to capture return from his enemy's hull. Feeling pressure to find the *Nagapasa* before it passed, he considered pounding the water with sound to increase the chance of a return but more so increasing the danger of counter detection. He opted for conservatism. "Yes. Set both drones to secure active search mode."

The sonar guru leaned sideways towards two apprentices who controlled tethered robots, examined their consoles, and then replied. "We've set both drones to active search, sir."

"Very well."

Forty-five minutes later, a sonar technician fingered his screen, curled forward in his seat, and pressed muffs against his ears.

Volkov glared at the man while the sonar guru leaned into him, beheld the man's screen, and then listened on his own headset.

Satisfied his underling heard something important, Anatoly twisted in his seat. "We hear it, sir."

Incredulous about his good fortune, the *Wraith's* commander sought confirmation. "The *Nagapasa*?"

"Yes, sir. Drone one hears its propeller blades, bearing three-three-one."

Volkov's tensed torso relaxed with his welcomed advantage. "So, you have blade rate?"

"We do, sir." Anatoly glanced at his stirring subordinate, exchanged quick verbal information, and then reported. "It's making turns for eight knots on a seven-bladed screw."

"Very well. Any active return?"

"No, sir. It's too far away for an active return."

"It doesn't matter. We've been gifted our adversary, and there's no need to announce ourselves. Secure active transmissions from both drones."

After relaying the order to his team, the sonar guru shared the status. "Both drones are in passive search mode, sir."

"Very well. Do you have a solution yet?"

"Almost…we're entering it in the system now. Assuming eight knots, the *Nagapasa* is on course zero-four-nine, range seven and a half miles."

"How far is it from drone one?"

"Three-point-seven miles, sir."

"Very well." Volkov stepped to the central plotting table to talk with Sergei and the Indonesian rider. "What do you men think?"

The rider replied. "The range of your drone's hearing is longer than expected. It should be a quieter ship than that."

Fiddling with the *Nagapasa's* known sound emissions files, Sergei fingered a window on the table and examined it. "At eight knots, I was expecting detection at about two-point-six miles from the drone, sir. He's right. Three-point-seven miles is generous."

Volkov frowned. "But not unbelievable?"

"No, sir."

"But still unusual, especially with a skilled captain."

Sergei rationalized. "A commanding officer's skill can't change the laws of physics, sir. He's in a hurry, but I'm not sure why it's a bit louder than expected."

Volkov folded his arms. "Neither am I. But we hear what we hear, and sound profiles are far from guaranteed predictors."

Revealing his submission to the time pressure, the executive officer shrugged. "Yeah. They can vary from day to day. It's half science, half black magic."

"Alright then, we're beginning our approach to *Nagapasa*."

The executive officer offered an optimistic smile. "Another victim of the *Wraith* awaits."

Lacking other useful emotions, Volkov let himself enjoy the advantage for a moment. "Alright, then. We'll shoot off its beam on a lagging line of sight. Plot me a course."

"With pleasure, sir."

Forty minutes later, Volkov admired the iconic geometry he'd created by placing himself in a perfect launching position, but he felt a mental tickle preventing his acceptance of good fortune.

The Indonesian rider studied him. "What's wrong, commander?"

Although he desired to neutralize the *Nagapasa* immediately, Volkov hesitated. "It's a shadow of a threat in my mind, but I'm having trouble putting it into words."

"You've only got four, maybe five minutes, before your geometry degrades and the *Nagapasa* gets away."

"I know. Damn it!" The *Wraith's* commander shifted his eyes around the chart, noticed a problem, and pointed at an annoying icon with a number 'twenty-seven' beside it. "Here."

From the charting table's other side, Sergei opined. "The *Nagapasa's* been trailing Contact Twenty-Seven since we've been tracking it. I think the *Nagapasa's* using Contact Twenty-Seven as a potential decoy for any torpedo that might come his way."

The rider snorted. "I'd do the same thing, especially knowing there's a ninety-nine percent chance you're going to shoot a slow-kill weapon."

"Yeah. That's what I'd do, too." Volkov applied words to a growing ugly thought. "But what if the decoy isn't the ship, but the ship is towing a decoy?"

The exec eyed his boss. "You mean we're hunting a ghost?"

"Yeah."

Sergei nodded. "I didn't want to say it, but I couldn't get the idea out of my mind."

"It's possible." The rider folded his arms. "But you can't let that stop you."

Volkov shot the Indonesian an 'it's-my-ship-not-yours' glance.

Against the silent challenge, the rider doubled down. "There's not enough time to gather the data to tell the difference. You've got to try the shot."

Volkov released the harsh glance. "Agreed. The best way to resolve this is with a torpedo seeker." He then turned towards the seated sonar guru and raised his voice. "And I believe tube two is ready?"

Anatoly took the hint and replied. "Tube two is ready for the *Nagapasa*, sir."

"Shoot tube two."

Five minutes later, Volkov watched his torpedo's icon blink and grow a textual appendage displaying the seeker's active state.

Anatoly announced the change. "Our seeker is range-gating."

"Very well." The *Wraith's* commander grew anxious. "Anatoly?"

"Yes, sir?"

"There's no active return, is there?"

"Not yet. No, sir."

Volkov shifted his gaze between the rider and his executive officer. "And the *Nagapasa* hasn't run yet."

Sergei shook his head. "A towed decoy?"

The Indonesian scowled. "I'll have a boarding party pay a special visit to that so-called neutral civilian ship, if you'll allow the communications buoy."

"I'll allow it." Volkov aimed his voice towards the gray-bearded veteran seated at his panel. "Download the last ten minutes of Subtics data into a communication buoy with a note about Contact Twenty-Seven towing a decoy. Launch it when ready."

Three minutes later, Anatoly curled forward, pressed his muffs to his head, and then barked. "Torpedo in the water! Bearing zero-seven-four!"

"Very well!" Volkov's stomach twisted, but he forced a cool announcement. "Remain calm. Analyze it. Give me a bearing rate or at least a drift."

Anatoly announced over his shoulder. "Bearing drift is to the left, sir. It's a low bearing rate. The weapon's leading us on a possible intercept course."

Adrenaline flooded Volkov and brought him clarity. Duped into shooting towed hydrophones, he'd revealed his position by his launch noises, his torpedo's blades, or both. He'd walked into a trap, begetting the *Nagapasa's* accurate shot.

His first move was to complete his mission–share data about the incoming weapon with friendly combatants and aircraft. Even with ambiguity of the enemy's launch distance, the hostile torpedo's presence tightened the search area by a factor of ten.

Volkov addressed his gray-bearded veteran. "The hostile torpedo's data will help the others find the *Nagapasa*. Update a buoy with the last two minutes of Subtics data and launch when ready."

"Aye, sir!"

Communications resolved, the *Wraith's* commander shifted his attention to his evasion. "Anatoly, do you have a bearing rate yet?"

"Yes, sir! Left zero-point-four degrees per minute. It's an intercept course."

"Very well, I'll turn to place the weapon on a lag line of sight." He raised his voice. "Helm, left full rudder, steady on course one-nine-zero."

His helmsman acknowledged the order, and the deck tilted.

During the turn, Volkov kept his submarine slow enough to hear the incoming doom. "What's happening, Anatoly?"

His eyes closed while listening to the dangers through his earmuffs, the guru lifted a finger.

Volkov deferred to his ace. "When you're ready."

Anatoly shook his head, lowered a muff to his jaw, and faced the submarine's captain. "Up-Doppler."

"Towards a new leading line of sight?"

"Yeah."

Terror numbed Volkov's blood. "It's got us."

The guru nodded. "We're being tracked, and that weapon's being guided to a new intercept course as we turn."

"*Blyad!*" Volkov raised his voice. "Attention in the control room. We are being tracked by the *Nagapasa*. It's guiding a torpedo towards us. Stealth is lost. We'll flee at flank speed."

A hush overcame the room for several heartbeats.

Volkov barked. "Helm, all-ahead flank. Cavitate."

As the ship shuddered towards its top speed, the gray-bearded veteran yelled from his control panel. "Pierre just acknowledged receipt of our second communication buoy."

"Very well." The *Wraith's* commander slid his gaze across the table and read Renard's trickling words. His boss could say little to encourage him except reminding him that people were more valuable than hardware. Volkov took the reminder as a recommendation to spare his crew, if possible.

As the Indonesian rider had foreshadowed, Volkov realized the *Nagapasa's* commander had proved his brilliance. He'd fooled him with sonic lies, and then he'd fired a kill shot.

He lifted his chin towards his exec. "Sergei?"

"Sir?"

"Prepare to abandon ship."

# CHAPTER 11

As her boss announced her husband's death sentence, Danielle stopped breathing. The hairs on her arm stood, and the air pressure dropped within the *Xerxes'* bridge dome.

Beside her, Taylor offered solace. "He'll find a way out."

Overwrought, she began assigning railgun rounds to the fishing ship which had lured Volkov to his doom.

The former British submarine officer tried again to soothe her. "He always does."

She snapped. "What if he doesn't?"

The Indonesian rider behind them interjected good news. "We've vectored a helicopter from the *Diponegoro* to establish a line of sonobuoys east of the *Nagapasa*. The data Commander Volkov shared on its torpedo shot will guide our air support."

Danielle hissed her intent. "The mission now includes revenge against that bloody trawler." She raised her voice to the open microphone. "Port and starboard weapons bays, I've targeted twenty rounds at Contact Twenty-Seven. Prepare to fire ten rounds each."

"Aye, ma'am. Ten rounds from the port railgun."

"Aye, ma'am. Ten rounds form the starboard railgun."

Eyeing his console, Taylor protested. "Ma'am, these rounds are aimed at the bridge, maneuvering, and living areas."

Her voice was fiery. "And?"

"And...the *Lepu* is on the way there."

"My rounds will hit well before it gets there."

"Well, yes. But–"

Her voice was icy. "But what?"

His response was a soft concession. "Nothing, ma'am."

Staving off a veto, she glared at the Frenchman's image.

"Pierre?"

Renard appeared gloomier about her decision than Taylor but acquiesced. "I can't fault you. Go ahead."

She glanced at her executive officer. "Mike, I want you guiding these rounds on the phased array from launch to impact."

"I'll guide all twenty rounds on the phased array from launch to impact, ma'am." He tapped keys to obey.

She raised her voice. "Port and starboard weapons bays, commence fire."

As the first pair of hypersonic rounds cracked overhead, her adrenaline spiked with vengeance.

Speaking Malay into his headset, the rider stirred. "Contact Twenty-Seven is not responding to the *Lepu's* hails."

Danielle craned her neck over her shoulder. "Do they know what I'm sending their way?"

Agitated, Commander Lestari toggled the languages of his speaking. "One moment, commander."

She nodded, watched her screen, and listened with bloodlust to another cracking salvo racing overhead.

Taylor leaned into her. "If we can get a bearing from the fishing boat to the torpedo, we can send it to Dmitry to triangulate its location."

Halfway through the volley, she ratcheted her angst down two notches and considered clemency. If she let the fishing boat's crew live, they could help her husband. "He could then try an anti-torpedo shot?"

Taylor nodded.

"Prepare to retarget all twenty rounds at Contact Twenty-Seven's propulsion gear."

Racing the rounds' hasty trajectories, the former submarine officer was curt. "Aye, ma'am." His deft fingertips hopped across his screen. "I've entered targeting coordinates coinciding with a best estimate of Contact Twenty-Seven's propulsion gear. I've not yet committed the update. You have twenty-three seconds before your first round hits."

"Very well." She again eyed the rider. "Anything?"

Lestari shook his head. "No, commander. The fishing boat is still disregarding the *Lepu's* hails."

"Have the *Lepu* broadcast an offer to spare the crew and only cripple the ship in exchange for information."

Confused, the rider scrunched his features. "Okay."

"Mike, commit the targeting of all twenty rounds to Contact Twenty-Seven's propulsion gear."

Taylor tapped keys. "I've retargeted all twenty rounds to Contact Twenty-Seven's' propulsion gear…the last pair has been fired, and all rounds acknowledge the update, ma'am."

"Very well."

The rider frowned. "You're crippling the fishing ship to inspire the crew's compliance?"

"Yes. Have the *Lepu* use this to make them share bearings to the *Nagapasa's* torpedo. It's so that Commander Volkov can triangulate its position and blow it up with his own torpedo."

"Right!" The Indonesian rider switched to Malay and spoke into his mouthpiece.

Taylor spoke. "If they agree to send bearings, will you have me splash the incoming rounds?"

"Yeah. Get ready to splash them."

"Aye, ma'am. Five seconds until the first pair hits."

Curious, she looked over her shoulder.

Lestari shook his head. "No response yet."

She watched her screen as two hypersonic icons merged with that of the civilian craft.

Taylor announced it. "I've lost telemetry with the first pair of rounds. I expect they were on target."

"Very well." She craned her neck towards her rider.

The Indonesian officer shook his head.

Seconds later, Taylor again reported. "I've lost telemetry with the second pair of rounds. I expect they were on target."

"Very well." Again, she eyed her rider.

Again, he shook his head.

Taylor announced the third pair's impact.

She heard rapid Malay and turned towards the Indonesian.

"They've responded! The ship's captain is begging for mercy."

Danielle vented. "My rounds helped that jackass find his radio."

"He says the rebels threatened his family, and he had no choice."

"He's got a choice now."

His voice tense, Taylor queried her. "Ma'am? The rounds?"

"Splash all the rounds you can."

"Aye, ma'am." His hands flew across his console. "It was too late for the fourth and fifth pairs, but I've splashed rounds eleven through twenty, ma'am."

"Very well." Her weapons idle, she turned her attention to the rider. "What's going on?"

Surprising her, he held a pocket-sized notepad in one hand while scribbling with a pencil. "Good information flow, commander."

Tension still gripped her. "Such as?"

"The fishing boat's dragging its hydrophones eighteen hundred yards behind its stern. Bearing from its hydrophones to the *Nagapasa's* torpedo is two-five-seven, timestamped at forty-two minutes, twelve seconds after the hour."

Taylor tapped keys. "It's a reasonable bearing."

Renard drew her attention to the monitor. "I agree. I'm sending the data to Dmitry over the low-frequency broadcast."

Proving his value as a submarine veteran, Taylor interrogated the *Xerxes'* rider. "Commander, what depth is the *Nagapasa's* weapon running at? Your fleet has a default setting, and the water's deep enough to support it."

"Our default is eight hundred, but we set it manually with each launch by procedure. I'd guess it's running anywhere between three hundred and one thousand feet."

Danielle glared at the image in her console. "He should send two heavyweights, Pierre. One shallow. One deep."

"Agreed, Commander Volkova. I'm having Henri type in that recommendation as we speak."

"Thanks, Pierre." She stole another glance at the officer

behind her. "Are we still getting bearings from the fishing ship? Commander Volkov needs to verify the weapon's speed."

"Yes." The officer tore a sheet from his small notebook and extended it. "Two more bearings with time stamps."

She examined the penciled characters and then announced them to her boss.

Renard confirmed them and then relayed them through Henri to the fleeing *Wraith*.

After half a minute, she asked for help. "Is there anything else we can do?"

Heads shaking, her comrades affirmed there was nothing more.

She summarized their status. "So, we wait."

Another half a minute later, Renard stirred. "Hah! I've received word via a communications buoy! Commander Volkov acknowledges receipt of our first bearing from the fishing vessel and requests continued bearings. He says he'll attempt the two-weapon anti-torpedo salvo as we suggested."

Waiting in silence proved insufferable, and Danielle sought data where none existed. She raised her voice to the open microphone. "Control room, bridge. Can you hear any sign of the *Wraith's* anti-torpedo shots?"

"Bridge, control room. No, ma'am. We're too far away. But we'll hear the explosions."

"Control room, bridge, aye."

Taylor continued his role as her therapist. "It should work."

As she nodded her agreement, appearing strong on the outside, her heart condemned her for lying with her body. She anticipated her husband's doom and sensed her pending collapse.

Behind her, ripping paper signaled the influx of new bearings from the fishing boat, and a fresh page appeared in the Indonesian's extended hand.

She delegated. "Handle this, Mike."

The former British submarine officer grabbed the sheet and relayed the numbers to Renard.

As the wait became interminable, a distant thunderclap rumbled. The seas brought her a muffled and lengthy boom, but Danielle couldn't discern if she heard more than one warhead. "Control room, bridge. Was that one detonation or two?"

"Bridge, control room. We're trying to figure it out, ma'am. It's either a single detonation or two timed closely. We'll listen to the recording and inform you when we know."

"Control room, bridge. Aye."

Serving as her voice of optimism, Taylor speculated. "That had to be Dmitry's. The *Nagapasa's* weapon was still too far away."

She lied. "I'm sure you're right."

"We'll hear from him soon. Give him time."

Until she heard from her husband, she'd struggle for breath. Her chest tightened as she forced the words. "Any time now."

From the loudspeaker, the sonar supervisor eased her fear. "Bridge, control room. We're sure it was two detonations, ma'am. Those were the *Wraith's* anti-torpedo shots."

"Control room, bridge. Aye. That's great news, but where the hell's the *Wraith*?"

"Bridge, control room. We won't hear it surfacing from this far away. We'll have to wait for radio contact, ma'am."

"Control room, bridge. Aye." She addressed the rider. "What does Contact Twenty-Seven hear?"

The Indonesian officer furiously scribbled notes. "I'm finding out now, commander. There was a delay in reporting after the explosions, but we've got a minute of bearings now. But they don't make sense." He ripped off and extended a sheet.

She read the bearings and timestamps, digested their strangeness, and then handed them to her executive officer. "He's right, Mike. These are weird."

Taylor tapped his screen and gazed at the updated positioning. "I concur. Maybe the *Nagapasa's* torpedo is still running with a damaged guidance system."

In her console, her boss became more animated than she remembered ever seeing him. "I've got a new communication from a buoy!"

Vicarious mortal terror escaped her pores. Although the evidence suggested her husband's survival, hearing from him soothed her. "Thank God."

Renard scowled. "Wait. It's mixed news. Dmitry says the *Nagapasa* steered its torpedo around his salvo."

She slumped. "Shit."

"I know. But don't give up hope. Dmitry's still fighting to evade. Let's keep our wits about ourselves and do what we must to assure his survival."

# CHAPTER 12

Frightened men staged life jackets near the *Wraith's* hatch, crowded the control room, and sent wafts of armpit stench over Volkov's nose.

Even with his thoughts riveted to the icons on the table's chart, the stink reminded the *Wraith's* commander he was scrambling to survive.

Sergei called his attention to tactics. "The *Nagapasa's* torpedo is back on an intercept course."

Volkov eyed the updated time to impact. "Our heavyweights bought us only ninety seconds."

"We have time to try it one more time, but there's no time to reload heavyweights."

Volkov snorted. "Then what's the point?"

"Try a bluff."

Recalling his discussion about the *Nagapasa's* commander, Volkov eyed the rider. "He won't fall for it, will he? He knows that my mission requires slow-kills and limpets."

The Indonesian's voice carried fear. "I'm not optimistic, but it might keep us alive, and you have to try it."

Volkov looked at his sonar guru. "Anatoly. I'm going to attempt a bluff to force another steer and buy us time. Assign tubes five and six to the *Nagapasa's* torpedo."

Anatoly tapped keys. "Tubes five and six, limpet weapons, are assigned against the *Nagapasa's* torpedo. Tube five is set to run shallow, tube six deep."

"Shoot tube six!"

"Shooting tube six!"

As air pumped the weapon and its surrounding slug of water

from the tube, excess pressure seeped into the submarine's atmosphere and compressed Volkov's ears. His voice muffled in his own hearing, he completed his launch. "Shoot tube five!"

"Shooting tube five!"

After the second limpet weapon carried his deception into the sea, Volkov forced a yawn to clear his eardrums. He lamented. "Even if this works, it buys us only another ninety seconds."

Sergei replied. "That could be enough to exhaust its fuel."

"Depending on where the *Nagapasa* was when launching."

The executive officer knifed his hand downward across an oval of uncertainty representing the enemy submarine's launch location. "If it was in the section behind my fingers, we're good regardless of this bluff. The weapon will run out of fuel."

Volkov inquired. "And if the bluff works?"

Sergei slid his hand forwards, shrinking the distance from which the *Nagapasa's* torpedo could reach its target. "Then I'd say it doubles our chances of evading."

Volkov watched the icons of his weapons approach that of the hostile threat. As they converged, he held his breath.

Then, the icons passed each other.

At the control room's front, a sweating technician emerged from the torpedo room. "We've got tube three reloaded with a heavyweight!"

Volkov shook his head. "It's too late. The bluff didn't work, and the weapon's too close. We'd damage ourselves."

Beads dripping from his chin, the technician became a statue while digesting defeat. "Too late?"

"Get your men out of there. Abandon ship!"

The technician turned, yelled, and gestured for the torpedo room's other sailors to join him in the escape.

Volkov eyed his executive officer. "Three minutes to impact."

"I know." Paleness fell over Sergei's face. "Damn it!"

Volkov jabbed his thumb towards the men mustering below the escape hatch. "It's time. Lead them off. I'm going to surface–"

Sergei flew into the table.

Volkov's jaw hammered shut, his vision blanked, and he

tumbled backwards while an awesome rumbling enveloped him in an endless boom.

A thunk on his skull preceded his loss of consciousness, and time stopped.

He awoke with a headache that billowed into a cloud of pain outside his skin. During moments of disorientation, he was a disembodied spirit floating in an immaterial realm of agony and despair. Conscious thought eluded him, reducing him to the sensations of bitterness, fear, and hopelessness.

"Dmitry!"

Hearing a voice added context and texture to Volkov's ethereal existence and beckoned him back towards reality. His rational mind groped for recovery, but pain and horror truncated and jumbled his thoughts into a cauldron of confusion.

"Dmitry!"

This time, a touch to his shoulder accompanied his name, allowing him to regain self-awareness.

He had not fallen into bodiless torment.

His torment was embodied and palpable, with electric icepicks ransacking the bones of his head. The anguished groan from his throat reverberated within his skull.

"Dmitry!"

Volkov achieved full consciousness and remembered he was a submarine commander. Instincts protected him from overstimulation and kept his eyes shut. But he recognized the voice. "Sergei?"

"You're awake!"

"Oh, my head. I can barely think."

"I'll think for you."

Volkov drifted away again.

"Dmitry!" Sergei shook his shoulder.

His eyelids flitting, the *Wraith's* commander returned to his control room and saw his executive officer. "Your face is blurry."

"Close your eyes. I can tell you what you need to know."

Obeying, Volkov heard men groaning. "Okay."

"I fell forward into the plotting table. It knocked the wind out of me. But I'm okay."

"Good."

"You fell backwards and hit your head against a console."

"Why did I fall?"

"The *Nagapasa's* torpedo exploded off our port stern."

"But we're alive. That should've been fatal."

"It was a command detonation, probably at the very end of the torpedo's fuel reserves. Far enough away that we survived the pressure wave."

A figure beyond Volkov's dim vision approached his executive officer and bent downward to speak. The *Wraith's* commander found the words inaudible.

Sergei angled his head towards the new interlocutor. "I'll visit them when I'm done with the captain."

"Aye, sir." The reporting sailor stood and departed.

Volkov was curious about what his executive officer had learned. "What news?"

"I've got a damage report. Are you ready, sir?"

"Yeah. Help me up."

"Do you hurt anywhere but your head?"

"I don't know." Volkov curled his torso forward. "Come on."

Sergei tugged his underarms. "Let's get you sitting first."

"Okay." Groggy, Volkov acquiesced and shifted his weight onto his buttocks. The improved perspective revealed victims motionless on the deck, and he feared others had suffered worse fates than his. "The crew?"

Sergei's tone was somber. "Two dead, both by head wounds. Delov and Kornev."

Shame flowed through Volkov's blood, condemning him for the first deaths under his command. The news stunned him into silence.

"Dmitry?"

Volkov's masculine instincts buried his suffering. "Yes, I'm fine. We'll mourn for them later. Whom must we help who are injured?"

"Ogarkov and Savvin are unconscious with head wounds. The corpsman is sure Ogarkov will pull through. Savvin is more critical and uncertain."

Volkov grunted. "So, we may lose a third man?"

"Possibly. The corpsman's moving him to the wardroom table for observation."

"What about everyone else?"

"Several fractures of limbs and ribs. Many bruises and flesh wounds, but half the crew remains able-bodied."

"So, we can still fight."

"Possibly. But there's nothing to fight. Nobody's shooting at us."

Tasting defeat, the *Wraith's* commander lamented. "The *Nagapasa* got away..."

"Not yet. We gave the Indonesians enough information to enclose its area of uncertainty with sonobuoys."

As his memory returned, Volkov sought an idea he'd been formulating during his evasion. While wrestling his headache to find that forgotten idea, he scowled.

"What's that look, sir?"

"I'm not sure. Something tells me we have another action to take before this is over."

Surprising the *Wraith's* commander, his Indonesian rider entered his vision and knelt beside his executive officer. He lowered himself slowly while cradling one arm in the other. "It's good to see you alive, Commander Volkov."

"And you. Your arm?"

"Broken, I think. Only a hairline fracture, I imagine. The corpsman hasn't had time to examine me yet."

On cue, the submarine's medical expert arrived, compelling Sergei to stand and give way. The corpsman knelt before his ship's captain. "You're the last head wound I need to treat, sir"

"Many suffered worse than I?"

The corpsman winced as he nodded his affirmation. "Two dead, one fighting for life, unfortunately."

"I know. Sergei told me."

"I'm sorry." The apology acknowledged Volkov's burden as a commanding officer and hinted he'd carry the emotional wound to his grave.

Seeking a distraction from the loss, the *Wraith's* commander eyed his examiner. "You're injured, too. I see it in your face."

Lifting a flashlight to his captain's eyes, the medical expert confessed. "I took it in my upper back."

"Bruised ribs?"

"I think so. Possible fractures, but that's unknowable until we get to X-rays. It's also irrelevant while I tend to our men."

Sergei interrupted. "I'll keep us deep to hold a steady deck while we treat the wounded, but I want to send a buoy to Pierre."

The comment triggered Volkov's tactical prowess. "Wait."

"Of course, sir. But I'm sure people are worried about us."

Volkov took the comment as a veiled reminder that his wife was considering herself a widow until he informed her otherwise, but a recommendation needed to accompany his update. "I think the command detonation has a clue we need to share."

"It will be shared with our Subtics upload, sir. I'll include all the system data since our last buoy."

The corpsman took his turn at demanding his boss' attention. "Hold your head still and watch my finger."

Observing the moving digit, Volkov remained silent and cringed against the flashlight aimed at his corneas.

Sergei played his trump card. "Dmitry, I'm sure Commander Volkova would appreciate knowing you're alive."

"She's strong!" Catching himself, the *Wraith's* commander immediately apologized. "I'm sorry. I mean, the clue with the command detonation. I think I remember…"

Accepting his tether to the conversation, Sergei knelt close enough to the Indonesian rider to resemble his conjoint twin. "Okay."

Remembrance rose within Volkov as he spoke. "The detonation came at the end of the torpedo's fuel." Referring to the *Nagapasa's* commander, he eyed his rider. "I'm sure he's smart enough to have waited until the last moment."

The Indonesian was cynical. "Agreed. If you wanted to make him become irrational, it didn't work."

"I'm not so sure."

"How so?"

"He didn't have to shoot. He'd already escaped, but he thought he could defeat me and earn a big trophy."

The Indonesian officer opined. "I see. He did give up clues about his position by shooting us, but his gamble might pay off. There's no word yet of our aircraft finding him."

Volkov remembered his idea. "We know the course, speed, and position the *Nagapasa's* torpedo took for much of its run. We can assume it was detonated at zero fuel and can backtrack it to where it had full fuel."

Raising an eyebrow, the Indonesian concurred. "It seems so obvious in retrospect. Of course…we can simulate the *Nagapasa's* torpedo's run perfectly on our combat systems."

"Get that recommendation to Pierre in a communication buoy immediately." Volkov lifted his gaze to his executive officer. "And tell him about our two dead colleagues so he can tell their loved ones they died under my command."

# CHAPTER 13

The *Xerxes'* bridge became a silent dome of despondency in Danielle's understanding. Numbness pervaded her, and her bones and sinews became mush.

Then a smoldering flame of fury throbbed in cadence with her pounding pulse.

Contradicting her growing fire, her pierced soul bled glaciers, and her desolate heart became ice.

Now numb, now hot, now cold, now bodiless, she phased in-and-out of space-time and between multiple psychological realms. But everywhere her tormented consciousness arrived, she suffered hellish agony.

A moment of sensory awareness anchored her to her warship, and an uncaring force–muscle memories–flicked her hand into action as she whipped her finger across a touchscreen.

Her fractured announcement arose from something foreign she'd once recognized as her own throat, and it rolled beyond the cloudy mist surrounding her as a growl of grief and rage. "I..." She cleared her tightening throat "Twenty splintering rounds... to Contact Twenty-Seven."

"Dani?"

Hearing a voice added context and texture to her ethereal existence and beckoned her back towards reality. Her rational mind groped for recovery, but grief and rage truncated and jumbled her thoughts into a cauldron of confusion.

She felt herself dissolving into the same nothingness she feared had swallowed her husband.

"Dani!"

This time, a touch to her shoulder accompanied her name, allowing her to regain self-awareness.

She had not fallen into bodiless torment.

Her torment was embodied and palpable, with unseen forces shredding her innards.

"Dani!"

Her instincts protected her from overstimulation with a lethargic return to full awareness, but she recognized the speaker. "Mike?"

"Yes! You're okay, ma'am?"

She noticed her shallow and rapid breathing. "What?"

"You're about to hyperventilate, ma'am."

Rays of the *Xerxes'* commander punched through the cloud of anguish surrounding her. "So, I'm a 'ma'am' again now?"

"I called you 'Dani' because you wouldn't respond."

Widowhood's desolation choked her, and she locked eyes with his but found no hope.

"We...I..." He lowered his gaze, recovered himself, and then faced her. "I'm sorry."

Shock and mourning skewed time, and the hostile warhead which she knew had killed her husband detonated both a moment and an eternity ago. Desperate, she looked to her monitor. "Pierre?"

Renard shut and reopened his eyes. "I, too, am terribly sorry. I myself am stunned, but I can't imagine how you must feel."

She felt gentle tears flowing down her cheeks.

The Frenchman continued. "But punishing a fishing boat's crew won't solve anything."

Her anger swelled, and it felt better than misery. She rode it as a wave of energy in reasserting herself. "It brings me some bloody justice." She aimed her nose towards the open microphone. "Port and starboard weapons bays..." Hearing the roaring pain in her voice frightened her enough to stop talking in mid-order.

Over the loudspeaker, the port bay's gunner replied. "Ma'am? Orders to the weapons bays?"

She folded her arms and pursed her lips.

Taylor raised his voice and answered. "Port and starboard

weapons bays, stand by."

"Port weapons bay, standing by."

"Starboard weapons bay, standing by."

Her body quivering, she fought to remain standing.

Taylor moved to her. "This operation is over, ma'am. Things are quiet now. I can handle the bridge, if you'd like some–"

Renard's pitch rose an octave higher. "A buoy from the *Wraith*! A buoy from the *Wraith*! Dear God, I've got a buoy from the *Wraith*!"

Unwilling to accept her husband's salvation, she feared the *Wraith's* commander had sent a heroic farewell with whatever tactical data he could. "What's it say?"

"Sorry...I was reading it while announcing it. Two dead. Delov and Kornev. One fighting for his life. The ship is intact."

Her hopes rose.

Facing his camera, Renard finished his report. "Many are injured but otherwise safe, including Dmitry."

She collapsed to her knees, pressed her palms against her face, and wept with heaving breaths.

Her husband was alive.

Minutes later, she was planted on a seat unfolded from the bridge's aft bulkhead. Through her blurry vision, she saw the Indonesian rider crouched by her side.

While aboard the *Xerxes*, Commander Lestari had shown himself a man of goodwill. He accepted her scrunched and moist tissue and then handed her a dry one. "I thought we'd lost him, too."

Relief dominated now, and she released a cathartic chuckle. Then she caught herself. "I should be more reserved. We lost two, maybe three of our own."

"No. It's okay to rejoice. We still have everyone else, including your husband. After a call that close, you're allowed to vent an emotion or two."

"Well, shit. I think I vented every one of them."

"Who could blame you?"

A chime filled the small bridge.

Standing at his console, Taylor replied. "Bridge?"

"Corpsman, sir. I request permission to enter the bridge."

Taylor pressed a key unlocking the door. "Enter!"

While hearing the medical professional's footsteps echoing up the steel stairs, Danielle protested. "I don't need the corpsman."

"Just a precaution, ma'am."

"Bloody hell, Mike. I'm not a little girl."

Ushering the rider aside, the corpsman knelt before the *Xerxes'* commander and intercepted the question Danielle had aimed at Taylor. "Not a little girl, ma'am. A commanding officer in combat. Then widowed. Then un-widowed. All in less than three minutes. That would've driven anyone bonkers. I need to examine you." He lifted a blood pressure cuff to her bicep.

"Is this really necessary?"

"Yes, ma'am. I won't take long."

"Fine."

While the cuff squeezed her, the corpsman recorded her temperature and felt her pulse. "Your body thinks it's running a marathon, ma'am."

Her heart pounding, she confessed. "I've been through worse."

"Not with me as your corpsman, you haven't, ma'am."

Noticing her trembling hands, she clasped them in her lap. "What do you need me to do?"

He reached into his shirt pocket and withdrew a pack of pills. "Take one of these. It's a Xanax. It'll calm you and help bring your vitals back to the normal range."

"Oh, come on! Please! I don't need narcotics."

"It's not a narcotic, ma'am."

"Whatever. I'll be too sloshed to think."

Lifting his nose, Taylor countered. "We're just observers, ma'am. It's Indonesian naval air versus the *Nagapasa* now."

Although she wanted to remain a lioness, the Niger River champion who'd earned the title 'Ghost Queen', she saw the truth. She'd been a mere observer since the final undersea detonation, and her client's air power had to manage hereafter.

"Fine. Give me my water, Mike."

He extracted her cup from a holder and then extended it. "Happy to, ma'am. I'll feel better if you do this."

She accepted her pill and swallowed it with a swig. "You won't feel better. I'll feel better in about five minutes, right doc?"

The corpsman nodded. "More or less."

"Okay. So, we're done here?"

Standing, the medical professional protested. "You should go to your stateroom and lie down, ma'am."

The comment pressed her deeper into her seat's cushion. She feared her crew's stares of pity, which would indicate doubt in their commanding officer, and she rubbed away smudged mascara. "I look like a mess."

"I'll walk with you, ma'am."

She eyed her caretaker. "So I can look like a weak mess under the corpsman's supervision? No."

Unhappy about discussing his patient's charisma, the corpsman sighed. "I urge you to–"

Wagging a finger at his headset, Lestari infused the dome with glee. "We found the *Nagapasa*!"

Danielle sprang to her feet. "Already?"

The Indonesian officer nodded. "A helicopter on active dipping sonar. It was searching only two miles from where Commander Volkov said to look."

Pride in her resurrected husband's skills warmed Danielle, making her wonder if good news or medication comforted her. "Fantastic!"

"We're sending another helicopter in support. "It's just a matter of time. No matter how resistant the *Nagapasa's* captain is, he'll need to snorkel before Papua."

"And then?"

"And then a helicopter shreds its head valve with twenty-millimeter rounds. Then we escort it back to its legitimate home port with cannons aimed at it. The *Lepu* and the *Pattimura* are en route. We're going to get that bastard!"

Despite Lestari's confidence, Danielle was unwilling to declare victory. "This could take hours. Your helicopters need to stay on top of it."

"They will. They train for scenarios like this. In fact, they've trained with the *Nagapasa* itself in multiple scenarios, and it couldn't escape."

Taylor interjected. "Once a helicopter has you, it has you."

"I'm still not willing to declare–"

Again wagging his finger, the rider looked downward while digesting the report in his earpiece. After a quick reply in Malay, he exposed wide eyes and a growing smile to the *Xerxes*' captain. "He surrendered."

Her jaw dropped. "Seriously?"

"The *Nagapasa* has surfaced!"

Taylor again interjected, but silently. He aimed his finger at an image of the capitulated submarine as photographed from above.

At her console, Danielle saw the photographer's boot and the helicopter's open door give the picture its perspective.

Lestari smirked. "He knew better than to tempt us to shoot him."

Enjoying the digitized image of victory, Danielle replied over her shoulder as her mind raced to make sense of the rapid developments. "Yeah…"

"And we're sending a medivac helicopter to the *Wraith*. As Mister Renard implied, one of its crew needs urgent trauma care for a head wound."

Taylor nodded his balding head towards a handset. "Now's a good time for an update to the crew, ma'am."

Agreeing, she lifted the handset and depressed its key. "Crew of the *Xerxes*, this is your captain. A lot has happened in a short period of time. Two men died aboard the *Wraith* after the *Nagapasa* command-detonated a close-aboard torpedo. Our thoughts go out to Delov and Kornev and their families."

Taylor nodded his approval as she paused and considered the grief she'd been spared.

She continued. "But our colleagues aboard the *Wraith* sent

accurate data about the *Nagapasa's* location, and Indonesian naval air proved its mettle. The *Nagapasa* has surfaced and surrendered. Let us remember our two fallen comrades as having given their lives in victory. Carry on."

The corpsman remained diligent. "Now may I escort you to your stateroom?"

At the bottom of the bridge's stairs, Danielle muscled open the watertight door and preceded the medical professional through it.

A dozen pairs of eyes stared back at her.

Some sailors' features showed joy in victory.

Some showed sadness in the young Russians' deaths.

Some showed uncertainty in processing success over the rebel submarine against the rebels' killing two of their own.

But to Danielle's relief, none showed her a shred of pity.

# CHAPTER 14

Feeling like a zombie, Terry Cahill examined the screens of the *Goliath's* bridge. He felt nothing, he recognized nothing in his tactical data, and nothing but doubt occupied his mind.

His pregnant wife was a world away, and the comforts of a Western-inspired Israel seemed less like home than it had before he'd dreamt of marrying one of its army officers.

Working closer to his native Australia than ever since departing its navy heightened his sense of no longer belonging there. The woman he'd loved in Perth long ago had rejected him, and the submarine fleet he'd loved serving had treated him no better.

A new reality of Ariella Dahan as his pregnant wife and Pierre Renard's fleet as his vocation had once enticed him with the promise of fulfillment, but they'd begun to feel like vapid replacements of his past dreams.

Loneliness crept up his spine.

He considered his new companions–friends, as he'd seen them before this mission's darkness haunted him.

Jake Slate struck him as a man of purpose. Without a mission, the American was a wayward soul, and the serene man convalescing in Renard's estate was a galaxy away from retaking command of the *Specter*. Cahill sensed their friendship breaking faster than Jake's mind had seemed to shatter in Nigeria.

Dmitry Volkov, a man he judged more docile and pensive than Jake, had offered a potential friendship–until a striking former British destroyer commander had stolen the Russian's heart.

And, of course, the distance.

Cahill was the only fleet member living in Israel, a long flight to the nearest mercenary companion.

He felt worse than alone. He felt unreal.

And after death's icy claws had clutched him a day earlier, after mortal terror had forced demonic hallucinations, he wondered if the living entity known to itself as 'Terrance Cahill' had ever existed.

While questioning the fabric of reality, he found himself doubting the existence of his own consciousness.

As the only undead creature commanding a warship, he glanced at the human form whose recent words had evaporated as unintelligible utterings. "Huh?"

Before his console, Walker replied. "I asked you what you think about testing the air defenses of the rebel tanks and artillery?"

Tactical machinations coaxed Cahill's mind back into gear. "Yeah. Why not?"

A French accent issued from a console. "Are you okay, Terry? You seemed distant during this discussion."

The *Goliath's* commander blinked. "No. No, I'm fine."

"Regardless, let me recap. Liam's referring to the recent movements of rebel hardware in preparation for a major offensive into the loyalist regions. This offers you free shots at the biggest pieces of their army. You could undermine their morale, and you could slow their progression as well."

Cahill's mind shifted into full speed. "Right, mate. But by meself without Danielle. It's going to be tough getting hits."

"I would have preferred you attacking together. However, the Chinese tankers drew you one way, and the *Nagapasa* pulled her another. So be it. Take your free shots."

Behind Cahill, the Indonesian rider reported. "We'll provide you extra air coverage. Between your MICAs and the SAMs of the *Bung Tomo*, we have plenty of ordnance to counter the anti-ship missiles of our shadows."

Icons showed the rebel frigate, *Yani*, which had protected the Chinese tankers, steaming with two smaller anti-ship missile escorts between the *Goliath* and the shoreline. Cahill lifted his gaze through the dome and saw the enemy frigate's masts jutting above the horizon. "Do we have targeting coordinates and eyes downrange on the targets?"

Commander Pasaribu answered. "We've got two drones ready to track the targets with radar and cameras. Between the two drones, we can expect sub-meter accuracy on the coordinates, even for moving targets."

"Can you send those visuals over the data link?"

"One moment." The Indonesian officer shifted to Malay, spoke into his headset, and then returned to English. "Try channels twelve and nineteen."

Cahill called up the channels and saw aerial views of trucks, tanks, artillery, and other towed equipment. The army rebels used a civilian highway which it had cleared of nonessential traffic. "Yeah. Let's do this. I don't see much chance of collateral damage. So, what can it hurt?"

Walker's tone was upbeat. "Want me to pick some targets?"

"Yeah, mate. Have at it."

Thirty minutes later, the *Goliath's* commander saw the friendly *Bung Tomo* stationed between himself and the shadowing rebel combatants. Confident any rebel retaliation against him would fail, he thought aloud. "I'm thinking of using only two rounds, one from each railgun, as a surgical test."

A French accent filled the dome. "Surgical test. An appropriate term. I agree with two rounds."

Cahill eyed Walker. "You briefed the gunners?"

"I did, sir. Two splintering rounds are ready for a ballistic intercept flight to Ground Target Eleven."

Cahill studied a screen framing two dozen pieces of heavy equipment moving as a convoy towards the loyal province of Central Papua. The eleventh target, a Harimau lightweight tank, marked the column's center. He cast his voice upward. "Port and starboard weapons bays, raise your railguns."

Icons showed the primed weapons as speakers carried the gunner's voices. "Port railgun is raised and ready... Starboard railgun is raised and ready."

Cahill studied the graphic prediction of the rounds' flights. "Looks good, Liam."

"Aye, sir. We're ready. Shall I, on automated control?"

"Launch two splintering rounds on automated control."

Walker obeyed, and hypersonic cracks thumped the bridge dome.

With a pair of drones monitoring the convoy, Cahill watched the army column continue its highway trek.

As the projectiles approached their halfway point, Walker expressed optimism. "They're not reacting."

Cahill was realistic. "They're watching. They'll react."

Ten seconds later, the aerial footage showed a gap forming in the column as vehicles forward of the rounds' predictable impact point continued onward while those behind it stopped.

Walker snorted. "A simple defense. Stop and let our rounds land on the pavement."

Cahill narrowed his eyes. "So, they're alert and tracking the sky. Let's see if they're jamming."

"Our phased array is in standby. We need to invoke guidance in twelve seconds to adjust the rounds' flights. Shall I wait until the last moment?"

The *Goliath's* commander shook his head. "No. Do it now. Maximum guidance power. Let's see what they do."

Walker reached for his screen. "I'm energizing the phased array with maximum guidance power…phased array is up… guidance is locked! The rounds have accepted our guidance!"

His gaze upon a live video feed, Cahill watched three tanks in the column race forward. "Looks like they're adjusting to our rounds' new trajectories. Check our guidance now, Liam."

Walker folded his arms. "Damn it. The *Yani* is jamming on all guidance frequencies. It's fourteen miles closer to our rounds, sir. I don't think we'll burn through it."

Cahill sensed the futility. "We won't."

The rider compounded the bad news. "Friendly ground observers are also sensing jamming from a towed radar suite."

Cahill eyed his boss' image. "Well, Pierre. No need to cry over it. This is expected, isn't it?"

"Indeed, it is. But at the cost of two cheap rounds you've illuminated our adversary's defensive readiness. This helps determine our plans going forward."

Through a drone's camera, Cahill watched his hypersonic buckshot ricochet off empty pavement and scar the highway. After the failed volley, he realized he could unload his entire ballistic arsenal for naught. "Yeah, mate. It means we need to conduct the landing, which means spilled blood."

A silence followed the dour statement, making Renard's throat-clearing cough seem loud.

Cahill tried to liven the dome he'd depressed. "We have some of the cellular-guided rounds that Danielle took to Nigeria. Shall we see if they fare any better?"

Walker opined. "It's worth a shot, sir. The gunners will need half a minute to load them."

"Do it."

Ninety seconds later, two cellular-guided rounds raced towards Ground Target Eleven.

Again, the army column split to allow the rounds a safe landing zone free of its equipment.

Cahill tried to get his rounds into his control. "Make the call, Liam. Connect to our rounds."

Walker tapped his screen. "I'm making the call..."

Seconds ticked away before Cahill replied. "And?"

"Nothing."

The rider clarified. "Our ground observers report that the army radar system is flooding the cellular spectrum."

Twenty seconds later, Cahill again watched a pair of unguided rounds ricochet off empty pavement.

The failed test underlined his limited power to thwart evil. Ambitious elites had taken half an island, declared it a country, and oppressed it. He'd nearly died trying to solve the problem, and now his four-round test of his enemy had borne no fruit.

Issuing from a console, Renard summarized the experiment.

"Our adversary is alert and ready to evade our railguns. And they've done their homework for jamming our guidance. I believe this constrains our usefulness for ground combat."

Walker kept a positive tone. "As planned from the beginning. We only tried this since we happened to be here after the tanker run. It was worth an attempt."

Cahill voiced a weak attempt at optimism. "Yeah, mate. It was."

An hour later, the *Goliath's* commander reached for the laptop on his foldout desk. As his stateroom's bulkheads created a newfound claustrophobia, he wanted to run away.

But there was nowhere to go.

As his walls moved inward, constricting his confines, he craved the metaphysical impossibility of escaping himself.

Unable to leave his own skin, he sought a sympathetic listener for solace, but his inner cry for companionship invoked vivid memories of a demonic desolation.

Who could comfort a lonely in-theater warship commander?

His wife, he thought.

But if he gave himself the privilege of telecommunications while denying it to his crew, he'd be worse than a weak leader. He'd be a hypocrite, and Ariella would know it.

He laughed through his nose wondering how fast she'd divorce him if he abused his privilege and called her.

Ephemeral joy rose with thoughts of his spouse, and then it vanished, leaving him emptier than empty.

Then, finally, the first suicidal thought of his life.

Realizing how instant and comforting he perceived death frightened him almost as much as oblivion itself.

He sought a distraction but couldn't concentrate.

He stood, moved to the door, but then reconsidered escaping his stateroom's confines. He refused to spread whatever evil oppressed him.

Instead, he turned and paced his room like a caged rabid dog.

Fearing he'd claw away his own flesh, he darted back into his seat when a hailing chime rang from the computer.

He invoked Renard's image. "Pierre?"

The Frenchman frowned. "You seem short of breath, my friend. Are you well?"

Cahill hadn't noticed his shallow breathing, which bordered on hyperventilation. He stretched the truth. "I was just pacing back and forth...for some exercise."

"Well, I'm glad you're sitting now. I have good news. The Indonesians have committed to a landing plan."

Finally, Cahill had a distraction. Better yet, he had a portent of the mission's end. "Excellent. Where? When?"

"Sorong. In three days."

Cahill envisioned the island. "That's as far from the land battles as you can get. And there's a nasty isthmus between Sorong and the main rebel forces."

"But that's the only downside. Everything else is positive. The shore is approachable, if Sorong falls the rebel fleet falls, and it's located in the most vulnerable province. Even taking the most distant province counts as a win. It would even the score, so to speak, with three Papuan provinces to each side."

"That's true only if the Indonesians can secure it before the other two provinces fall."

"True, the timing will be tight, but the plan is promising, and victory will shift morale on both sides. I was quite content with the choice of Sorong."

Cahill pondered what effect the landing would have on his morale, but his mind drifted in an opaque future.

"Terry?"

"Yeah?"

"You and your escorts need to transit to the Sorong staging area. I'll be sending your staging coordinates over the datalink."

"Okay. Good."

"Terry!"

"Yeah, mate?"

"You seem distant. Are you well?"

Cahill wanted to share his darkest fears to another person, but he stayed his tongue. His superior during a military campaign was the wrong confessor.

Unsure if he lied or merely encouraged himself, he dismissed his troubled appearance and forced a smile. "I'm fine, Pierre. It's nothing a good meal and a cup of coffee won't fix."

# CHAPTER 15

Rear Admiral Hakim gathered his thoughts before replying. "Like you, general, I regret the capture of the *Nagapasa*, but–"

His voice booming from the phone, Purnomo squashed the rebuttal. "You deployed that submarine to stop the mercenaries, but you sank only one old corvette before losing it. You now have to take on the railguns and humane torpedoes without it. That's a blunder, and it's yours."

Hakim bolstered the armor shielding his ego and protested. "I have plenty of undersea drones, sir. In fact, the *Nagapasa* was only a small part of my undersea defense."

"You expect Chinese robots to protect you?"

"They probe where my surface combatants can't go."

"And then what? Even if your drones detect targets, what can they do? They carry no weapons."

"They automatically inform my fleet, and we will prosecute any submarine in our waters."

A nasally laugh revealed the general's doubt. "And you've trained with these drones for how long? A week at most?"

"Sir, I..."

"Don't bother. You have bigger problems."

Assuming the open-ended comment was an obligation to read his boss' mind, Hakim guessed. "If you mean the railguns, I showed an effective defense during the tanker run, and we just combined my maritime assets with your ground assets to nullify the *Goliath*'s attack against one of your convoys."

"The *Goliath* was conducting a limited test. I'm concerned when I would face four railguns, and not just two."

"Of course, sir. But I'll be doubling up my combatants with close-in-weapon-systems to screen my forces from the railguns."

"Which limits your coverage area."

Hakim sensed his world becoming brittle. "We are maneuverable, sir. Nimble."

"So are they. When they come, they'll move swiftly, and we have no idea where they'll attack."

Tired of his boss criticizing his leadership, Hakim was happy to switch subjects to the loyalists' landing. "You must have some inkling from our spies."

"Too many inklings. I've heard of a dozen possible landing sites. Jakarta's overloading our spy network with disinformation."

The admiral wondered if the reply was a misdirection, and he suspected a chasm growing between himself and the junta's head. "Sir, can you tell me anything about the landing or perhaps your land movements, to help me deploy my assets?"

"Not on this line. The spy network is too strong. Beginning at the top of the next hour, I'm shifting to hand-carried cryptology. You and my other command outposts will communicate through USB sticks that I'll send you daily via armed couriers."

The daily reliance upon envoys widened the fearsome chasm separating Hakim from his boss. "I understand, sir."

"Good. My courier is en route. I'll contact you when needed."

After the line went dead, Hakim succumbed to a nagging desire to despise his leader. As the pressure of battle and nation-forming loomed heavy, it compressed that hatred into knots of twisting diaphragm muscles. Angry, he whispered to the empty office. "I'm replacing that man."

Thoughts of political alliances danced in his head.

He questioned which provincial governors would favor a naval officer heading their junta instead of a soldier. With reliance on a maritime economy, the politicians would welcome a shift from ground strength to a seaborne leader once the loyalist provinces' resistance was stomped out.

He brooded over the burden of supporting General Purnomo in solidifying their nation, compounded by his newly perceived need of supplanting the incompetent army officer.

For a moment, he wondered if his personal ambition blinded him, but then he flushed such defeatist ideas from his mind.

Opportunity had placed Purnomo in charge of a new nation's military government, but fate would soon dictate his dismissal, when the general's services were no longer needed.

A new leader would need to lead, and Hakim began to accept himself as that person.

Thoughts of running a nation unsettled him until his ambition overpowered his doubts and fueled his newfound waking dream of becoming its second head of state.

But accomplishing that required appearing obedient to its junta's first head of state, the general, while assuring there remained a country to govern.

Finally, in desperation, he tried to banish his political thoughts. He'd followed a godman in creating a new state, and a godman is never wrong.

He decided to keep trusting his boss as his secretary's voice accompanied a knock on the door. "Admiral, General Purnomo's couriers are here."

Hakim checked the time and realized he'd been comparing his rise to the presidency against his continued loyalty to Purnomo for nearly half an hour. "Enter."

A young lieutenant escorted into the office a younger looking army captain and a sergeant with a small, reinforced plastic case chained to his wrist.

The lieutenant gave a hasty greeting. "I've checked their IDs, sir. They're from General Purnomo's staff and say you need a new encryption device."

Hakim grunted and nodded.

"Shall I stay and learn how to handle this encryption on your computer, sir?"

"Yes." The admiral stood. "I'll take my leave."

Forcing a smile, the lieutenant played his role of obsequious servant. "Of course, sir. We'll have you online soon."

As Hakim passed through his door into the command center, movement caught his eye.

The cowardly captain running his surface and subsurface naval operations stirred upon seeing his boss and then carried his hefty frame around the tactical table.

Hakim disliked his underling's dour visage. "Something's wrong, Captain Moeljadi?"

"There's been a hit to morale from the *Nagapasa's* loss, sir."

The admiral narrowed his eyes. "That's understandable."

"But you praised me for sending it out to attack the loyalists. Now, we must look like blunderers for its capture."

Hakim embraced his first instinct of correcting the captain for attempting to share blame. "We who?"

The challenge sent the craven into a moment of indecision. After squirming for courage, he replied. "Us. You and me, sir. I sent the *Nagapasa*, and you publicly praised me and its crew. You awarded them medals they have yet to receive."

"I know all that. I mean, why blame yourself?"

As understanding settled upon the nervous officer, his features relaxed. "I see. You blame its commanding officer."

"Of course, I do. What idiot can't bring a submarine home with all that open water and tactical support?"

"But we called him a hero."

"He got arrogant. Leave it at that. Blame him."

"I see, sir. When the subject comes up again, I'll be sure to speak along such lines."

"Good. Anything else?"

"No, sir. Thank you." The captain turned.

Hakim stopped him. "Wait."

"Yes, sir?"

The admiral leaned forward. "Be confident when speaking of this. Any doubt will only worsen that morale problem you noticed."

"Yes, sir. I can handle that."

Hakim was unsure of the man's mettle but needed it to hold. "Good. Dismissed." Assuming he'd given the couriers time to update his computer, he pivoted back into his office.

The army couriers stepped back while the naval lieutenant

contorted his torso to operate the admiral's workstation without getting in his way. "Sir, I've installed the security program and have placed today's encryption stick in your USB drive. I'll be doing the same daily for our data center's server to allow a data link."

"Good."

"This places you on the general's virtual private network."

Hakim sat. "Now what?"

"Sir, you can hail the general's staff by clicking this icon." The lieutenant pointed at the screen and then leaned back, allowing his boss space to maneuver his arms.

Impatient, Hakim tried the icon.

A young army officer's face appeared on his screen. "Good afternoon, Admiral. I'm the command network's watch officer. My station will always be manned. How may I help you, sir?"

"How does this work?"

The soldier cleared his throat. "Sir, you may want to staff your computer twenty-four-seven. The general's staff will contact you through less secure means if necessary, but that would be only to direct you to this network. All future classified information will come over this network."

"Yes. I see." He glanced at his secretary. "Lieutenant, set up a watch rotation of junior officers to monitor my workstation when I'm not in my office."

The young naval officer nodded. "Of course, admiral."

Hakim returned his attention to the monitor. "When should I expect the general's next briefing?"

"That's scheduled for eighteen hundred hours, sir. Due to the hand-delivered encryption, you'll have to participate using the computer in which you've inserted the security dongle."

"Very well. Can I use my computer as I wish otherwise?"

"Yes, sir. But you need to guard it as you would guard a top-secret document."

"Nobody has access to this office except me and my secretary, who has the proper clearance."

"Excellent, sir. There will always be a team in this vault to answer any hails."

Hakim noticed the stark wall behind the army officer. He then noticed a phone-like graphic in a panel of his workstation's new security software. "So, I'll click on this green icon if I want the general's attention?"

"Yes, sir. It's the hailing button."

Hakim glanced at his monitor's clock and tallied almost half an hour until the briefing. "Thank you, captain. You'll excuse me." He stood, gestured towards the door, and addressed his secretary. "Lieutenant, please escort our visitors away. I'm sure they have to get back to their base."

The secretary led the army couriers from the admiral's room, leaving his boss alone.

Welcoming his solitude, Hakim gathered his thoughts.

As the complexity of his world overwhelmed him, he stood, moved to a window, and gazed upon the naval base's grounds.

A row of clipped hedges lining a manicured patch of grass distracted him from considerations of death, battle lines, and warfare. The respite felt instantaneous, but when his computer issued a chime and disturbed his calm, he calculated that he'd stared through the glass for twenty minutes.

He sat and saw the familiar image of a young army officer seated in a stark room. "Hello, admiral. The general will begin his briefing in ten minutes."

"Very well. I'll gather my staff." Hakim lifted a remote controller from his desk and sent his monitor's feed to a wall screen. He then sent an instant message from his workstation hailing his secretary.

His secretary's familiar voice accompanied a knock on the door. "May I enter, Admiral?"

"Enter."

The lieutenant opened and jutted his torso through the door. "What can I do for you, sir?"

"Get Captain Moeljadi, Colonel Soebijakto, and Colonel Pardi in here. They have five minutes."

"Aye, aye, sir!"

Five minutes later, the admiral's surface, air, and land bosses were seated in aging leather chairs facing the wall's screen. To Hakim, their banter while awaiting the briefing seemed empty beyond haughty chatter.

They fell silent when the general's visage appeared.

Hakim gasped, held his breath, and ogled the dubious godman.

Purnomo's skin seemed worn, like he'd aged a decade since the rebellion's inception, and his eyes seemed black but burning with a dark fire. "You must all maintain the utmost secrecy of what I'm about to share. It involves everything we know about our enemy and how we'll overcome them."

As a map replaced the general's image, Hakim leaned forward and pressed his elbows into his desk.

Purnomo narrated while a cursor moved across the new nation and its maritime areas. The arrow settled in Cenderawasih Bay, which squeezed the border between the eastern four and western two provinces into an isthmus. "We'll attack Central Papua. Once we take it, the final loyalist and only landlocked province, Highland Papua, will be surrounded."

Hakim recognized the potential lessening of his surface fleet's burden. The blockade within the blockade, his combatants' denial of seaborne supplies reaching his enemy, would become needless if the loyalists lost Central Papua's harbor. He welcomed the expected reduction in burned fuel and fatiguing sailors.

But he became wary of the potential diminishing of the navy's importance, as ovals with aircraft icons appeared over land and water to Purnomo's narration. "Admiral Hakim!"

The admiral replied. "Here, sir."

"Your air patrols will cover these two areas."

Flight ovals paralleled the province's northern and southern borders, leaving Hakim unimpressed. The assignment was obvious, given the geography.

Purnomo next addressed the sea presence. "I'll leave the

details up to you, admiral, but I want these three major combatants guarding air and sea access from the northeast."

Hakim held his breath as an anti-submarine-warfare corvette and two of his five anti-air-missile ships appeared in Cenderawasih Bay, north of the provincial capital city of Nabire.

The general continued revealing what the admiral considered an overconcentration of his sea power. "And I want these four combatants to the south."

Hakim's chest tightened as two more anti-submarine corvettes appeared beside two more anti-air ships.

Before he could protest, his fat surface fleet boss crinkled his seat's leather upholstery while facing him. "Sir, that leaves the rest of the nation practically unguarded."

Hakim scowled at his underling. "Silence."

Haughty, Purnomo spoke. "Is there a problem, admiral?"

"No, sir."

"I'll allow questions when I'm done." The general next showed the land forces, with icons of infantry, artillery, and tanks appearing to the north and the west.

Hakim noticed a discrepancy.

The marines, moving from Sorong and the west, had a long trek through sizable cities–homes to strong militias–towards the province's largest city of Timika. But the army, moving from its base in the north, would cover a short distance to the capital of Nabire against minimal opposition.

While swallowing bile, he watched his lean, grizzly colonel face him. But with a quick head shake, he silenced the marine officer before he could protest.

The general stated his goals. "We'll destroy loyalist morale by taking the capital and their largest population center, Nabire and Timika, respectively."

Hakim risked a challenge. "General?"

Purnomo's visage was stern. "Yes?"

"The timing. You have a larger force covering less ground to Nabire, which has a smaller resistance than Timika. It should fall faster than Timika, maybe days earlier–"

"I'll stop you there, admiral. Once Nabire is secured, we'll send all available forces to Timika as reinforcements. Surely, your marines welcome the challenge of softening the resistance and perhaps taking the city before needing assistance?"

Hakim diverted his gaze to the mountains running lengthwise across the island's center. Since the army would go the long way around the highlands, the marines taking the largest city would encounter fierce resistance for days before relief could join them.

The marines would take a beating until the army arrived to claim victory, and the admiral likened the plan to swallowing a turd through a feeding tube.

He stifled his anger. "Of course, sir. Understood."

"And to allay your fears, we'll shift close air support assets to offering your marines whatever firepower they lack."

Hakim recognized the words 'fear' and 'lack' as a verbal attack, but without leverage to counter, he played defense and steeled his voice. "I'm sure our marines will impress us as always, but I appreciate the insurance policy, so to speak."

"So to speak." Purnomo smirked. "Now, I'll turn the presentation over to Colonel Yasin to demonstrate the timing."

The general stepped away from the camera, and an army infantry officer took his place and narrated a frame-by-frame advancement of the plan over time.

As the colonel droned on about troop movements against expected resistance, Hakim checked his underlings' body language for attentiveness. Convinced they'd learn the details, he set himself free to forecast his future.

Emotions flooded him, but the frustration of his conclusions left him angry.

He judged the multitude of decisions compromising his maritime assets as Purnomo's plot to undermine his admiralty, weaken his forces, and supplant him with a puppet after solidifying his grasp of the nation. By depleting the defense near Sorong, the general had exposed the navy to Jakarta's landing.

If the loyalists enjoyed good fortune in bringing their landing craft ashore, they'd take the headquarters of Papua's navy, provided they brought the will and tenacity to bleed for victory.

Barbs of doubt pricked Hakim's soul. He inwardly wrestled with his response to the general's gamesmanship, trying to convince himself he'd see a path through it.

But a path to where?

A world under Purnomo suddenly seemed sickening, and Hakim's fervor of loyalty died.

Any doubts about his destiny as the future president evaporated while the general's selfish agenda unfolded on the large screen. He vowed it to himself–for the good populace who deserved his leadership–even if he had to violently remove the general.

But first, Hakim needed to meet the challenges of the pending ground offensive and the expected loyalist landing, and he returned his attention to the wall screen.

Purnomo replaced the colonel in the display. "We'll position our assets immediately, and we'll begin our offensive, with all ground personnel moving towards their targets weapons free, at zero-six-hundred hours tomorrow morning. That is all."

Hakim noticed the general left no time for questioning. With less than two days until the offensive and unknown time until the loyalists stormed unknown shores, Purnomo had leveraged the ticking clock as a weapon against dissent.

The three chairs of the admiral's underlings swiveled around, converting the general's former audience to his.

Hakim bought time to think by asking his staff to expose their grief. "What do you think of that?"

The air boss went first. "No complaints on the air operations, sir. But I see chinks in the rest of the plan."

Encouraged by the opening, Colonel Pardi opined. "I welcome the challenge, and my marines are up to it, sir. I'll get the men loaded and moving. It's tight timing to reach our starting points, but they'll be there in time."

"But what do you think? Speak feely."

"I think it's a textbook trick to make my marines expendable and give the glory to the general's army."

Hakim snorted. "Don't hold back your true thoughts!"

The cynicism lightened a tense mood, and the chubby surface fleet leader spoke after nervous chuckling. "I agree with the colonel, sir. But it's bad for us, too. The general wants us to overload our ships around ground movements at the expense of protecting everything else. He's even leaving this very base at risk."

Rapid knocks on the door preempted Hakim's retort. "Enter!"

Moving with rare audacity, the secretary strode to Hakim's side. "Sir, you need to see this."

"What?"

The lieutenant reached for the remote. "May I?"

"Go ahead. What's going on?"

"Jokowi." As the young officer twiddled the controller, the Indonesian president's image appeared on the screen.

In an unannounced press conference, President Widodo spoke to his nation and created a pit in Hakim's stomach. "Let's see what lies this man spins."

Meeting Hakim's expectations, Indonesia's president spent a boring fifteen minutes vilifying the rebel junta, and the admiral commentated. "Blah, blah, blah. Does he really believe anyone cares about his damned opinion?"

His subordinates chuckled.

President Widodo slowed his speech and hammered home words which nailed Hakim to a tree. "As a gesture of peace, I offer pardons for all rebel civilians except for the provincial governors and for all military personnel except for those of flag rank."

The brilliant move hit Hakim hard, and he sensed a steel wedge forming between himself and the underlings.

Widodo continued. "Governors and flag officers will stand trial for their crimes, but any such person who surrenders before the deadline will be spared from capital punishment. My offer expires in seventy-two hours from midnight tonight. Anyone who fails to surrender before the deadline will stand trial without this clemency."

After the president bid his farewell, Hakim ripped the remote from his secretary's hand and shut off the broadcast. "I trust none of you are foolish enough to believe him."

His audience reassured him of their loyalty.

"Good. Go to your staffs and make sure they also doubt Jokowi's lies. And make it clear that cowardice will not be tolerated."

As the officers shuffled through the door, a frantic naval commander stood in their way and barked. "Captain Moeljadi!"

The hefty officer stopped. "What?"

"The *Kaisiepo* has abandoned its patrol area and is not answering our hails, sir."

"Damn it!"

His world shattering with cruel revelations, Hakim felt heaviness crushing him. "Captain, I give weight to your opinion. Do you really think the *Kaisiepo's* captain is capable of treason? Convincing his crew to join him?"

The craven's glassy stare revealed the unspoken irony that every warrior in Papua had committed treason against Indonesia. "Yes, sir. If I had to guess, he expected Jokowi's message and waited until a public commitment before running. I didn't think he'd turn against us, but in my mind, he was a risk."

Hakim recalled his surface ships' patrol areas. "You've got enough firepower nearby to prevent the escape, don't you?"

"I do, sir."

"Very well. Destroy the *Kaisiepo*."

# CHAPTER 16

After watching President Widodo's speech, Cahill silenced his console and spoke over his shoulder. "Did you know about this?"

His ankle crossed over his leg, the Indonesian rider in the foldout seat of the rear bulkhead shrugged. "People were talking about it, but I was ordered not to mention it until it happened."

"Well, shit, mate. It just happened."

"I know. And I–" The rider raised one index finger and pressed the other against an earpiece. He exchanged short sentences in Malay into his boom microphone. Shadows cut across his features but then receded as his eyes widened. "The corvette, *Kaisiepo*, is defecting."

Cahill's stomach twisted. "No shit?"

Standing beside his boss, Liam Walker intercepted the question. "Check out the data link. It's accelerated to flank speed and has turned towards the quarantine boundary."

The *Goliath's* commander viewed an upper screen which showed icons of nearby ships, and he noticed the *Kaisiepo* pointing towards a weak spot in the loyalist blockade. "What do you know about the commanding officer?"

Behind him, the rider replied. "Nothing abnormal. A clean sheet. But after a third of our navy committed treason, it's hard to judge."

Cahill eyed the distances between combatants near the fleeing corvette. "The *Kaisiepo's* going to stay out of cannon range of any combatant, but there's plenty of missile shooters that can reach."

From a console, Pierre Renard quipped. "Hostile and friendly shooters, that is. You're within twenty miles, and I must remind you of our rules of engagement, that you may defend a defector but not counterattack or provoke the rebels."

Though Cahill knew the rules were clear, the Indonesian officer felt compelled to confirm them. "I concur with defense but without permission to counterstrike or provoke."

Walker advanced the conversation. "We're just outside of MICA range, sir. But if we accelerate to flank, we can reach–"

As Cahill watched his screen, unwanted information appeared, and his blood ran cold. He shouted the memorized vernacular he'd learned during operations with NATO-trained colleagues. "Vampires! A patrol aircraft has detected three in flight!"

Commander Pasaribu spat rapid Malay into his headset and then translated the exchange. "The *Bung Tomo* confirms anti-ship missiles on its air search radar."

Cahill verified his radar was void of hostile data. With low mast heights, the *Goliath* would be last among friendly assets to detect the sea-skimmers. But the feed from Indonesian sensors kept tally on the rebel weapons as their changing geometries exposed them. "We see five vampires now, from at least two shooters. It's a coordinated attack."

Two seconds later, Walker commented. "Now we see seven vampires, sir, from three shooters. I'm going to call it eight vampires and assume three minor combatants unloaded their arsenals."

After banter in Malay, the rider agreed. "The *Bung Tomo's* commander tracks eight vampires from three missile boats targeting the *Kaisiepo*. Vampires one and two are C-802's from the *Layang*, three and four are C-705's from the *Alamang*, and five through eight are Exocet Block 3's from the *Kerambit*."

Walker's furrowed brow cast shadows over his eyes. "The *Kaisiepo* has only eight Mistrals, sir. And the vampires are set to arrive on four separate axes."

With the operation's first anti-ship warheads in flight, Cahill's heart pounded. He closed his eyes and saw the memory of a waking nightmare, a vision of sagging and torn skin that had taunted him during his earlier brush with death. He rubbed his eyes and blinked. "Shit, mate. There's not a bloody thing we can do."

The rider was somber. "If it comes to it, we can help the survivors."

From the console, Renard agreed. "Indeed. You and your escorts must prepare for rescue operations, should a missile find its mark. Keep your anti-air defenses ready, but above all, hold back your offensive fires. No retaliation unless attacked."

Wanting time to think, Cahill delegated. "Liam, coordinate with the *Basri* and the *Bung Tomo* to position ourselves to render assistance to the *Kaisiepo*."

Half a minute later, the *Goliath* pitched with the waves of the gentle seas, following the spreading wake of the accelerating escort corvette, *Basri*.

Nobody on the bridge spoke, and cooling fans provided the audible background for the men's silent viewing through the glassy dome.

Lowering his binoculars, Walker shook his head. "I can see smoke rising from the nearest Exocets, for what it's worth. We're too low to see anything else."

Pasaribu added. "Even the *Bung Tomo's* crow's nest is too low to see, but we can watch on the drone."

"We're just out of range to help. This is cruel." Cahill lowered his gaze to a screen showing the desperate *Kaisiepo* from the western sky. The corvette's forward Mistral launcher spat exhaust fumes while sending its first supersonic missile into the air. "God help them."

Eyeing the drone's feed, Walker whispered his compassion for the *Kaisiepo* and its crew. "Come on."

In one display, contrails from the supersonic Mistrals raced from the *Kaisiepo* offscreen. In another, icons of the protective missiles merged with those of the incoming vampires.

Seconds ticked away, and icons vanished.

In Cahill's peripheral vision, flashes burst from the horizon as tiny warheads directed metal towards the fuselages of the anti-ship menaces. Eight flashes bloomed in the missile-versus-missile engagement.

Five vampires disappeared.

But three escaped their pursuing Mistrals' defensive blasts and continued toward the target.

"Shit." Cahill sighed and watched the *Kaisiepo's* point defenses rise to life. The cannon cracked, the twenty-millimeter guns chattered, and decoy launchers popped chaff clouds.

Tense, the rider yelped. "Splash Vampire Four!"

Shifting his eyes between icons and the video of the threatened corvette, Cahill whispered. "Six down. Two to go." As the *Kaisiepo* drove underneath its directed chaff cloud, he watched one of the remaining missiles race over the vessel.

Then the other raced over it.

Walker was reserved. "Chaff worked once, but those vampires are doubling back."

Cahill lamented. "Doubling back with real-time adjustment. They won't be fooled again by the chaff cloud."

Anti-air gunfire belched metal towards a surviving vampire, and the rider announced success. "Splash Vampire Two. Only Vampire Six, an Exocet, remains."

Then the unthinkable happened.

The Exocet punctured the *Kaisiepo* amidships and detonated.

Watching the drone's feed, Cahill imagined himself witnessing a sales video of an armaments demonstration.

As countless engineers had designed the destruction, the Exocet's warhead performed to perfection. An explosion burst from the entrance wound in the corvette's hull, ripping metal outward.

Cahill imagined the carnage within the penetrated compartment. In his mind's eye, sailors closest to the explosion disappeared into mist while a scorching pressure wave pancaked others against buckling bulkheads.

Those were the lucky ones.

Sailors more distant from the warhead would survive to endure charred flesh falling from their burning bodies.

And the remainder of the crew would fight secondary fires, busted pipes carrying high-pressure fluids and gases, toxic fumes, and flooding from cuts below the waterline.

Cahill faced the rider who was standing behind him. "I'm sorry. The crew was brave and defended their ship well."

The Indonesian officer nodded somberly.

Walker added his condolences. "Yeah, mate. We'll do whatever we can for the survivors."

From a console, Renard advised. "Remember defense only. Create a shield of anti-air protection around the *Kaisiepo*, but don't let your emotions compel you to aggression."

Cahill examined icons. "There's nothing left for the shooters to shoot. They unloaded their anti-ship arsenals, and they're driving away. This is over except for helping our mates on the *Kaisiepo*."

After exchanges in Malay, the rider updated the mercenaries. "We're awaiting damage reports, but my superiors fear the *Kaisiepo* will be lost."

Walker opined. "Yeah. I don't think it can handle an Exocet."

A history lesson from a classroom in Jervis Bay Australia bloomed in Cahill's head. "In the late eighties, the USS *Stark* survived two Exocets."

Walker countered. "I remember that, too. Persian Gulf."

"Yeah."

"But only one of them exploded. So, it was really only one Exocet, plus burning fuel and kinetic energy from the other."

"Still, a frigate survived an Exocet."

"Yes, sir. But the *Kaisiepo's* only a third as big as the *Stark*."

Cahill grunted.

"The ship's going down, sir. May as well accept it."

"The *Basri* and *Bung Tomo* can help survivors. We're not needed for that, and I'm sick of doing nothing."

Renard challenged his employee. "Terry?"

"Yeah, mate?"

"What's on your mind?"

Cahill wrestled with ideas, trying to merge abstract thoughts and tangible images into a meaningful act. "Not sure yet."

With the damaged combatant over the *Goliath's* horizon,

the rider remained in constant touch with his countrymen to receive updates and shared the latest news. "The *Kaisiepo's* captain is flooding starboard compartments to mitigate his list to port and to reduce transverse stresses on its hull."

The *Goliath's* commander shot back. "But can he stay afloat?"

"He hasn't made that decision yet. Damage and casualty reports are still coming in."

An idea gelled in Cahill's head. "I didn't leave me pregnant wife behind in Israel to watch a friendly corvette sink."

Walker glared at him. "I know what you're thinking, sir. And I don't like it."

Seeking solace, the rider queried. "What's he thinking?"

"He wants to dive below the *Kaisiepo* and lift it."

Cahill replied. "I'm not sure how this could play out, but I need to act fast to keep it out of Davy Jones' locker."

Betrayed in his voice, the rider's hope rose as he eyed the empty cargo bay. "You can put the *Kaiseipo* in there?"

"I haven't figured that out yet, either, but we've done something similar before in this fleet."

Walker raised an eyebrow. "The *Tarantuls*?"

"Yeah. The *Xerxes* lifted one in rehearsal and another in combat."

"But a *Tarantul's* three times smaller than the *Kaisiepo*. You're exaggerating your arguments by a factor of three, sir."

"We lifted the *Tarantuls* almost all the way out of the water, mate. But we don't need to with the *Kaiseipo*. We only need to nudge its hole higher."

Walker was adamant. "We could tilt the ship if we try, sir, making their damage control efforts–"

Cahill quipped. "If all arguments were straightforward, Pierre could replace me with an AI. But when that happens..." He extended his finger towards the smoke rising from the warhead's damage. "...he needs command decisions."

Renard accepted the segue. "And what's your decision?"

The *Goliath's* commander thought aloud. "I'm still making it. I won't be saving any lives by lifting it, but our mission is to spare

Indonesian military assets, human and machine."

With his profit motive tied to Indonesian losses, Renard revealed his skewed opinion. "You'd preserve hundreds of millions of euros worth of hardware by saving the *Kaisiepo* for repairs."

Cahill drew encouragement from his boss' tone. "Then I'm doing it. Liam, we've got twenty minutes before we arrive on station. Get with our loading team and review our procedure against our design and a schematic of the *Kaiseipo*. Make sure it can fit without us worsening its list."

Accepting the command, Walker turned and scurried down the bridge's stairway.

Twenty minutes later, Cahill aimed his ship at the bow of the listing corvette. He faced the *Kaiseipo* bow-to-stern so he could examine the port-side wreckage from the bridge dome.

In the low sun, he saw evidence of destruction where smoke from solid propellant and secondary fires billowed from the combatant's belly and from the twin smokestacks of its ventilation system.

Three horizontal fountains showed the crew's effort to supplement the bilge drain effluence with portable pumps, but men in lifejackets gathering topside betrayed the fear of many sailors.

Beside the combatant, a *Dorang*-class patrol boat abandoned its quarantine duties in favor of shooting high-pressure seawater through the open wound. Two horizontal streams injected fluid into the *Kaisiepo* where hydraulic fluid burned above the Cenderawasih Bay's sea level.

The rider stepped to the *Goliath's* commander. "I have a damage control update. May I show you?"

"Use Liam's station."

Extending his arm, the Indonesian officer invoked a menu of the *Kaiseipo's* schematic and then pointed. "The missile hit here, in the Port Machinery Room. The blast broke through every boundary of that room except the deck. The overhead was compromised, which is sending smoke into the ship. The forward bulkhead buckled, which flooded the Port Auxiliary Room."

Cahill followed the lesson earnestly. "Above Port Auxiliary is a berthing area."

"Yes, and fortunately, it was empty while at general quarters. The port bulkhead is beyond shoring and is allowing free flooding into Central Machinery."

Cahill drew a conclusion. "And the captain flooded Starboard Machinery to reduce stresses on the keel."

"Right. But here's the big problem." The rider pointed to the port engine room. "Port Machinery's aft bulkhead is losing its watertight integrity."

"Flooding in the engine room. The worst place."

"And the captain reports that bilge pumps and portable pumps aren't keeping pace. The water level in Port Engineering is rising. If that doesn't change, the ship is lost."

"Damn it." A gentle chime directed Cahill's finger to a communication circuit. "Bridge."

From the *Goliath's* Control Room, Walker sounded eager. "It's the executive officer, sir. I request permission to enter the bridge."

Cahill tapped an icon unlocking the door, which his enthusiastic exec threw shut behind him before trotting up the stairs.

Pasaribu stepped aside and let Walker have his console.

Cahill sought news. "What do you have, Liam?"

"We can stabilize and support the *Kaiseipo*, but not in our cargo bed. Its keel is shallower and broader than I'd thought, like our *ANZAC* frigates. So, our cargo bed won't tilt it any worse. We'll hold the underbelly from both sides."

"Directly on our hulls?"

Walker shrugged. "Yes, sir. That's the bad news. We'll probably rip off all twenty-four hydraulic rams and a few external cameras. But any other damage would be superficial."

From the console, Renard intercepted the question. "Since the decision seems more financial than tactical, allow me. Do it. You described no more than two million euros of damage to the *Goliath*, and that's a rounding error on the value of saving that ship."

The *Goliath's* commander gave his order. "Liam, get the crew ready for this loading operation and prepare to submerge the ship."

"Wait!" The Indonesian officer raised his finger and pointed at his earpiece. After an exchange in Malay, he gave an update. "The captain declares the ship lost. He's ordering his crew to life rafts."

"No! This will work. Tell him we have a plan." Cahill looked skyward in search of answers, and the hidden sun emerged from behind low clouds. He hoped that fate bathed him in nature's light as a positive sign.

The rider nodded. "I'll ask again."

While the Indonesian officer again chattered in Malay, Walker opined. "He may fear structural damage if we try."

The *Goliath's* commander retorted. "Torpedoes and mines snap keels. Missiles hit well above waterlines."

"But on a ship that small–"

Cahill refused inaction. "I don't care. If I want to put me ship underneath one that splits in half, that's up to me." He shifted his gaze to the Frenchman's digital image. "Pierre?"

"I'm not stopping you. It's dangerous, but it's a sound decision. Your ship's built for it, and I trust you."

Appreciating the support, the *Goliath's* commander craved success. "Can you intervene?"

"I'll hail the admiral in–"

Pasaribu interrupted. "The *Kaiseipo's* captain agrees to let you try, but he's concerned about the list. If it gets to thirty degrees, he'll abandon ship."

Cahill snapped. "We have two hulls. We'll hold him like a baby in a cradle. Tell him!"

Nodding, the officer spoke in his native language. After a silent pause, the man's smile revealed the answer. "The captain will continue damage control efforts while you try it."

Twenty minutes later, sunlight broke through the submerged but shallow dome. Cahill spied a bright icon on a console verifying his full-speed, two-way communications with his boss and his clients, which a raised mast from his starboard weapons bay retained.

Skilled operators in the compartment below handled his four outboard motors and slid his ship underneath the damaged *Kaiseipo*. The *Goliath's* commander enjoyed an upward perspective of the listing corvette's hull.

As Cahill passed the combatant's sonar system, it served as a signpost below the keel marking progress towards the damage, and he shifted his gaze ahead. The patrol boat had paused its firefighting to give the submerged transport vessel maneuvering space.

Seconds later, outwardly torn metal shaping a three-meter-wide and five-meter-tall hole appeared above.

A dark shape jutted through the opening and rested on the lower lip of ripped metal. Shimmering water toyed with the perspective, and Cahill imagined he saw a human head.

Still aching from his narrow escape from torpedoes, he thought he saw a face charred to its sinews and frozen in a scream, and he gasped. "What the hell is that?"

Calm, Walker replied. "I can't tell. But if I had to guess, maybe a block valve from a hydraulic actuator."

Cahill lowered his gaze. Grateful as the ripped metal slid behind him, he closed his eyes. Again, the memory of a waking nightmare, the sagging and torn skin of infernal origin, tormented him.

For unknown time, he battled his inner demon to a stalemate until his starboard hull bumped the corvette.

Walker announced the status. "We're pushing the *Kaisiepo* up."

Cahill's mind returned to reality. "Yeah. Good work, mate."

"As long as the swells cooperate, we may keep our hydraulic rams, sir. So far, they're bearing the strain."

A minute later, the rider spoke. "The list is improving! Half a degree already."

Ten minutes later, the *Goliath* held the *Kaisiepo* level atop its twin hulls. Cahill then had his rover camera sent towards the damage to verify it was safe for a repair team.

Then the patrol boat returned to the firefight and deployed two divers into the compartment.

After a long half hour, the report came through the rider. "The divers say they can make enough repairs to minimize the flooding into Port Engineering for the pumps to keep pace."

Cahill was bullish on his effort's success. "And the ship can be salvaged?"

"It's hard to say until it reaches a dry dock for examination, but I'm hearing a lot of optimism in the background chatter."

The *Goliath's* commander realized the cost of his salvage effort. "I may be stuck underneath for a while."

From the console, Renard soured the success. "For days."

Cahill protested. "Is that an estimate, or is that a decision?"

"It's a decision. There's too much damage for the *Kaisiepo* to trust patchwork repairs. I want you to stay with it all the way to port. Unfortunately, I'll have to remove the *Goliath* from the landing."

Cahill slumped his shoulders. "I compromised our mission?"

Renard scowled. "No! I could order you to abandon the *Kaisiepo* to its fate, but I imagine a bulkhead giving way or bilge pumps failing. It's one casualty from seeing its winning battle to stay afloat become a defeat."

Pasaribu consoled the Australian. "This isn't exactly your mission parameters, but it's the sort of action we needed."

Part of Cahill knew he'd done the right thing, but a darker part lamented yielding his part in the contested landing. He'd wanted to prove himself in combat after the jolt two torpedoes and a diabolical vision had delivered.

But inner demons told him he'd salvaged the corvette just to sidestep danger, leaving him cold and empty.

# CHAPTER 17

Hakim released a sardonic laugh and then praised his underling, raising himself for having issued the order. "Congratulations Captain Moeljadi. Your ships performed wonderfully."

The obese officer beamed. "Thank you, sir. The *Kaisiepo* won't be creating any more problems for us."

Hakim enjoyed the feed from a drone which showed the still-burning corvette drifting below the setting sun. As his surface fleet's first trophy cast long shadows, he drew extra motivation from the mercenary combatant stuck underneath it. "This is better than sinking it. The *Kaisiepo* and the *Goliath* will both be unavailable to challenge us."

Captain Moeljadi's smile waned. "Sir, we do need to address the gap this leaves in General Purnomo's plan. He wanted the *Kaisiepo* in his northern maritime defenses."

Success fueled the admiral's courage. "I will inform him of the unfortunate loss to his plan. I'm not whittling down our defenses here in Sorong to replace it. In fact, I'll call him now and inform him of our victory."

"Good idea, sir."

The admiral gave a vapid order. "See what you can do to compensate for the loss of the *Kaisiepo*."

"Of course, sir."

As Hakim turned towards his office, he saw his secretary marching to him. "Admiral, the general is hailing you. He's on the line waiting, sir."

"Ah, good timing. Tell him I'll be right there." Hakim bragged over his shoulder while walking away. "He must be calling to congratulate us. I'll be back with good news soon."

Hakim was haughty as he sat and used the encrypted network. "I was just going to call you, sir, to tell you about my fleet's flawless reaction to the *Kaisiepo*."

"I'm not interested in your bragging, admiral. I'm calling to inform you of a new problem."

The general's immediate dismissal of his success angered the admiral. He grit his teeth and then replied. "I'm listening, sir."

"The families of the *Kaisiepo's* crew are trying to escape. My spies have seen key crewmembers' families boarding a chartered deep sea fishing boat."

Hakim inwardly raged against the families–not for escaping, but for necessitating the difficult decision for which he'd be judged, and he vilified them. "The *Kaisiepo's* crew has placed their families in danger."

"And their fates rest squarely upon the shoulders of the treasonous crew. I'll let you deal with it, but make sure you give a clear message to other would-be traitors."

Hakim prodded for clarity on his orders, which seemed less like a command than a wink. "A message about the consequences of disloyalty?"

"Precisely. The fishing ship's name is the *Blue Fin*, and it's leaving from Amamapare."

"Amamapare. The *Blue Fin*. Understood, sir."

"Take care of it, and remember, they brought this upon themselves." The screen went dark.

Hakim whispered obscenities.

His boss, a failing godman, attempted to reassert his deity by killing dozens of innocents, and within his iron fist of tyranny he'd squeezed Hakim into the role of triggerman.

Trapped in cognitive dissonance, Hakim wrestled with his shattered conscience until he banished the soft inner voice harkening his rejection of Purnomo's order, veiled in cryptic ambiguity, to kill the *Kaisiepo's* crew's families.

Survival instincts concocted phantom threats, political and military, that would destroy him if he resisted. Feeling helpless, he justified his actions by condemning the innocent.

By having placed him in this predicament, they were guilty, and after shallow deliberation, he accepted his path– and the embellishments and crafted lies that would mark it.

Stradling blurry lines between sailor and statesman, between servant and master, forced Hakim to rationalize his choice. He needed to obey Purnomo now, do the difficult task, and trust himself to manage the fallout. But the only way to protect himself was to sacrifice a lackey to take the fall.

He strolled across his office's worn carpet to its door, opened it, and jutted his head through the frame. "Lieutenant?"

The subordinate stood. "Yes, sir?"

"Have Colonel Soebijakto report to my office."

"Aye, sir."

"But tell him to wait five minutes before reporting. I don't want anyone to be alarmed."

The young officer gave a knowing look. "I'll handle it, sir."

Five minutes later, Hakim was seated at his desk. "We've got a problem, and I need one of your aircraft to fix it."

Seated opposite his de facto boss, the short pilot replied. "Just one aircraft, sir? I'm getting the entire airwing ready for the offensive. What's going on?"

I just heard from the general." Knowing that lying would get easier as his deception unfolded, Hakim uttered his first untruth. "A group of traitors has commandeered a sport fishing boat and intends to attack one of our major combatants."

"You're serious, sir?"

"Yes. And they'll feign a fire and request evacuation assistance to dupe the *Harun* to come close. Then they'll attack."

"How, sir?"

"Anti-tank missiles. Stolen or perhaps taken with unspoken permission from the loyalist military. Enough warheads to cripple or even sink the *Harun*."

"Stolen?" The subordinate's eyes narrowed. "So, it's not a military operation?"

"No, sadly. Civilian extremists have gone rogue, and the worst of it is they're using human shields."

"No! Who? How?"

"The general said they've taken prisoners aboard, mostly women and children."

"Women and children?"

"Yes."

"This is a lot to take, sir. Something like this can't end well."

For effect, the admiral nodded slowly. "The responsibility is upon their shoulders for what must be done. And because of the sensitive nature of this order, I want you to use just one aircraft."

"Of course, sir. Do you expect any anti-air missiles?"

Embellishing his lie, Hakim conjured an answer. "No. These cretins extended their luck far enough by grabbing the anti-tank weapons."

"Then one aircraft will be sufficient, sir. Do you want the engineering spaces strafed to cripple the vessel for boarding?"

"You'll notice that Captain Moeljadi's not in the room."

"I don't follow you, sir."

Hakim insulted the underling to divert his focus from his deception. "I don't think you understand me, colonel. We're supporting a major offensive tomorrow while defending against a possible landing. We have no time for prisoners, nor can the junta tolerate the attention such prisoners would garner."

Accepting the discomfort, Colonel Soebijakto folded his arms, furrowed his brow, and brooded. Then he snorted and joined the admiral in a shared world of rationalized violence. "I get it, sir. We can minimize the number of people who'll know about this. I hate it, but the deaths of human shields rest squarely on the shoulders of those who exploit them."

Hakim coaxed his accomplice with pandering words. "It takes a strong man to see that."

"Let's get this done before they can cripple the *Harun*, sir."

"Call up a southern drone and find it on visual. The ship's name is the *Blue Fin*, and it's leaving from Amamapare."

"Amamapare. I see. The *Harun* is the nearest major

combatant."

"And it's one of our largest and most modern ships. It would be an unacceptable loss, especially to such an underhanded attack."

"It would be disgraceful. It can't happen."

Seeing his fiction digested, Hakim felt a childish pride for having duped another. "No, it can't."

"I know the right pilot. He's young and ambitious, and he'd do anything for career advancement. He's hungry for approval and will jump at this."

"Excellent. Where's he now in your flying rotation?"

"He's the wingman for my Alert-Five sortie."

"Bump one of your other aircraft to his position, and get him ready for this."

"Of course, sir. When do you want him airborne?"

"Ten minutes. But first, brief him on a private line."

"And file the sortie with flight control after he agrees?"

"If you must."

The colonel smirked. "Since you and General Purnomo were wise enough to remove my incompetent higher-ranking officers, it's my air force. I can have flight control grant him the airspace while knowing nothing about his mission."

The ease with which he manipulated the colonel made Hakim wonder if Purnomo had done the same with him. "You're proving our decision to trust you."

The colonel pulled a cell phone from his pocket. "Would you like him on speakerphone?"

Hakim stood. "No. Talk to him alone while I inform Captain Moeljadi. His surface commanders need to know about this, since they monitor the air space."

"Understood. The Air Force will see it done, sir."

Hakim placed his palm on the colonel's shoulders while marching past him. "I know. It's a difficult order, but I am one-hundred percent certain you can handle it."

In the control center, Hakim gestured for his marine and surface bosses to join him in a private conversation. Obedient,

Colonel Pardi and Captain Moeljadi stepped away from the charting table and joined him beyond the earshot of others. "We have a grave situation."

The officers nodded.

Using another lie, Hakim clarified. "A young pilot is attempting to defect with his aircraft."

Gasps and frowns.

"Colonel Soebijakto is trying to talk him out of it, but I'm afraid it may be too late."

The marine replied. "When will it be too late, sir?"

"An excellent question. I don't want him escaping our airspace, which leaves us little time, but I fear the stakes are higher than that."

The naval officer queried. "Violence, sir? You fear he may employ his weapons against us?"

Hakim eyed the pudgy man. "Against us or even random targets."

"That's terrorism, sir, and we can't allow it. Do you need me to shoot him down?"

The swallowed lie encouraged the admiral. "Let him show aggression first, either a weapon's firing or maneuvering for a strafing run."

"I'll have all my ships watch for him. If he shows hostile intent, do I have permission to bring him down?"

"Yes, but wait for aggression. I want to let Colonel Soebijakto resolve this without losing an aircraft, hopefully before the man takes off."

"He's still on the ground?"

Hakim nodded. "In an Alert-Five aircraft, fully loaded, and there's no stopping him from taking off. He'll probably head south or southwest if the colonel fails to change his mind."

"He won't get by my ships, sir, but I need to inform my unit commanders. Will you excuse me?"

"Not yet. First, I want you to call me on my cell immediately when you gain the aircraft on radar."

"Aye, sir! I'll call."

As the captain waddled away, the marine glared. "You want me here for some other reason, sir?"

Another slow nod preceded the next untruth. "Colonel Soebijakto had evidence of this pilot's disloyalty for some time, but he still put him in an alert aircraft. He ignored the signs, and he's trying to wiggle out of the responsibility in my office. But he put a psychologically unstable pilot on the tarmac."

"That was foolish at best."

"And disloyal at worst. I believe the colonel's expecting me to empathize with his errors, but he miscalculated and has lost my confidence. That's why I need you."

"Whatever you need, sir. Disloyalty is intolerable, especially on the eve of battle."

"Station military police by my door and be ready to take him to the brig when I call on you or if he tries to leave."

While sorting through implications, the marine hesitated before replying. "I'll need something to charge him with, sir. Since we've stuck to our former code of military justice, incompetence isn't a jailable offense."

"No, it's not. But treason is, which he's all but confessed in his ignoring of the warning signs."

"Understood, sir. I'll station my military police at your door."

"I suspect that Widodo's dangling carrot of a pardon captured the young pilot's imagination and has confused the colonel."

"That's possible, sir."

"I'll want him bound and gagged so he doesn't spew propaganda on the way out."

Colonel Pardi winced. "He didn't show any signs, sir. I've been working beside him for weeks."

Hakim folded his arms and pretended to reflect upon the quandary unfurled within his fiction. "Stress and doubt can turn weaker men into jellyfish. I need your support in ridding us of his cowardice."

"I'll see to it, sir."

Five minutes later, the admiral sat at his desk and eyed his deceit's victim. "Where is he?"

"He's just become airborne, climbing to five-thousand feet."

"Good." Hakim's phone rang, and he lifted it. "Go ahead."

Close to the admiral's ear, the speaker carried Captain Moeljadi's voice. "We've got an F-16 on radar, sir. It took off from the alert response runway, as you predicted. Several ships are tracking it."

"Very well." Confident he'd duped the surface commander into shooting down the unwitting pilot, the admiral hung up and returned his attention to the colonel. "How long until he's on target?"

"Two minutes, sir."

"You've got visual?"

"Not anymore, sir. I verified the *Blue Fin's* location within a large swath of water so that the drone operator wouldn't get suspicious, and then I had him immediately return the drone to surveillance."

"Good thinking." Seconds passed like eternities as Hakim wanted his problems to disappear into a forgettable past.

The colonel twisted, revealing the earpiece and microphone dangling down the side of his neck. As his fledgling air force's senior officer, Soebijakto apparently enjoyed privileged phone communications. "The pilot has a visual. He's passing far behind the *Blue Fin* to identify its name on its stern."

"What's needed to confirm the shot?"

"Only my order."

Hakim's heart pounded with fear and shame, a shame beyond bearing that he painted over with the pride of being strong enough to carry out difficult deeds. "Well?"

Colonel Soebijakto raised a finger. "Understood. Target is identified as the *Blue Fin*. You are weapons free. Take the shot." He lowered his finger. "We have one Maverick missile launched, and it's locked onto the target, sir."

Unable to speak, Hakim nodded.

Springing to his feet, the colonel yelped. "What? Get out of there. Evasive maneuvers!"

Feigning ignorance, Hakim also stood. "What's wrong?"

"Surface-to-Air missiles, sir. Two Sea Cepters on his radar."

The admiral pretended to blame the loyalist ship shadowing the *Harun*. "From the *Muda*?"

"He says it's from the *Harun*, but that's illogical."

"Keep him calm. Help him out of this." Hakim stormed by the colonel to his office's exit. He opened the door and saw Colonel Pardi standing with four military police. "Arrest Colonel Soebijakto for treason."

"Arrest Colonel Soebijakto for treason, aye, sir." The marine colonel led his detail into the admiral's office.

Closing the door behind him, the admiral strolled towards the tactical table, pondering the intricacies of his lies. Bending to his will, reality became misty as he joined the animated captain. "Is it over?"

The captain steeled his face, but his rosy cheeks revealed his excitement. "Splash one F-16 and its traitor pilot. We got him, sir."

Hakim slapped the man's fleshy back and patronized him. "Well done, Captain Moeljadi."

"Thank you, sir. Unfortunately, our anti-air assets weren't in range to destroy the hostile missile. Jamming is failing also. It's going to hit."

Hakim had ignored the disparate flight times of the airborne weaponry, with the smaller anti-air missiles flying faster than their anti-ship counterparts. After hearing of the Maverick's expected detonation, he sighed in relief but feigned compassion. "Do what you can for any survivors."

"Of course, sir. I'm sending small boats."

"Good."

"I've also vectored a drone camera toward the target, sir. It's a fishing boat." Fat fingers danced across the table, and a black-and-white video of the *Blue Fin* appeared.

The image went white with the Maverick's impact. Then the *Blue Fin*, a luxurious fisherman the *Kaisiepo's* crew had rented, rolled to its starboard side and slipped lower into the water.

Secondary fires burned, and smoke hid much of its hull.

As the ship settled into a foundering death, pulled straight down by its flooding weight, a fiery figure appeared on its fantail.

Hakim discerned a female human form carrying an infant in its arms while scorching fuel and clothing traced dancing flames around its victims.

Dusk's failing illumination backlit the Madonna and Child into a stark juxtaposition of silhouette and fire. Seeking water to soothe her unquenchable agony, the woman faltered and fell to the deck.

Unable to grasp his reaction, much less voice one, Hakim watched in silence as water rose to the burning corpses, quenched their fire, and swallowed them into the abyss. He then forced his next lie. "This is on Colonel Soebijakto. He could have stopped this, but he didn't."

Stunned by the horror, the captain said nothing.

"See if you can find survivors."

Emotional, the captain responded weakly. "Aye, sir."

Hakim needed solitude. "I must show Colonel Soebijakto his shame. I will make him watch the recording."

Captain Moeljadi scowled. "An outrage."

The admiral shifted his gaze to the most senior Air Force officer. "Lieutenant Colonel Sinurat, I've had your former superior arrested. It's now your air force."

"Aye, sir. I won't let you down."

Sensing his escape, Hakim marched away. While out of earshot of others, he whispered to himself. "Be hard, my heart. Be hard."

# CHAPTER 18

Dmitry Volkov's head throbbed, but seeing his sailors returning his ship to combat readiness comforted him. "It's not broken, is it?"

"You'd be on the medevac helicopter if I'd even suspected."

"Then why's it pounding?"

"Pain is a good sign."

From his folded-out captain's chair on the *Wraith's* elevated conning platform, Volkov chided his medical expert. "So says the guy whose head isn't pounding."

The corpsman scowled. "Your thick Russian skull took the blow, sir. You're lucky compared to some others."

The *Wraith's* commander lamented his two dead crewmen and the many serious injuries. "Don't remind me."

"None of us will ever forget."

"True."

"Do you want pain medications?"

Volkov declined. "I can't cloud my mind with opioids."

"Try this." The corpsman grabbed two white pills from his black bag and extended them.

"What are they?"

"Acetaminophen."

"Fine. Thank you." Volkov swallowed his pain killers with a gulp of tepid tea and then returned the cup to its holder.

"Tell me immediately if you have dizziness, shortness of breath, trouble seeing, or excessive fatigue."

"That describes most of my day."

"You know what I mean. Don't be a hero."

Volkov nodded his compliance to the only sailor aboard who could give him an order. "Okay."

"You're going to need some sleep soon."

Volkov dismissed the advice with a noncommittal response. "I'll see to it when I can."

"When's that going to be?"

Caught within the medical professional's unyielding inquiry, the *Wraith's* commander equivocated. "We have more than a day's journey to the staging point."

"Most of it atop the *Xerxes*, I assume. So, you'll have time."

"Yes. But I've got scenarios to review."

"Dmitry, please."

The *Wraith's* commander conceded. "I'll get six hours before the landing. I promise."

"Good, sir. I'm holding you to that." Continuing his visits with the injured, the corpsman departed.

Alone with his pounding skull, the *Wraith's* commander mentally replayed recent events.

He studied a strategic display spanning from his location near the Philippines to the rebel nation's southeastern edge.

Enemy ground forces staged themselves for attacks against Central Papua, and seaborne combatants overloaded the targeted province's northern and southern maritime areas.

By gathering to protect an offensive, they'd left the naval headquarters at Sorong weak.

In contrast, his Indonesian clients pinpointed Sorong for the landing, expecting to overpower its defenses and decapitate the navy. But they offered nothing beyond boosted air support, most of it unmanned, for bracing the loyalists in targeted Central Papua.

The *Wraith's* commander judged each side as seeking rapid victories, but they both trusted their attacked vulnerabilities to hold without further bolstering.

A battle of offensives.

A race to victory.

A test of wills.

An unspoken desire to limit the violence, pitting strengths against weaknesses.

Volkov groaned and caressed the tender flesh-egg protruding from the back of his skull.

Distracting him from his reflections and soreness, his executive officer stopped and blurted out an update. "Sir, Diesel Four is out of commission, but Diesels One through three are fully ready."

Volkov recalled the warhead's toll upon the generator. "The air intake?"

"Yes. It got bent and pulled off in the explosion, and it's not going to fit. It needs to be replaced."

"We've got a spare but not enough people to replace it?"

Sergei shook his head. "Right. At least, not before the landing, sir. And unless you want to trust our lives to duct tape…"

Remembering a Chinese *Ming*-class submarine's diesel suffocating the crew by instantly gobbling their air, Volkov would avoid transforming his sailors into asphyxiated corpses. "We won't risk duct tape unless…well, we won't risk it."

"Right." Sergei plopped his buttocks into a seat in front of his boss. "I could use a breather. I've been trotting up and down this ship for hours."

"You and the half of us who are capable." Eyeing his rugged exec, the *Wraith's* commander saw battle-tested strength, but stress and fatigue wore upon the hardened man's features. Seeing the deep strain upon the man helped him grasp his corpsman's perspective. "The crew needs to sleep tonight."

Sergei voiced an understatement. "It's been a tough day."

Volkov shifted his awareness to the map. "We're about six hundred nautical miles from the staging point."

"But only thirty-one from our rendezvous with the *Xerxes*."

"This may be the best use of the *Xerxes* yet, taking us into battle while we sleep and lick our wounds."

"What's our drop-dead arrival time?"

The *Wraith's* commander recalled his latest update. "Renard said forty-eight hours, but I think he meant roughly two days."

Showing his quick mind, Sergei calculated. "We can do this, sir. If she keeps all MESMA plants online, Commander Volkova will carry us at twelve to thirteen knots on average. That should get us there in time."

"I'll check the numbers to make sure."

"She could always surface and sprint to make up time…"

"Let's keep the rebels doubting our status."

"Right, sir. We'll make it." The exec glanced around the space as if seeking something or someone needing his attention. "Do you mind if I check the torpedo room?"

"No. Go."

Sergei darted away.

Examining his subordinate, Volkov saw new life rising from the man's frame. Moving with purpose, Sergei seemed unbreakable despite his fatigue, like a mountain of mortal danger had wrung out any weakness, leaving a core of supple durability.

In a moment, he realized his underling had grown capable of commanding his own warship. Sergei was ready to replace him as the commander of the *Wraith*.

But not today.

Stretching his frame, Volkov stood and reached for the piping above. The *Wraith* was his, and he would lead it limping and bruised into combat once again.

Movement caught his eye, and he spied his Indonesian rider swiveling a chair towards a small crowd which had formed around a sonar technician.

Stepping from the conning platform, Volkov joined the half dozen onlookers surrounding the sonar technician and the corpsman kneeling before him. "What's going on?"

His splinted arm resting on his lap, the rider replied. "He's going to reset his dislocated shoulder."

Volkov winced. "Ouch. That's–"

The corpsman interrupted. "Not as bad as it used to be. There's a new technique that gently shakes it back into place. It takes about three to five minutes."

Concerned about his pain, the sonar tech protested. "But you gave me muscle relaxants and codeine."

"That's to relax you so you don't fight me."

"Oh. Okay. I'm not, am I? Fighting you?"

"No, you're doing fine."

Medications slowing his speech, the sonar tech inquired. "When are you going to do it?"

"I've been doing it for over three minutes. It's a gentle pull-and-rotate motion. It'll slide back in any minute now."

"Oh, that would be–"

A thudding thunk made the patient yell, and the corpsman released his arm. "*Blyat*! You said that wouldn't hurt! But that hurt!"

"Not compared to the old technique of one big nasty yank. Standing, the corpsman deadpanned. "Be thankful I knew the gentler version."

Four hours later, Volkov brought the *Wraith* to the *Xerxes*.

A slow, careful docking procedure placed his submarine within the cargo bed, and he secured his engine room.

He even sent his tactical staff to their bunks, trusting the *Xerxes*' team to listen and watch for distant dangers.

As a passenger aboard the transport vessel, the *Wraith's* commander began the new day's wee hours anticipating needed rest for himself and for his sailors.

Sitting at his stateroom's desk and needing sleep, Volkov first wanted to see his wife. A huge yawn stretched his scalp and yanked his throbbing bump while he grabbed his laptop.

She was already in her stateroom on the *Xerxes*, waiting for him. In her practiced Russian, she joked, but gentle tears streamed down her cheeks upon recognizing him. "Where've you been hiding? Your ship's not that big."

"Anatoly needed cajoling to separate his ears from our hydrophones."

The comment appeared to lift her from her recent emotional torment, and she wiped her face. She spoke English into her phone and then replied in Russian. "Did you have to restrain him?"

Volkov laughed. "No. He was so tired and traumatized–like all of us–that he yielded after a single protest."

"Poor Anatoly."

"I'm sure he's snoring now and hardly cares about hydrophones."

"If I know him, he'd hear any threats in his sleep."

The *Wraith's* commander chuckled. "Probably."

She changed the subject. "Did you see the videos from Terry?"

He had, as had his crew. After taking their beating, his sailors needed a dose of success. "I keep it running in a loop in the crew's mess area. We all love it. It was incredible." He reconsidered. "Actually, it was very credible. Somehow, I believe that Pierre and Jake envisioned long ago when designing the *Goliath* they'd use it for something like this."

"And Terry acted decisively. I'm sure they would've gotten all the survivors off the *Kaisiepo*, but it was a financial and motivational win."

"You would've done the same."

"Probably. But Terry did it. Give him his due."

"Yes. Of course. God bless Terry. But part of me wishes he was available for the assault."

"Stop second guessing. It won't help."

He found her advice sage. "Yeah. I agree. And I have enough to think about. Any updates to our landing plan?"

"Since we can't use the *Goliath*, it's just you and me for submerged assets. The Indonesians still don't want to send in their submarines with heavyweight torpedoes."

Volkov had expected as much. "Good. And our only hidden enemies are the drones, right?"

"Right. So, our allies won't be attacking anything submerged, and our chances of friendly fire are nil."

"That's good, but what's our tasking after losing half our railguns?"

"Unchanged. Soften but preserve the rebel combatants."

"If you try it, they could shoot down or evade every round."

"I don't want to talk about it now. We've got all night to plan."

"I wish I had forty torpedo tubes."

She smirked. "You get what you have."

Sensing emotional warmth from the cold steel surrounding him, the *Wraith's* commander admired his submarine. "It's a tough ship, deserving my respect."

"Right."

"It's still a difficult mission."

"But you and I will have some flexibility to plan this out ourselves. No constraints of having to coordinate with surface and air assets, although they'll be available if needed."

"Easier said than done."

"But easier without an enemy submarine, thanks to you."

Stifling an unidentified thought rising from nowhere, Volkov cleared his throat.

During an uncomfortable silence, Danielle appeared stuck for words, struggling uncharacteristically to share her thoughts.

Discomfort spurring him, Volkov voiced a confession. "I found the *Nagapasa* by making myself a target and getting within a whisker of being vaporized."

She frowned. "But you succeeded."

"I almost died. I almost lost my ship. I lost two men and subjected the rest to trauma."

"But you won. You accomplished your mission, and you saved your ship and most of your crew."

"True." Faces of the dead tormented him. "But my men. I remember them. They should still be alive."

"Why?"

Her challenge confused him. "I was their captain."

"And you're perfect?"

"No, but–"

Showing her strength, she crushed his self-pity. "They're dead because of countless factors beyond anyone's control. But I know one thing that wasn't one of those factors."

"Uh, what's that?"

"A bad captain."

"I rerun scenarios in my head automatically. I can't stop it. I keep wondering if I'd turned too late or too soon, drove too slow or too fast–"

"Stop it."

He scowled. "I just said I can't!"

Easing up, she shifted from harshness to tenderness. "Time will help. You're still in shock."

"Yes. Perhaps you're right."

Her shoulders rose as she inhaled an anxious breath. "As long as you're in shock."

He glared at her. "Yes?"

"I…"

"We're going into combat, my love. Please share with me whatever you must."

"Oh, bloody hell, Dmitry." She looked downward but then refocused earnest eyes on the screen. "I'm pregnant."

# CHAPTER 19

Twenty-four hours later, a short nap had taken Admiral Hakim into the new day, the day of the ground offensive, placing him and his staff on high alert.

A young ensign yelled from the doorway across the office. "It's zero-two-hundred hours, admiral. You'd asked to be woken at this time, sir."

Groggy, Hakim grumbled. "Status?"

"Sir, Captain Moeljadi reports all ships are positioned at the northern and southern offensive operations areas." Hesitant, the ensign paused for a reply.

Hakim obliged. "Very well. The Air status?"

"Sir, Lieutenant Colonel Sinurat reports all aircraft ready for the offensive. Army air will handle ground support, but Air Force assets will begin combat air control patrol sorties at zero-five-thirty."

"Very well. Ground status?"

Rustling paper revealed the junior officer's wisdom in having scribbled notes. "Sir, Colonel Pardi reports that the Third Marine Force will land three kilometers west of Mimako in three hours to begin its advance over the plains towards Timika."

"And the Army?"

"Landing twelve kilometers west of Nabire in one hour, sir."

"Very well. Where's Colonel Pardi?"

"Sir, he's sleeping in his office."

Hakim wanted the marine colonel close for protection, leading his defensive battalions around Sorong, while his larger infantry and artillery brigades sought Timika. "Very well."

"That's all I had, sir."

Rolling from his sofa, Hakim grumbled. "Dismissed."

A clicking latch signaled solitude.

Hakim grabbed a toiletry bag from his desk and then left his office. The low lights in the control center confirmed the early hour, as did the smaller crowd of midnight watch subordinates seated at consoles and surrounding the plotting table.

He walked into the men's room and freshened himself like an airport traveler. When finished, he returned his bag to his desk and then reversed course again towards the plotting table.

A naval commander, the senior watchman, greeted him. "Good morning, admiral."

Hakim was gruff. "Any sign of the landing?"

"Nothing offensive yet, sir. We're still tracking a cluster of warships fourteen miles off the western side of Salawati Island."

Hakim had conceded the loyalists lurking within a whisker of his nation's waters.

Salawati's geography pushed the invading force into a five-hour trek to Sorong, followed by another two hours to reach beaches south of the urban center where enemy assets could move towards the naval base, the marine base, or both.

That concession included a rational assumption that loyalists would avoid the minefield he'd ordered planted between Salawati and Papua.

Having ordered the mines set with seventy-two-hour active lives, Hakim expected them to seal the chokepoint south of Sorong and force the invaders to meet his vessels to the north. A notice to mariners warned wary commercial ships while informing his enemies to stay away.

"How's the minefield?"

"It's eighty-two percent deployed, sir. It'll be complete before the loyalists can reach it."

After grunting his acknowledgement, the admiral examined icons. As he'd ordered, the requested ships supported General Purnomo's offensive in Central Papua while the remnant protected approaches to Sorong.

Concentrating his combatants left half his nation's borders exposed, but he conceded the rougher terrains. If the loyalists stormed coastal marshes and forests, then so be it. There would be time to react, and the expected ground victories at Nabire and Timika would solidify the junta's dominance.

At least, that's what Hakim told himself.

He also told himself that Purnomo embodied this belief, and that the general retained enough charisma and prowess to hold Papua's warriors and civilians within his revolutionary grip.

Expecting successes on offense and defense, Hakim retired again to his office to nap during the calm before predicted storms.

His slumber passed in an instant, and the young ensign's voice returned Hakim's awareness to the couch.

"Admiral? Admiral?"

"I'm awake."

"Colonel Pardi informs you that surface-to-air-radar detects hostile aircraft flying in formation twenty-five miles northeast of Sorong."

"Very well." Hakim rolled to his feet. "I'm coming."

At the command center's plotting table, Pardi looked as disheveled as a marine could. Dark skin under his eyes and a ruddy pillow mark on his cheek revealed the untimely end of his slumber. "Ground radar north of our marine base at Klaurung detected six aircraft moving in formation towards Mesewo."

Hakim examined the new icons on the table. "They're staying away from our SAM sites."

"Intentionally, sir. Given the subsonic speeds and trajectories, I don't believe them to be attack aircraft. I expect they're cargo ships dropping paratroopers."

"Logical. What's our defense's status?"

"I'll send Charlie and Delta Companies from the Fourteenth Battalion to intercept them, sir. Given the distance and terrain, the enemy forces won't get by Charlie and Delta any time soon."

Hakim smirked. "This all but confirms where they're landing. Unless this paratrooper drop is a bluff, they're targeting Sorong."

"Agreed, sir. And that all but confirms they'll attempt to take the beaches west of Klamesin, which is what we've prepared for."

"Very well. Review your defenses for me."

Pardi tapped the chart. "We've got enough SAM sites to keep aircraft from overflying our shores. It starts here at Sorong's northwestern tip, and a battery of fourteen sites plus your capital ships will deny enemy flights southward through Klamesin down to here, just south of Jeflio."

"Air control is crucial. This is good, even with the Air Force committed to the offensive, we can hold."

"If they approach Sorong, we'll have parity in the air, sir. Stopping the assault landing vessels will come down to gunnery and ground-based missiles, and we've got a hellish arsenal awaiting them." Pardi pointed to icons of tanks, howitzers, rocket launchers, and entrenched infantry units.

Hakim admired the network of weaponry spanning twenty miles from Sorong across vulnerable beaches, stopping at a chokepoint where he'd have sea mines laid. "Good. We're ready."

The marine gave a slow nod. "We are, sir. But I noticed you're mining the approach from the south. Are you not going to mine the approaches to the north?"

"I won't bottle up my own navy, and even with remote-control mines, I'm hesitant to ask anyone to pass over them by turning them off with sonar pulse codes."

"Understood, sir."

"I recommend you get some sleep, colonel. We've still got a few hours before any enemy unit can engage us."

Fifteen minutes later, Hakim fell asleep again on his couch.
He dreamt.

Reliving his childhood, he watched his grammar-school-self labor with a heavy backpack laden with textbooks. Smarter than his peers in all his classes, he drew their unwanted attention while walking home.

Three larger boys outpaced and caught him, yanked his

backpack, and tripped him backwards.

When his head hit the sidewalk, his world turned bleach-white with a high-pitched whining in ears. Then the blue sky appeared above with the twinkling stars of a concussion, and he heard his assailants' jeers. Dirty soles scuffed and scraped his clothes before the attackers pranced away.

In his dreamscape, the boys reappeared over his stunned frame as he was teleported into a restroom stall. Cruel hands shoved his head into the toilet as flushing water swirled around his face.

Next, his feet dangled above the ground as taunters grabbed his ripping underwear from all sides.

In his dream, his tears formed a river which drained into a chasm the uncaring earth had opened to swallow all signs of his suffering. A child howling for compassion found only indifference.

Then his drunken father appeared in the white uniform of a one-star admiral. After guzzling his rum and coke, the elder Hakim slammed the glass to the table, turned his eyes from the television, and glared at his son. "You disgust me."

The words pierced the boy. "They bully me! It's not my fault!"

"Bullies only bully the weak. You're weak."

The dreamscape child sought his mother for solace, but she materialized as a statue with a brittle and cracking expression of anguish from her hopelessness as an abusive alcoholic's wife.

As the woman evaporated, the elder Hakim became real again, this time wearing his uniform pants and a white undershirt. After ripping the belt from his trousers, he whipped his son. "Weak. Embarrassing me. Making your mother cry."

Memories of stinging welts peppered the vision.

Shame.

Shame and desire to be ignored dragged his deepest inner self into a bottomless abyss.

Hatred.

Hatred of self and, therefore, hatred of all, became his

hermeneutic through which he ingested the world.

Loneliness.

Loneliness drove him to seek isolation from others despite his natural need for relations.

Reasoned experience convinced the child he was different. If human, whatever that was, he was abnormal. And since the shamed, hating, and lonely child carried a survival instinct, he had to prove his abnormality wasn't his flaw but a superiority.

Otherwise, his oppressing world was correct, and he was scum.

The festering, untreated trauma of victimhood governed the sleeper's relived life. The need to prove himself sharpened his wits and fueled success, but the emotional damage remained within the grown man's core.

Echoing his younger self, the sleeping Hakim shrieked within his soul. "Curse all fate! Curse my creator! Curse all existence!"

Next, the boy doubled in age and carried upon his growing frame the strength to challenge his father. But the young man also professed wisdom, a secret and questionable wisdom, that nothing was beyond consideration to protect himself.

Now the slumbering illusion was his father snoring in a bed made empty by his wife's suicide. Carrying two full bottles of rum and a funnel, the young Hakim crept to the admiral's side, shook him, and confirmed he'd passed out drunk.

Blaming his father for his mother's death, the boy who became a man that night ripped the covers from the drunkard, pulled down his pants, and slid the funnel into his anus.

He showed an adult's patience as he poured the alcohol into his father's digestive system as the lower intestines absorbed it. While halfway through the second bottle, Hakim heard his victim's breathing slow, sputter, and stop.

After killing his father, he disposed of the evidence and retired to his bedroom.

Unable to sleep that night, his dreaming self recalled his

younger self daydreaming about escaping his childhood's agony. His acceptance to the Indonesian Naval Academy promised deliverance, and he pondered the infinite possibilities while squashing guilt for murdering the elder Hakim.

But the recurring vision of his father, angry and burning with hell's fire, came back to life every subconscious night. Tormenting him, it reminded him of the pounding inner pain.

"Weak. Embarrassing me. Making your mother cry."

Hakim awoke, sensed himself on the couch, and realized his subordinate's voice had stirred him. "Yes?"

The ensign addressed him. "Captain Moeljadi reports a traitor discovered aboard the *Martadinata*, admiral. He's been woken up and requests to speak with you."

His slumber having already angered him, the admiral growled. "Send him in immediately."

"Aye, aye, sir!"

Hakim wiped dream visions from his memory and transferred their lingering ire into contempt for a new enemy. As the ensign opened the door for the captain to waddle through, the admiral had mentally condemned the traitor. "Sit, captain. Report."

Looking like an unshaven walrus, Captain Moeljadi spoke from behind puffy eyes. "The operations officer of the *Martadinata*, Lieutenant Commander Darmawan, requested to resign his commission and to seek asylum with the loyalists."

Hearing of the audacity kindled the admiral's angst. "Oh, he did, did he? A coward wishes to run from the battle."

"The first would-be victim of Jokowi's supposed pardon."

"Supposed, indeed. Only a fool would believe."

"Darmawan claims that his sister, nephew, and two nieces died aboard the *Blue Fin*."

Word of the chartered vessel he'd ordered destroyed flushed ice through Hakim's heated blood. "What were they doing aboard the *Blue Fin*?"

"His sister married Lieutenant Commander Prakoso, the

engineering officer aboard the *Kaisiepo*. Prakoso met Darmawan at the academy, and they also served together as junior officers aboard the *Malahayati*."

"Personal loss is no excuse."

"Agreed, sir. And it gets worse."

"How could it get worse?"

"Sir, he's been stirring up dissent with other crew members. He didn't report this to the *Martadinata's* commanding officer, but word surfaced that Darmawan has been vocal about the order to destroy the *Blue Fin* coming from higher than Colonel Soebijakto."

A pit formed in Hakim's stomach as he questioned which truths had leaked from framing the jailed Air Force colonel for retribution against the *Kaisiepo*. "That's wild speculation. Who could believe such lies?"

Calculating his response, the chubby captain hesitated before replying. "Of course, he's just speculating, sir. I think your observation of cowardice explains it."

Hakim liked the answer and compounded the traitor's condemnation. "So, Lieutenant Commander Darmawan's brother-in-law gambled away his family through treason, and he's suddenly lost his mettle for combat."

"I can't argue that perspective, sir."

Hakim pounded his desk and yelled. "Nobody will argue my perspective! Not heading into a war!"

Moeljadi's puffy face flushed pinker. "Aye, sir."

The veins of his neck throbbing, the admiral called out. "Ensign!"

A moment later, the young officer stuck his head through the doorway. "Sir!"

"Get word to the *Martadinata* that Lieutenant Commander Darmawan will remain in the brig. If the ship goes down, I don't care if he goes with it. If he survives, he can come here for Court Martial hearings."

An unknown span of time lapsed after Hakim again rested.

Pitch black emptiness filled his dreamscape, and he again awoke to the ensign's voice.

"Sir, you're being hailed."

His mental fogginess evaporating, Hakim heard the gentle, repeating chime from his workstation. "Who is it?"

"General Purnomo, sir!"

A pit formed in Hakim's stomach. "Very well. Dismissed."

As the ensign departed, he left the admiral alone and laboring towards his workstation against stiff and weary legs.

Sitting, Hakim lifted his gaze towards the screen and silently begged providence for good news. "General Purnomo, sir. To what do I owe the pleasure at this hour?"

The junta's leader looked sick and angry. Under stubble, his cheeks shifted from an ugly gray to a muddy sanguine, betraying his stifled rage as he skipped pleasantries. "First Lieutenant Solossa is alive, in critical condition, and in a loyalist hospital."

Hakim had no idea who Solossa was. "Sir, I–"

Raising his voice, Purnomo discharged verbal venom. "I know you don't recognize his name, because you paid him too little attention! He's the accursed pilot you ordered to destroy the *Blue Fin*! He's now in the hands of the enemy!"

"But we watched him on a drone, sir! He was dangling from his ejection seat's parachute, and he was lost at sea."

"Don't tell me he was lost when I just saw him on YouTube!"

Hakim hoped the pilot's video was fake because otherwise he couldn't bear it. "Our best observations determined he was lost, sir."

"Your best observations were wrong!"

Having assumed his world could get no worse, Hakim slipped further into an abyss. Silent questions berated him.

Had his plan to destroy the *Kaisiepo's* family been flawed?

Had he erred in its execution?

What dangers did a captured-rescued pilot pose?

"Is he talking, sir?"

"No, he's still unconscious, but that's the only solace from this mess you've created."

Losing control, the admiral blurted out an emotional protest. "I created? You ordered me to take out the *Blue Fin*, and I did what I had to do!"

Purnomo's countenance became haughty. "I don't remember it that way, and you seem to be struggling to accept the consequences of your actions."

His boss' easy denial informed Hakim of his quandary. An Air Force colonel in the brig, an Army superior leading his junta, and an unconscious aviator in enemy hands contained enough knowledge to condemn him as a monster. And each man was motivated to publicize the truth in his own defense.

His pulse racing, Hakim sought a path to protect himself. But his mental machinations left him empty and unable to see a way out, and he felt weak.

Weak, furious, and desperate.

# CHAPTER 20

Later that morning, Danielle completed her first day of transit with her husband's submarine in her cargo bed.

Welcoming hours of low stress and routine seafaring, she swallowed the last of her sliced melon and glanced at the clock.

Taylor needed relief on the bridge, but she had ten minutes to linger and sought information from her rider. "Commander Lestari, how certain was the admiral's confidence in the landing plan?"

The Indonesian officer powered through a mouthful of potatoes, swallowed, and then wiped his lips. "It's as certain as it can be, ma'am. The plan won't change again. Unless, of course, it has to."

She'd expected the wiggly answer. "Fair enough. That's as good as it's going to get."

"You seem content with that."

"I am. I'm liking the tentative idea we've been kicking around with Commander Volkov and his team. I think it's our committed course of action now."

Lestari straddled the proverbial fence between fear, bravado, and self-mocking sarcasm. "Wonderful! I've always wanted to navigate a minefield."

She'd concocted the idea during last evening's dinner, and after running it by experts on both ships, she found a growing excitement for the challenge and the fruits of its success. "There's no better ship ever designed for it. We've got enough side scan sonars to count the gills on a fish."

"I'm sure we'll be fine, ma'am." His tone revealed homage for her and her vessel but still betrayed modest doubt.

Danielle wondered how many of her crew and her husband's

sailors had heard about the plan. She wondered how many shared Lestari's apprehension and had suffered nightmares from having heard.

The same nightmares she'd endured overnight of a moored warhead slipping past her defenses.

Five minutes later, she stood beside Taylor on the bridge. "Are you ready for some rest?"

"Yes, ma'am."

"The final briefing for the minefield begins at fifteen hundred. If I see you out of your rack before fourteen hundred, I'll have the corpsman drug you and throw you back in."

"I don't think it'll be a problem, ma'am."

"Good. Enjoy your rest. I relieve you of the deck and the conn."

Taylor disappeared down the steps, and she glanced around the dome.

As the rising sun illuminated the seas, she and two escort vessels turned towards their staging point. Morotai Island, the last major landmass separating her from the assault force, revealed lush tree lines hiding subdued government offices that seemed to shake off sleep under the day's new light.

She turned her attention to a console and read an update on the rebel's ground campaign in Central Papua. Troop movements had revealed a split between a northern offensive targeting Nabire and a southern assault against heavier expected resistance in Timika. The province's governor called for aid, and Jakarta told him help would arrive within a week.

But despite her scouring of plans, reports, and calculations, Danielle saw nothing showing Indonesian troops reaching Nabire or Timika within a week. The intent was to land at Sorong, decapitate Papua's maritime military, and to stage further troop movements through the littoral waters, the air, and the rugged terrain.

Beyond the landing awaited a great unknown of countless variables upon which myriad voices had pontificated.

Her brain full of naval tactics, she paid minimal heed to such post-landfall affairs, but she recognized possibilities and would allow her clients the opportunity by neutralizing the rebel ships.

But more than a day separated her from them.

So, she emptied her head of concerns, watched the gentle waves, and enjoyed the appeal of the ocean's infinitude, leaving her to wonder if anyone was untouched by the sea's call to be awed.

As Morotai Island slid behind her sterns, she enjoyed the quiet solitude which had accompanied seafarers since antiquity.

But she realized she wasn't alone and probably wouldn't be for the next eight months.

Two days earlier, she'd felt a compulsion to verify her suspicions, and a test kit had proven her intuition true. Per her math, the tryst in Port Said had procreated the baby, and she gestated the fleet's first member conceived during a mission.

Allowing a moment of giddiness, she chuckled at the Indonesia campaign's souvenir growing inside her. But everything had changed overnight. Her every idea or impression now centered on someone else, leading her to unfamiliar mental patterns, including an odd one challenging her vocation.

An apparent moment ago, she'd been a fierce warrior. Now, contradictions arose within her, like the image of a nursing mother holding a baby in one arm while shooting missiles with the other.

Something had upended her worldview, and it needed correcting.

After the minefield.

After the surrender of rebel ships.

After she could experience a forgotten reality far from warfare.

But another calm day at sea awaited her, and she hoped to resolve her inner contradictions before reaching the staging point.

That evening, Danielle stood alone on the bridge.

The day's quiet contemplation gave way to edginess as the

*Wraith*-*Xerxes* tandem joined warships lurking off the western side of Salawati Island. As she scanned her full horizon, the running lights and silhouettes of friendly combatants verified the iconic information on her radar.

A landing force had formed.

She slowed the *Xerxes* to a crawl and joined a multiple-mile-long ovular racetrack pattern with her Indonesian clients. Each scheduled vessel waited its turn with one of two refueling tankers.

To prepare for her turns, one each for the *Wraith* and the *Xerxes*, she submerged and removed the submarine from her back. She then surfaced and slipped to the starboard side of an old tanker while losing sight of her husband's ship being mated on the port side.

Slow but accurate maneuvering with her outboard motors pressed her vessel against the rusting gas pump, *Sungai Gerong*. Artificial lights flooded an expansive area where Indonesian workers tossed lines to waiting sailors on the *Xerxes*.

From her vantage on the bridge, Danielle admired Taylor, who moved with a confident authority as he yanked his tethered harness behind him atop the catamaran's port hull. She watched him raise his bridge-to-bridge radio.

His lips moved a fractional second before his words reached her ears under the dome. "Bridge, topside. Over?"

Danielle lifted a handheld, short-range device. "Topside, bridge. Go ahead. Over."

"Bridge, topside. Ma'am, I request permission to tie up to the *Sungai Gerong* for refueling operations. Over."

"Topside, bridge. Tie up to the *Sungai Gerong* and commence refueling operations. Over."

"Bridge, topside, aye. Out."

After nylon ropes mated the vessels, deckhands lowered a metallic gangway onto the *Xerxes* and then shouldered fuel lines across it. Trusting Taylor, Danielle left topside's logistical affairs to her capable exec, and she turned her attention towards a screen at her console.

She hailed the *Wraith's* bridge.

Sergei answered with his hair shooting horizontally from his head. "*Da!*" Eyeing Danielle, the *Wraith's* executive officer switched to broken English, yelling against the blustery wind. "Hi, Commander Volkova!"

She'd forgotten the submarine shifted its bridge to its conning tower when surfaced. Given the compactness of the tower's tiny standing area, she could see enough of Sergei's surroundings to predict the answer, but she had to ask, after probing her memory for Russian words. "Is Dmitry there?"

Sergei shook his head, scrunching his features as his nose faced the incoming gale whipping against the tanker's far side. He reverted to Russian. "No. You should try his stateroom."

Danielle recognized the words from many chats with Dmitry. "Thank you, Sergei. Goodbye."

"Goodbye!"

When her screen darkened, she selected her husband's private quarters and sent a hail through a wireless router aboard the tanker to the *Wraith*.

No answer.

She then tried the *Wraith's* wardroom. Then the crew's mess. Then the engineering spaces. But her husband remained elusive.

Stymied, she plopped her buttocks onto a cushioned seat and then folded her arms. She chuckled when she concluded that Volkov must have boarded the tanker to buy her a gift.

Whatever gift that could be was a mystery.

She doubted the *Sungai Gerong* had a gift shop, but she expected most naval vessels to operate a store for snacks and knickknacks, and given their spartan environs, she'd accept her husband's simplest gesture of appreciation.

A chime startled her, and she checked the monitor showing the opposite side of the bridge's door below.

With a goofy smile, her husband awaited permission to enter. "Dmitry?"

"*Da!* May I enter the bridge?"

Startled, she tapped a button to unlock the door. "*Da!*"

Seconds later, he completed his sprint up the echoing stairs and then withdrew something from behind his back.

More interested in Volkov than his present, she darted into his arms.

Deftly, Volkov whipped the hidden gift behind his wife's head while embracing her for the first time since learning of her pregnancy. "I missed you."

"I missed you too." She sought his language's word for 'swim' before interrogating him. "Did you swim here?"

"My clothes are dry, my love."

She crossed her arms, tried to restrain her joy at the surprise visit, and reminded herself to keep speaking Volkov's language. "How did you get here so fast?"

"If you think I'm Superman, that's okay."

She released him and then examined his features.

He beamed with new zeal.

Numbers danced in her head, reconstructing the elapsed time since her ship had mated with the metallic gangway. At most five minutes had passed. "You flew?"

He giggled, and as he calmed himself, his panting from exertion became obvious. "Nope."

Her next volley required linguistic help, and she pulled out her phone. She uttered her intent and then extended the device while it spoke and displayed the Russian words. "You leapt from the *Wraith* to the tanker, sprinted across the tanker, ran across my gangway, and then crawled through the tunnel in world-record time?"

He shrugged and blushed. "And then jogged the length of your hull! My knees still hurt. I crawled through the tunnel very fast!"

"You romantic fool."

"Yes! That's me. Oh, before I forget." He lifted the stuffed teddy bear he'd carried from warship to warship.

"You found that on the..." Russian for 'tanker' escaped her, and she used the formal name. "...on the *Sungai Gerong*?"

Seemingly happy with her appreciation, Volkov burst with pride. "Nope! I bought it before we deployed. I hoped to need it.

I'm happy now that I do."

She examined the stuffed animal and recognized most of the Cyrillic characters. "What does it say?"

"It says 'Mommy', of course."

Ten minutes later, she handed him a cup of coffee from a fresh pot in the *Xerxes*' wardroom. She stayed in a public space out of respect for her crew.

The joy of reuniting with Volkov waned, and the edginess of pending danger surfaced. "Have you talked to Pierre about the minefield?"

"Thanks." He accepted the coffee, sipped, and then answered. "I haven't talked to him since we last briefed him."

"Then he still agrees with the plan?"

His scowl surprised her. "I don't think he ever approved."

She blurted her reply, referring to the afternoon's planning of the minefield run. Renard had led the planning, but he'd remained passive to the married couple's ruminations. "What? He never protested?"

"I think he's afraid to contradict a pair of spouses with a baby growing inside one of them."

His words surprising her more than his scowl, she sat opposite him with her steaming mug and protested. "Pierre's not afraid of anything."

"*Da!*" After the strong counter, Volkov carefully crafted his English retort. "He's afraid of assigning a family to such danger."

"You're overreacting."

"Am I? Could you send us into a minefield?"

She conceded. "Well, no. But I'm not Pierre. That's his job."

"I think the fleet has outgrown him. I don't think anyone should bear his burdens."

Although she prepared her Russian to pivot the conversation from her husband's concerns, she silently admitted his observation of Renard's limits were accurate. "I agree it's a difficult decision. But we'll survive the minefield."

"Every new father wants his wife and only child to lead him

through a shadowy abyss of fatal explosives."

"You know what I meant."

"Unfortunately, I do. You're trying to be brave. You are brave. But that's no substitute for prudence."

She mulled over his meaning but found it too bizarre to her understanding to accept. "What are you saying?"

"This isn't our only child. It is our first of several."

"Don't I get a say in this?"

He eyed her with a knowing look. "We've agreed to race your... I forget what it's called."

"My biological clock."

"*Da!* I want us to be parents of as many as we can have."

"Yes. Yes, we agreed. Let me get used to this one. Things are moving so fast."

"After this mission, I won't risk creating an orphan by putting us both in the same mortal danger. One of us must quit the fleet."

Unable to concoct a counter argument while thoughts of battle distracted her, Danielle let the subject die.

Then she accepted her husband's opinion. Risking one's life was one thing, but doing so with dependents was another.

But she'd committed to the minefield and her new destiny, either as a corpse or as a hero and mother. Or as a mother and a hero. She wasn't sure of the priority, and it bothered her.

Unsure how to resolve her conflicting desires for glory in combat against those of mundane motherhood, she sipped her coffee and wondered if marrying Volkov had been a mistake.

# CHAPTER 21

Admiral Hakim stood before his subordinates at the command center's plotting table. "I trust you all appreciate how truly great the glory of this moment is."

The obsequious faces he'd grown accustomed to now instead revealed a hardness for battle.

Hardness at something random and personal for each man.

With invisibly thin threads, the admiral believed he united his hardened warriors under a new nation's banner. But heavy ground resistance in Central Papua, a landing force approaching Sorong, a captured pilot he'd tricked into slaughtering innocents, and President Widodo's lingering offer of pardon challenged his control.

They challenged his slipping sanity.

Tenuous as his grip felt, he felt they would follow him. His command presence and charisma would assure it, and if nothing else, they owed him obedience for having taken them this far. To think otherwise was unthinkable.

He stuffed a chorus of doubts into his soul and caked a layer of oozing confidence over his visage. "Let's first look at the offensive in Central Papua. The army is now surrounding Nabire and placing the city under siege."

Steeled eyes around the table gazed upon icons showing the rebels' dominance in the targeted province's capital city.

Hakim shifted his focus southward. "Meanwhile, our marines are driving hard for Timika. They've already met unexpected resistance from militia along the route, but they're advancing on our timetables."

Across from him, the lean marine colonel opined. "We've taken twenty percent more casualties than expected, sir, but it would be worse if my marines fought one whit below their capabilities. They're not. They're fighting like marines."

"Of course, Colonel Pardi. I, too, am proud of them, especially given the challenges you met crossing the Mimika River."

The marine officer recounted the resistance. "Loyalist militia got their hands on a few anti-tank weapons, and they struck from a well-hidden ambush site on the riverbank. Although they had only a few missiles, they hit the most vulnerable target, which was a mobile bridge layer. They destroyed one, but we had a spare. Otherwise, we'd still be talking about getting across."

"But we're not, because you had a spare."

"Right, sir. And we've still got one more river to cross. So, the mobile bridge layer will be well guarded."

"I'm sure." Hakim pivoted subjects again. "The Air Force is holding off loyalist attempts to encroach our air space."

Having replaced his jailed superior, the de facto air boss accepted the praise and kept quiet among his higher-ranking compatriots.

Hakim completed his assessment of the offensive. "And as expected, we have more than enough seaborne firepower to reduce the enemy's navy to observers." He eyed his overweight underling. "And Captain Moeljadi has earned my confidence in using that firepower to keep the loyalists at bay in Central Papua."

The heavyset officer blushed. "Thank you, sir."

"Of course. Now, more to our immediate needs, we look to our defenses. None of our ground victories will matter if we lose our navy and marines. That's what's at stake here."

Anxious eyes glared at the chart.

Hakim panned the map to its upper left edge. "We've prepared our defenses from Sorong to Jeflio, where the coastline becomes too rugged for landings, and we also have an active minefield preventing the enemy's approach from the south. It's a brilliant defense, and it will hold."

Hints of bravado appeared on his frightened staff's features.

Hakim continued. "And we can confirm the strength, or dare

I say weaknesses of the enemy's landing forces. Let's start with what's already landed. Colonel Pardi?"

The marine grabbed a remote controller and slid the cursor into the eastern forests. "Yesterday, the loyalists dropped a company in the woods. Charlie and Delta Companies are blocking their approach, but they're awaiting the landing before moving. That lets me keep our other defensive forces positioned along our shorelines, as you can see on the chart. That's it, sir."

"Very well, colonel." Hakim eyed his heavyset underling. "This brings us to the brunt of the enemy's forces, which per our latest intelligence, remain well within our strength to resist. Share what you've learned, Captain Moeljadi."

"Our intelligence is excellent, sir. We've got eyes in the air, land, and sea watching them."

The admiral disliked his cowardly underling's rising bravado. "Very well, captain. Skip ahead to the data."

"Aye, sir." As his chubby finger tapped capacitive icons, windows popped up showing photos and statistics of each enemy ship. "The loyalists have dedicated most of their amphibious vessels to the effort. We track four major combatants and twelve landing ships moving around the north end of Batanta Island, along with nearly forty small combatants ranging from missile boat to patrol craft."

Hakim opined. "They were smart enough to avoid the narrows between Batanta and Salawati."

Colonel Pardi confirmed the wisdom. "I've got a few guns on Salawati, in case they were stupid enough to try it, sir."

"They're not idiots."

The marine was proud. "No, sir. But I'm moving all my guns on Salawati to the eastern shore. So, if any loyalist ship tries to back away from the heavy fire of our Sorong batteries, there'll be no safe retreat except to flee back north to open water."

"Very well colonel. Keep going, captain."

Captain Moeljadi scowled. "Speaking strictly in terms of naval firepower, we're outnumbered and outgunned, but only slightly."

Hakim was gruff. "General Purnomo took too many ships into his offensive, but the advantage is still ours with shore support."

A pudgy finger moved across the fifteen-mile-wide entrance between Papua and Salawati which gave access to Sorong and the Papuan northwestern coastlines. "That's why I want to delay engaging the combatants until they reach our gunnery kill zones. I'm tempted to be assertive, but this situation demands patience. Let them come to us, and we'll shred them."

"Very well, captain. With coordinated fires between our coastal batteries and our major combatants, we'll outgun the enemy."

Finding untapped courage, the heavyset captain was confident. "We'll pick the location, and we'll have guns from both islands optimized. We'll force a conflagration–nothing of theirs gets by–among all naval vessels, including the small combatants, starting here." He tapped the screen six miles southwest of Sorong, near the top of a funnel that Salawati Island carved in the sea with Papua.

A funnel capped with a southern minefield.

Hakim was haughty. "We'll meet them there. We'll neutralize them. And then we'll whittle away their landing forces before they can threaten our shores."

Captain Moeljadi replied. "Sir, I'm sure they'll still bring their forces, even under heavy fire. We're looking at two waves, with the first eleven ships consisting of four *Teluk Bintuni* landing ships-tank, five *Teluk Gilimanuk* landing ships-medium, and two *Makassar* landing platform docks. Nearly three thousand troops, twenty-five tanks, and thirty-five heavy vehicles."

Pardi opined. "That's serious, and those forces alone outnumber what I could commit to our defenses. But even if the entire first wave landed, we could hold, based upon the advantages of defending turf as opposed to having to advance."

Moeljadi gave the marine a sideways glance. "But the second wave will come from a single ship, the *Tanjung Kambani*. That's another fifteen hundred troops, fifty tanks, and one hundred and fifty vehicles. That is, hypothetically, if they survive my ships."

"Your ships and my guns."

"Of course. But, hypothetically…"

The officer answered like a marine. Candidly. "Hypothetically, if their first and second waves land intact, we'll be overrun. I can slow them for at most a week without reinforcements…"

Considering his own safety, the admiral interrupted. "We won't get any. General Purnomo wants his victory in Central Papua."

"I assume so, too, sir. Without reinforcements, the marine base and this naval base would be overrun, and the navy and the marine corps would fall."

Although Hakim knew each man had drawn the conclusion during briefs, small discussions, and in the recesses of his frightened soul, the first enunciation of possible defeat brought the room to silence.

He broke the silence. "Then they must think they're getting through. Why? What do we not see?"

Captain Moeljadi replied. "The submarines, sir. That's what we don't see."

Hakim had almost forgotten. "The *Wraith*?"

"The *Nagapasa* hit it badly enough that sailors required medical evacuation. That could mean anything from a mission kill to a ninety-percent capable warship, sir."

"And you've not heard or seen it?"

"Not a peep, sir." The chubby finger walked over the table. "I've got two undersea drones guarding the seas west of Sorong. And I just had a sonobuoy field laid from Sorong to Salawati. If the *Wraith* tries to slip through that tight net, we'll hear it."

Hakim decided he had bigger problems than a damaged and distant submarine. "Very well. What about those railgun-shooting abominations?"

"Sir, the *Goliath* is still underneath the *Kaisiepo* in the Banda Sea on its way to the Surabaya shipyard for repairs. That removes two railguns from our concerns, but we've lost track of the *Xerxes*."

"It's not moving around Batanta Island with the landing force?"

"Not on the surface, sir, although it could be submerged and keeping pace with the rest."

"Did we see it refuel?"

"No, sir. They refueled far enough away to stay hidden, and they didn't let anyone close enough for a look. We see everything moving north of Batanta Island, but if anything else got refueled, we won't know about it until we encounter it."

"So be it." Hakim smirked. "Two big rifles and six torpedo tubes without reload capability. The *Xerxes* doesn't concern me."

Moeljadi folded his arms atop his protruding stomach. "Nor should it, sir. I've got a missile boat assigned to each major combatant to double-up the close-in-weapon-systems. Two railguns at six rounds per minute won't get through. They don't have the fire rate to outdo one close-in cannon, much less two."

Hakim enjoyed moments of serenity as he expected to survive the military combat and even the ensuing political battles within and around the junta.

An hour later, Hakim stepped before his office's full-length mirror admiring himself in his battle dress uniform. He sensed his hour of glory arriving.

But his sense was skewed.

Something else was coming for him.

Shame.

Life became a blur.

The door opened.

Colonel Pardi led six marines and again as many army policemen into the office.

Handcuffs chafed his wrists behind his back.

Captain Moeljadi's fleshy face glared at the admiral.

And Colonel Soebijakto, the disgraced Air Force officer, stood between his peers.

Pardi plopped a phone onto the admiral's desk and set it playing at high volume. Aircraft sounds and two tense male voices rose from the device.

Fury and horror focused Hakim. "What's the meaning of this?"

Pardi answered. "Sir, General Purnomo has ordered me to restrain you and hand you over to his security forces. The recording will explain everything."

"What recording? What madness is this?" Hakim froze as he heard Colonel Soebijakto ordering a young pilot to destroy the *Kaisiepo's* fleeing family on the *Blue Fin*.

Pardi revealed the admiral's sin. "There's a third man's voice on the recording, sir. Although you're quiet, it's you, talking like you're trying to remain hidden."

"Don't be a dunce, colonel. Even if you suspect something true about this...this audio show, it could be all a hoax. Technology allows such tricks. Don't be fooled, man!"

"The truth is, sir, the timeline aligns with my memory of where you were, in and out of your office, when First Lieutenant Solossa destroyed the *Blue Fin*, and then was himself conveniently shot down."

Moeljadi added to the admiral's disgrace. "I remember it well, since you had me shoot him down. First Lieutenant Solossa is no traitor. But you told me otherwise to make me do it."

The air force officer quipped. "And I remember every detail, right down to the moment you had me gagged and dragged away. Fortunately, General Purnomo was curious enough to commandeer my phone records, and that's why we have you on audio orchestrating a mass murder."

Terror and rage overcame Hakim. "It wasn't me! It was Purnomo! He ordered me to do it. I was just obeying orders, as any one of you would."

Pardi stuck his hard features inches from the admiral's nose and glared. "Sir, let's pretend I believe you, because I want to. I really do. So, if the general ordered you to do this, did you obey out of simple obedience, or because you wanted revenge on the *Kaisiepo's* crew for embarrassing you?"

Feeling his world crumble, Hakim howled. "They deserved it!"

Pardi stepped back, pasted disgust on his visage, and averted his eyes from the admiral. "Take him. Get him out of here."

As strong men pushed Hakim from the office which had been his privilege, he listened to the conversation trailing away behind him.

Pardi spoke. "Now we have a decision. How long do we have?"

Moeljadi answered. "About thirteen hours."

"It's your navy now, captain. Technically, we work for you."

The freed pilot added. "We don't have time to quibble about who's in charge, and I concur it's the navy."

His courage curing like concrete, the heavyset man accepted leadership's burden. "Each of you grab advisors whose judgment you trust and bring them here. We'll talk about it here, and we'll talk about it now."

Hakim felt chaos and misery flowing as poisons throughout him. His last thought while sinking into irrational despair was that of the once-cowardly heavyset captain sitting at his desk, condemning him for having made a difficult and complex decision.

He was the victim. Him. The noble and misjudged Hakim–not the women and children he'd blown up.

The man who'd been Mego Hakim became something subhuman, stripped of humility's dignity, by declaring himself a righteous victim for his evil actions' consequences.

His soul closed in upon itself in a self-inflicted hell.

# CHAPTER 22

Volkov leaned into his chair's back, balancing against the *Wraith's* thirty-degree down angle. The seatbelt pinched his hip. "I hate steep angles."

Fighting the same battle against gravity, the *Wraith's* English translator, a familiar crewman, deadpanned. "If it keeps us from getting blown up, I'll bear it."

Ogling screens of visual and acoustic data from the *Xerxes*, Volkov joined every free pair of eyes aboard both vessels in seeking signs of the first mine. The thirty-degree down angle gave the transport ship's side scan hydrophones a forward-looking vantage at the limit of their electronic steering abilities.

Designed to paint high-resolution portraits from acoustic data above the cargo bed, the *Xerxes'* side scan sonar system comforted Volkov in its ability to see mines in time to react.

Also, the *Xerxes'* wired rover drove three hundred meters ahead of the tandem vessels, giving a creepy, artificially illuminated perspective of the chokepoint's shallow and silty bottom.

When the rover's camera presented its first evidence of danger, the anchor to a moored mine, a dozen voices in the *Wraith's* control room sang the alarm in chorus with another dozen over the loudspeakers from the *Xerxes*.

Multiple languages erupted in a crackling, buzzing enthusiasm for discovering the first obstacle.

Then silence.

Commander Danielle Volkova announced her response. "Slowing to zero speed over ground on the outboards."

While the translator announced Danielle's words in Russian, Volkov admired the simplicity of the weapon seen through the remote-control camera.

One fluke of the admiralty type anchor pointed upward while the other disappeared into the sand. As a technician aboard the *Xerxes* commanded the rover shallow, the camera followed the cable from the shank upward and then stopped when the mine appeared below the surface as a silhouette backlit by the setting sun's rays.

Seated close to the *Wraith's* commander, the submarine's Indonesian rider repeated what he and his compadre aboard the *Xerxes* had affirmed during planning sessions. "This type is our standard moored mine. It's only a danger to us if we get within three meters. We can go around."

Before replying, Volkov waited to hear the report from a similar conversation he overheard in the *Xerxes'* control room.

When his wife's environs became quieter, she faced him and used the Russian translator beside her to state her agreement. "It's a moored mine. We'll go around it to the left."

Volkov digested nuggets of her English while her interpreter restated her meaning in Russian. Then, as the tandem ship's senior officer, he agreed. The natural channel between the islands of Papua and Salawati offered deeper water to the left. "I concur. Stay on depth and twist to the left. Stay at zero speed over ground until you've scanned the new track."

After translators relayed orders between the spouses, she replied. "I'm twisting us on the outboards to a new course of three-five-three. I'm taking the rover at maximum speed to three hundred meters ahead of our new track."

Translators translated, and Volkov answered. "Very well."

When the rover appeared at the limit of the *Xerxes'* titled side scan sonar system, Danielle returned the tandem to forward movement. "We're clear on course three-five-three for at least three hundred meters. I'm taking us to three knots on the outboards."

"Very well."

Stopping, repositioning the rover, and detouring around the mine added eight minutes to the prescribed journey. Twenty-two percent of the way through the channel's mined length, Volkov grew confident in his chances of surviving the hidden dangers.

But the fruits of survival taunted him with their dubiousness, and he voiced his concern. "We're two hours from sunset."

His rider completed the thought. "And four hours from the battle for the landing."

"I want to prevent that. That's why I'm here, but we planned on having to maneuver around three, at most four, mines."

"We may arrive after the anti-ship missile exchanges."

"That's the destruction we're trying to avoid."

"We can still get there in time. We don't know how well this field is laid, and I'm sure they didn't expect us to run it."

"They laid it well enough to divert us once already, and we're barely one-fifth the way through it."

"Even if we're late, enough ships on both sides will survive the early attacks to warrant our intervention. Sneaking up behind the enemy with twelve torpedo tubes and Commander Volkova's railguns will still matter."

Volkov swiveled his chair against the *Wraith's* down angle and braced his weight on his lower leg. He glared at the chart, wiggled a cursor through time, speed, and distance scenarios, and then folded his arms. "But if we fail to arrive when planned, lives will be lost in the surface battle that don't need to be."

"We'll have to hope that our arrival will be welcomed, no matter when we get there."

"I thought you'd be more anxious about your navy and your countrymen's lives."

"Predicting what happens when missiles fly and guns fire between that many ships is anyone's guess." The rider glanced around his tight confines and then opined. "But I'm quite certain what would happen if we trigger one of these to go off. So, please don't rush."

Twenty minutes later, the rover found its second anchor, roughly forty percent through the mined channel.

Another cautious and flawless detour to the left, and another eight minutes of delay.

Then another ten minutes brought Volkov to an impasse.

As Danielle slipped the tandem vessels to the left of the third moored mine's anchor, the rover's camera caught an ugly threat on the channel's silty floor.

Glaring through the camera, Volkov–along with dozens of silent sailors aboard both ships–watched an anchor's short cable holding a cylinder deep in the channel. He grunted. "*Blyad*. A rising mine."

In his tilted seat, the Indonesian officer's frame stiffened. "Passive acoustic, with a torpedo payload. It's there to stop submarines like us."

"They aren't making this easy."

"Not at all. The acquisition cone is too wide to go around. We'll have to neutralize it."

Volkov nodded a silent affirmation while listening to his wife's rider share similar information on her ship. Awaiting confirmation from the *Xerxes'* team, he recalled the tactics the riders had alluded to earlier for neutralizing such an impediment.

None were good.

Through translators, Danielle shared her recommendation. "I want to cut the tether with the rover's cutting rod."

Unsure how to proceed through the unwanted surprise, Volkov thought aloud. "That will take…however long it takes. And it will release the captor cylinder to the surface." He eyed his rider for confirmation.

While the translator turned Volkov's words into English, the rider nodded and clarified. "We could hope they're not looking, but that's a fool's hope. If they're paying attention, it's a dead giveaway."

The translator interrupted. "Should I say that in English?"

Volkov nodded. "Yes."

A quick exchange between warship commanders judged the

dangers worth accepting, and Danielle set the rover to cutting the rising mine's cable. While electrodes weakened steel with a burning arc, valuable time elapsed.

Twenty minutes.

When the cylinder with the torpedo snapped its tether and floated to the surface, Volkov let out a shallow sigh. He ordered Danielle to recommence their crawl, and he watched on the side scan sonar as the current and the tandem's lethargic forward movement carried the harmless warhead wide of the *Xerxes'* starboard weapons bay.

Another fifteen minutes passed, and another anchor appeared in the rover's camera with the side scan sonar painting its tethered mine a few meters below the surface.

Volkov complained. "We're going to be late."

His rider shook his head. "I'm afraid so. Let's trust there'll be a landing force to protect when we get there."

Having been held irrelevant to safe navigation, the *Wraith's* sonar guru barked. "Dipping sonar, bearing one-six-six!"

By instinct, Volkov tensed his legs and hips to stand, but his seatbelt restrained him. "Dani! Get your MICAs ready!"

She replied in Russian. "I agree." She issued a quick command to her subordinates and then spoke English to the screen. "We'll try to evade, but–"

The translators became adrenaline-fueled mouthpieces while keeping pace with the Commanders Volkov. The *Wraith's* commander was adamant. "No! We attack. We can't evade."

"But we have no evidence of having been detected. Why give away our presence?"

"They know we're here. That's why the helicopter's investigating that rising mine we just cut."

"That's due diligence. It's just one helicopter."

Volkov glanced at the chart, the low-bandwidth feed, and then the chart again. An ellipse of uncertainty representing the enemy helicopter covered many square miles of water around the *Wraith-Xerxes* tandem. Accompanying the ellipse, a note from Renard asked his commanders if they'd done something to garner the attention of a solitary aircraft.

Danielle persevered. "If the helicopter doesn't find us in the next few minutes, it won't find us at all."

"But if it does find us, we won't have time to shoot it down before it attacks, and we won't evade. It's now or never!"

She folded her arms. "It's your decision."

He swallowed as he realized he disagreed with his tactically brilliant wife. Then he reminded himself he was a career submarine officer, and she was not. "Then I've made it. Get us to a level deck, optimize your ship for anti-air defense, and surface the tandem. You're weapons free for anti-air combat."

A minute later, the tandem surfaced, and Volkov likened himself to an infant in his mother's arms.

Helpless aboard his cradled submarine, he waited for his wife to protect him. Her close-in-weapon-system, her MICA missiles, and her railguns were mortal dangers to the helicopter's crew, and he commanded them.

But they all belonged to her.

He wondered if fatherhood portended similar frustrations of shared responsibility, where he and Danielle would need to power through differing assumptions, opinions, and control of resources in guiding their children.

His heart thumping, Volkov protested the lack of a weapon engaging the airborne enemy. "What's going on? Where is it?"

"Maybe it's too low beyond our horizon." Danielle's vexation carried the anxiety of sensing an unseen danger.

Her tone made Volkov question if he'd doomed them by surfacing. "Is your radar energized?"

She scowled. "MICAs don't fly without it! Yes, my radar is on! We don't hold the helicopter on any–"

Breaking the argument, Renard's voice rang from loudspeakers. "Nor will you hold it."

In her native language, Danielle inquired. "Why not? What's going on, Pierre?"

"While you were surfacing, the rebels surrendered, and that helicopter turned back."

After Volkov's translator expressed the sentiment in Russian, a wave of silent relief bathed the *Wraith's* control room. Men sank into their chairs, some exchanging fist bumps and high-fives, as the news settled into their reality.

But the *Wraith's* commander remained incredulous. "Just like that? Just now?"

"Just now, yes, as the timing was fortuitous. But not just like that. There was a buildup, and we're now only seeing the full picture."

"What are we seeing?"

"Check your data feed. I've sent you links to social media where a Captain Basuki Moeljadi is committing the entire rebel navy to President Widodo's offer of pardons. He says the air force and the marine corps will do the same, and those services' respective leaders are standing beside him as he speaks."

Volkov had Sergei broadcast the live feed on all screens. The heavyset captain looked both angry and contrite, the anger aimed at his former rebel leaders and the contrition aimed at those offering forgiveness.

On his either side, a grim-faced marine colonel and an air force colonel kept silent except to interject periodic agreement in the unified decision to undo their parts in the revolt.

Strikingly, the proper Indonesian flag covered the wall behind the trio.

The *Wraith's* commander turned to his rider. "What's he saying?"

Wide-eyed, the rider summarized. "So far, he's said that all navy, marine corps, and air force assets are now at the service of President Widodo, ready to follow all his lawful orders."

"Wow."

"No kidding."

"Why'd they change their minds?"

"Incredible." The rider absorbed the live feed.

Volkov let the man watch until he could no longer bear the

suspense. "It sounds like some important news?"

"He's talking about the pilot who claims he was tricked into destroying *Blue Fin* and the *Kaisiepo's* families."

Familiar with the attack, Volkov spat. "That was cowardly vengeance."

"Captain Moeljadi says he has incontrovertible evidence that the pilot was telling the truth. The order came from men of the junta, possibly from General Purnomo himself. He has a phone recording that implicates Rear Admiral Mego Hakim."

"So, the captain realizes he chose the wrong side?"

"And so do Colonels Pardi and Soebijakto. They've joined Moeljadi in allowing our landing and withdrawing their forces from Purnomo's offensive in Central Papua."

"Their warriors are obeying? Switching sides when ordered?"

"Apparently, the evidence of Hakim's tyranny is enough. Nobody wants to serve a monster."

"There may be outliers, but that sounds like it's enough evidence to sway enough men."

"If mob psychology can fuel a rebellion, it can undo one."

Volkov shifted his attention to his console and addressed Renard with his translator's support. "We're still in a minefield, Pierre. I'd like a way out without having to dodge more mines."

"Things are happening fast, my friend. The landing will happen, although uncontested. Then forces will unite. Some rebels will be detained. Some will be trusted immediately to fight. But none except those under Purnomo remain against us, and he will fall. It's now only a matter of time."

"So, everyone's too busy to help us out?"

"No, my friend. If you promise not to shoot it down, the helicopter that was searching for you has the proper acoustic codes to inert every mine in your path."

Volkov raised a finger and moved his eyes to his wife's image on the screen. "Danielle, secure all your weapons and stand down from anti-air defenses. Weapons tight."

Her reply revealed a confident regality with shades of the Ghost Queen. "My weapons are already secured, and I've stood down from anti-air defenses. I'm weapons tight."

Volkov shifted his attention. "We're weapons tight, Pierre. We're ready for our escort through the rest of this minefield."

"I'll get that helicopter to you as fast as I can."

"Sure. But Danielle's railguns could lend support to thwarting whatever resistance General Purnomo will still present."

Renard shook his head. "No. You'll rendezvous with Terry in the Surabaya shipyard. You'll undergo an examination for structural damage from your close-aboard detonation."

"That's far from Papua."

"But you'll have a couple days for your crews to enjoy some liberty." His skin sagging, the Frenchman looked mortally fatigued. "We've done enough here, and we have the cleanest, least stressful victory I can remember."

Volkov snorted. "We were due for a break."

"Yes, my friend. We were. Make sure my ships are seaworthy and bring my family home."

THE END

## Epilog 1

A month later, Danielle Volkova stepped from her Uber ride onto the curb where sandstone-colored walls framed a simply elegant and deceptively large edifice, her husband's church.

She walked around the building and descended stairs to the basement below the sanctuary. She pushed through a side door into an empty assembly hall with classrooms around its perimeter.

Her husband's voice droned from a chamber at the hall's far end. She marched toward it and heard his rapidly improving English.

She reached the glass door and stood until a catechumen noticed her and pointed.

Volkov stood and let her in. "Hi, Dani. Is everything okay?"

"Yeah. I just came from my ultrasound."

"Oh, yes. You seem well. All is well, then?"

"Oh, it's a very healthy pregnancy, especially for my age."

"Praise God! Since you came all this way to share good news with me, I assume I'm taking you to dinner?"

She hadn't thought that far, and given her limited culinary skills, she wanted to learn new styles of cooking. "I was actually going to try your mom's recipe for Pelmeni tonight."

"You spoke to my mother?"

"Yes."

"In Russian?"

"*Da!* Does she speak another language I don't know about?"

"No. Um, did she tell you to include..." He exchanged words in Russian with students ranging in age from young adult to elderly.

An old lady replied in English. "Garlic."

"Yes! Thank you." He turned back to his wife. "Garlic in the meat filling."

She noticed how volunteering to teach at his Orthodox church let him practice English with the safety nets of bilingual Russian students. "Yes, of course. Just like your mom makes it."

He folded his arms. "Then this is really my lucky day."

"More than you know."

"You have more good news?"

"Yes. In private please?"

He ushered her into the assembly hall and spoke in a hushed tone. "You said it's good news, right?"

"Yes. Would you like to know the sex?"

"Oh! Please. A boy or a girl?"

She yelped in elation. "One of each!"

"Two babies!" He hugged her. "Good job, Dani!"

"Thank God for fertility drugs."

"They worked perfectly!"

With her life pivoting towards destinations unthinkable only a few years ago, she stepped back. "I don't want to delay your class any longer. I'm going home to start rolling the minced meat."

Reentering the classroom, he called out. "Remember the garlic!"

After enjoying a dinner of meat pies with a side of beet soup, Danielle stood to clear the dirtied dishes.

In English, Volkov stopped her. "No. You sit. I'll clean."

After checking a word on her phone, she replied in Russian. "Is this going to be a habit?"

"I clean the table?"

"And do the dishes."

"Yes, at least while you're pregnant." His smile enticed her to challenge him into extending his cleaning role.

"While I'm pregnant and beyond."

"It's possible." As he lifted plates and utensils, he scowled. "Why don't we already know who cleans the dishes?"

She snorted. "Because we never do it."

"We're lazy. Everyone pays someone else to do their hard work."

Her concurrence came via a concrete example. "We need to stop ordering our food through Deliveroo."

Turning the argument around while he clanked plates into the sink, he opined. "We have all the money we need. Maybe it's okay to pay people to do some work for us. That's economics, after all."

She surprised herself with the strength of her conviction, a strength she'd sensed rising since the confirmation of her twins. "I want to serve food to my husband and children that I prepare with my own hands. It just seems proper. Neither of us needs to work. Shame on me if I can't make the time."

He ran the faucet and raised his voice. "But time and money are different things!"

Tallying their income from years in the fleet, she counted a net worth of independent wealth. But money failed to create time, the time needed for relationships, and she realized her loneliness. She mentally juxtaposed that sentiment against the pleasant sounds of a doting husband placing scoured dishes into the washer.

When he stopped the faucet, he froze in seeming thought over the sink. "You've gotten quiet."

"Yeah." She welcomed the silence as it enticed her deeper thoughts, but those thoughts led to an icy moment of candor. With minimal time together outside of maritime combat, she and Volkov related as warship commanders, but not as Danielle and Dmitry, parents raising children.

She thought she'd married a stranger. "We have to make time for each other if we want to be a family."

He strode around the table and sat facing her. "Of course. Did you want me to make some dessert?"

She folded her arms at his male denseness. "I'm trying to talk to you. This is important!"

His expression became one of knowing. "Ah. I see. It's very important. I misunderstood the subject matter."

His newfound zeal for a discussion unbalanced her. "It's a broad subject matter. How do you understand it?"

"It's our unfinished conversation. One of us, maybe both of us, must quit the fleet."

His first admission that both of them could retire from naval combat startled her. "If we both quit, we'll ruin Pierre."

"Maybe. But it's time to tell him. We've hidden from this conversation long enough." He stood. "Join me on the couch."

"We're going to call him now?"

He chuckled. "Nobody calls Pierre unless it's urgent. When you need help telling him something, you call Henri."

Trusting her husband, she lowered herself to the cushion, leaned into his shoulder, and eyed his phone. "You're calling Henri?"

"Texted him. Waiting for a reply." Volkov thumbed his screen. "Oh, there it is. He's calling on a video chat."

With the evening sky above him as he strolled between the rising fauna of a garden within Renard's headquarters, the handsome Frenchman appeared. At the fringe of the screen, Henri's wife joined her husband in a greeting. "Good evening, Commanders Volkov."

The Volkovs hailed their friends. "Hi, Henri and Karen."

After a quick exchange with his wife, Henri was alone. "I assume we need to speak of business?"

Recognizing her husband's delay in having to translate the English, Danielle answered. "We've got some great news, and some not-so-great news."

"Let's start with the good."

Danielle yelped. "I'm having twins. A boy and a girl!"

Henri smiled into the quiet night. "How wonderful! You must both be happy!"

She nodded. "Yes, of course. But that's why there's also bad news. Dmitry and I have talked it over, and one of us needs to take a leave of absence from the fleet to raise our children."

The Frenchman's eyes narrowed. "I admit I had foreseen this."

Encouraged, she sensed common ground in the discussion. "You've talked about this with Pierre?"

"Not yet. But he suspects it's coming."

"We haven't decided which of us should leave. I think Mike's ready to replace me. Dmitry thinks Sergei can replace him.

We tried to form a recommendation, but there are too many complexities. We'll be flexible."

Henri sounded more receptive than she'd feared. "I consider that a perfectly logical perspective. I understand completely and will bring your concerns to Pierre."

After bidding the Frenchman farewell, she looked to Volkov. "If Pierre decides he can't live without you, I'll miss being called 'Commander Volkova'. It's beautiful and powerful."

"So is 'Ghost Queen', and you can keep the title no matter what."

She wrapped her arms around him and squeezed him close against her body and their children. "No matter what Pierre decides, you can call me the 'Ghost Queen' forever."

## Epilog 2

A month later, an immigration agent threw a wrench into Volkov's travel plans. "Mister Volkov, you and your wife will need to accompany my supervisor to the interview room."

Beside him, Danielle asked for a translation. "I think I understood, but what's going on?"

Knowing the weight of his homeland's bureaucracy, Volkov spoke above a whisper in English. "He said we're going to spend the day being threatened and ignored."

She recoiled and eyed him.

He added. "Okay, it shouldn't be that bad, but they may separate us. Be calm and speak the truth about everything–except the fleet. Remain silent on that."

Her face revealed fear of worst-case scenarios ruining their first trip as spouses to his homeland.

He lied. "Don't worry. I'm sure we'll be okay."

"Should we call Pierre?"

"I'll text him and Henri. We won't have time to talk."

"They know we're entering Russia? You didn't forget?"

"Yes, I told them. That's standard procedure, and Pierre said it could be challenging but that we should be safe."

"So, why don't I feel safe?"

"Pierre's not perfect. And I don't want to keep relying on him. I want to enter my own country without a billionaire's assistance."

As the supervisor arrived to escort the spouses away, Volkov pondered the ransom a pair of Renard's commanders might earn.

Surprised to have kept his phone and his wife at arm's reach, Volkov sat across a cluttered desk from the supervisor. He risked a question. "May I ask why you've detained us?"

Young and determined, the supervisory agent appeared the type to double check everything. "Routine, I promise. Well, routine for you, given your history and the nature of you and your wife's employment. You may be pulled aside for questioning every time you enter or leave the country."

"Can we streamline this?" Volkov noticed his arm subconsciously moving towards his wallet to fund a bribe.

"No. We're almost done. Just a verification of your past travels." The agent put his nose in Volkov's passport. "What were your last two border crossings, and why, not counting your present travel?"

Volkov recalled the recent movements requiring his passport. "I flew from Heathrow to Charles de Gaulle for work, and then two months later, I flew from Charles de Gaulle to Heathrow between our home in London and our fleet's port in Toulon."

The supervisor switched to excellent English. "And you, Misses Volkova. What were your last two border crossings, and for what purposes, not counting your present travel?"

Danielle replied in English. "I traveled with Dmitry on the same flights and for the same purpose."

Delighted, the supervisor returned the passports and switched back to his own language. "You're learning Russian?"

She nodded.

The supervisor lifted his gaze and called two agents, and then three immigration officers stood before the detainees.

Volkov was unsure. "So, may we go now?"

The supervisor raised a finger. "Almost. Your travel itineraries don't show it, but you show up in crisis areas. Indonesia. Nigeria. Yemen. We are all observers and, dare I say, fans of the Commanders Volkov."

"Fans?"

"A former commander of a Russian submarine joins a do-gooder pirate fleet and punishes tyrants. And his wife is his partner called the Ghost Queen. You're a bit famous."

Volkov eyed his wife. "Should I be jealous?"

Before she could reply, the agents squatted between the spouses while the supervisor held a phone on a plastic stick. Blushing, he completed his transformation from immigration officer to pop culture fan. "After we get a selfie with the

Commanders Volkov, you're free to go."

Six hours later, Volkov indulged in a second Kartoshka cake pop. He shoved the entire three-bite dessert into his mouth and labored to chew it before his mother noticed.

At the table's end near the kitchen, his mother noticed. "Dmitry! Have your father and I not taught you manners?"

Volkov grabbed a snifter and sipped cognac to moisten his mouthful. While putting his molars in overdrive, he looked around the table. Accusatory eyes from two brothers, two sisters, two siblings-in-law, both parents, and one wife left him feeling like a toddler. He swallowed half the cake. "When they're made with so much love, how can I resist?"

At the table's far end, Volkov's father quipped. "Nice try, but it's all made with love in this house. It's no excuse for bad manners."

Volkov sipped more cognac, swallowed, and confessed. "Guilty!"

Narrowing his eyes, the elder Volkov changed subjects. "You and Danielle are leaving the decision to your boss?"

Instinctively, Volkov raised his arm and caressed his wife's back while answering. "We need to consider Pierre's needs."

"A decision that important needs trusted advisors."

"But Papa, we're financially solid for life. Don't worry."

"Not money, but callings." The elder's reply flowed like wisdom. "You found your dream vocations, but soon you'll be too old for it. Make sure the one who quits can bear quitting."

Thirty minutes later, Volkov sat on the patio with the men.

His middle brother lowered the ultrasound to a picnic table. "Two babies. Perfect, given your ages. I think it would be sad to have just one and then find out you're too old for another."

"I'll never be too old!"

"You know what I meant. Dani's eggs, you idiot."

"I know what you meant." Volkov filled his cheeks with cigar smoke and rested his eyes on the logs burning in the fire pit.

"How old is she?"

"Thirty-eight now. Thirty-nine before they're born."

The middle brother grunted. "She looks strong."

"She is. The fertility drugs helped, but she did this."

Interrupting, his youngest brother opined. "That Ghost Queen thing in Africa was cool. You guys were micro-hits on social media."

The middle brother quipped. "Not them. Just her."

Volkov backhanded his brother's chest, spilling his cognac.

"Sorry. I'll get you a refill." Volkov carried his brother's glass through the patio door into his parents' kitchen. He measured a shot and then poured it into the drinkware.

While returning to the patio, Volkov reheard his father's words. *Make sure the one who quits can bear quitting.* After handing off the replacement beverage, he walked off the patio and onto the cold grass extending towards the tree line. "I need to make a call."

Alone in the backyard, Volkov pleaded. "I can't let Dani quit. She's worked her whole life for this. I'll be a stay-at-home dad."

Henri sounded receptive. "That's perfectly logical. I'll bring your concerns to Pierre, but…"

"But?"

"I said the same thing three minutes ago to your wife. She's on hold with me."

"Huh?"

"I wouldn't have betrayed her, but given the coincidental timing, I had to tell you. You and Danielle need a candid conversation."

Volkov stepped to the window and looked inside his parents' living room. Seated among his mother, sisters, and sisters-in-law, his wife seemed at ease in communicating in their tongue.

But she seemed impatient with the phone below her ear, as if she waited for an interlocutor to recommence a paused conversation.

He rapped on the window and then pressed his device against

it to expose his discussion with Henri.

Danielle walked towards the pane, leaned forward, and examined the pixelated text. She covered her mouth while laughing, turned away, and then hung up on her paused call.

Volkov yelled through the glass. "Did you tell him to let me stay in the fleet?"

"Yeah. Did you just call him, too?"

"Yes, but I'm the man. I'm supposed to sacrifice for you."

"Oh well. Too bad." She shrugged. "I thought of it first."

Volkov bid Henri farewell and slid his phone into his pocket. Unsure of his professional future, he was surer of his choice in marrying Danielle than ever.

## Epilog 3

Six months later, Terry Cahill watched his wife lower their infant son into his crib. Having given birth a month ago, Ariella seemed a healthy mix of exhilaration and fatigue.

After escorting her to their bedroom, he helped her into the bed.

Leaning back, she protested. "I'm fine, Terry. Ever since I became a mother, you think I'm going to break."

"I want you to be comfortable."

"I'm fine."

He pulled the covers over her shoulder and then rounded the bed to his side. "How fine?"

"Terry!" her voice trailed off.

Cahill chuckled and murmured to himself. "I guess we're not working on another baby tonight."

Her deep breathing mocked his request.

"Okay. I guess not. Bedtime for Daddy, too."

His head buzzed with the excitement of fatherhood, and he couldn't sleep. For some reason, anxiety gripped him, and he stirred under the covers for two hours.

He relieved himself in the bathroom and then returned to the bed to attempt slumber. As he dozed off, his awareness drifted until cruel fate trapped it between reality, memory, and horrors.

Cahill's floating mind replayed his hellish vision of seeing Liam Walker transformed into a demon. His executive officer's face became a twisted aberration of sagging and torn skins atop a body of scarred and blighted leather.

Then came recent memories of wanting to commit suicide.

Cahill curled forward and yelped, waking his wife.

Ariella mumbled. "Are you okay?"

"Yeah. It's nothing." After considering the intensity of the episode, he altered his assessment. "Actually, it is something."

"Can we talk about it in the morning?"

"Can you stay awake while I summarize?"

"Go ahead."

Cahill explained the vision he'd never shared.

"That's deep, Terry. But I wouldn't worry. Maybe you ate something that upset your stomach."

He snapped. "Impossible! It was too real for that."

"Okay. The mind can do bizarre things under stress. I'm sure there's a natural explanation."

He disagreed. "I wasn't sure if I was alive. I wasn't sure I wanted to be. Am I becoming a coward?"

She propped herself on her elbow. "I didn't marry a coward. Do you think I'd let a coward father my children?"

"No."

"But if it's still bothering you in the morning, we'll talk."

"Yeah. Right. I'll let you get back to sleep."

Later that morning, Cahill awoke with the compromised lethargy of a half night of sleep.

With Ariella still dozing, he decided her Saturday morning routine for her by making a pot of coffee, crafting two egg omelets laden with cheese, and frying thin cuts of lamb bacon.

Sounds of doors opening indicated her rising and checking on their son, Daniel. After visiting the infant, she entered the kitchen. "You cooked?"

"I'm no dunce around breakfast foods." He lowered a plate to the table. "See if you like it."

She sat. "I can't wait."

He sat opposite her with his plate. "Enjoy." He shoved a forkful of egg and cheese into his mouth.

She took a bite and indicated her approval with her expression. After swallowing, she opined. "Very good, Terry."

"I may do this more often. Not just weekends."

Her phone rang, and she frowned while lifting it.

Cahill protested. "You're still on maternity leave."

Ignoring his comment, she addressed her digital interlocutor. "Lieutenant Colonel Dahan." While hearing the news, she opened her eyes wide, gasped, and then sprang from the chair. She stopped in the kitchen and became a statue frozen in horror.

Cahill darted beside her. "What's wrong?"

Her raised palm silenced him as she tensed, and a tear flowed down her cheek.

He waited until she hung up to talk. "Ariella?"

"Massacres. Gang rapes. Babies ripped from wombs. It's still happening as we speak."

Ice ran through Cahill. "An attack?"

Unable to speak, she nodded but collected herself. "Hamas."

"It's that bad?"

With resolve, she eyed him. "The worst in decades."

"Oh, bloody...you're sure it was Hamas?"

"Yeah. They're already taking credit."

Something clicked inside Cahill. Suddenly, his universe shrank from anywhere the *Goliath's* railguns could reach to one wife and one son.

Then another epiphany struck him.

Australia had been home, but it had vomited him.

Renard's fleet had then been home, but it was distant, dispersed, and dormant. They were a sort of family, but forces beyond them were pulling them apart.

The epiphany's conclusion—he was Israeli.

And he wanted to defend his family.

Ariella interrupted his ruminations. "I'm ending my maternity leave and going to fight this. I've got three days of milk in the refrigerator and another week's worth of formula." She marched towards their bedroom.

He called out to her. "I'm enlisting in the army."

With her uniform blouse in hand, she returned to the kitchen. "You're enlisting?"

"I have to. I can't sit by idly while this happens."

"You're already a warrior."

"Not like that. I can't protect distant strangers when my wife and child are threatened."

She slid her blouse over her undershirt. "You're at least six months away from mastering Hebrew enough, and that's if you study intensely."

"I can do that. I'd like to. You have courses?"

"Of course, we do. But do you want to throw away everything else to become a grunt?"

"How can I deploy far away while Hamas tries to kill my family? It would be like running away."

Ariella agreed. "Okay. I'll enroll you in Hebrew today."

"Thanks. I can really do this, can't I?"

"It'll take resolve, especially since you're turning forty before you become fluent in Hebrew."

Cahill had ignored his age. "Oh. I hadn't…"

"Don't worry. Forty isn't a magic number. You're married to an officer, and we need patriots. But you'll have to give up your Australian citizenship."

"I can visit my family as a foreigner. Not a big deal."

"Okay. Then the only question is, will you keep your resolve?"

"I have to. That's what my life's adding up to."

"Good." She turned. "I need to get moving."

An hour later, Cahill held a bottle to his son's mouth. "Enjoy mommy's milk. You need to get strong to protect your country."

Daniel burped onto his bib.

When the fluid again flowed from the bottle in one hand, Cahill used his other to lift his phone, dial a number, and place the device on speaker.

Henri answered. "Terry? To what do I owe the pleasure?"

"You've heard the news of the Hamas attacks?"

"I've just seen it. I'm sorry."

"No, Henri. I'm sorry. It's…" Cahill sought the words. "I can't come back to the fleet. I'm going to get my Israeli citizenship and join the army."

"That's a huge decision, and it sounds, dare I say, hurried."

"It is, but it's right."

"I can't imagine having my home attacked like that."

"I can't either, even while it's still happening. I need to do something."

"I don't like it." Henri's tone shifted to one of compassion. "But

I understand completely and will bring your concerns to Pierre."

## Epilog 4

Three months later, Jake Slate sat alone in the newly constructed adoration chapel of Saint Thomas Chaldean Catholic Church.

On the one-year anniversary of his entrance into the seminary, he wavered on his decision to become a priest.

Unable to receive new perspectives, or even inklings of them, while sitting in contemplation, he sighed, stood, and closed the monstrance's door to the heavenly host's viewing window. "No answers today, I guess."

He stepped into the grotto's foyer to light a candle.

His pensive, slow movements contrasted those of a man in his twenties who scurried into the grotto and also reached for a candle.

Jake offered an instinctive greeting. "Hi."

Edgy, the young man launched his request. "I was looking for someone to talk to, but there's nobody in the church."

Glancing through the foyer windows, Jake saw an empty parking lot separating him from the sandstone-colored bricks of the main edifice. His first wave of thoughts was about lacking time to talk, lacking interest, and escaping the needy man's pending ramblings.

His second, seasoned thoughts recognized someone in distress who'd benefit from someone caring about him for five minutes.

Jake gave his troubled interlocutor an opening. "What are you looking for?"

Unable to hold eye contact, the jumpy man gave vague but significant clues. "I wanted to talk to someone, but I couldn't find anyone in the church."

Jake saw the speaker as an uncomfortable source of discomfort and wondered how many years had elapsed since anyone had listened to him without an agenda.

A silent voice offered wisdom. *You can serve him by paying attention. There is nobody else.*

The inner voice had become a frequent visitor to Jake's head since his combat in Nigeria, pushing him in the priesthood's general direction. He was learning to trust it. "Tell me what's going on."

The grotto's latest visitor seemed stunned by Jake's interest. But desperation fueled his plea, and he stammered while conveying his misery. "I've been diagnosed with paranoid schizophrenia, and they make me take medicine."

Jake's soul ran away and harkened his body to follow, but he corrected his wimpy instinct. The silent voice issued advice. *A conversation can't hurt you.* "Your mind is yours, no matter what other people say. 'Paranoid schizophrenia' is just a label."

"I don't like it."

"That's okay. You don't have to." Jake raised his gaze to the crucifix above the candles. "But whether or not the diagnosis is accurate, it's your cross."

The schizophrenic looked at the symbol hanging on a cobblestone wall above the candles' glowing flames.

Jake felt the responsibility to probe. "You said you're being made to take medicine. Is someone forcing you?"

"At the hospital they made me. They held me down."

"I'm sorry you went through that. That's horrible."

The man pondered the empathy in hushed serenity.

Jake continued. "Is anyone still forcing you?"

"No. Not since I left the hospital last week."

"Okay. Hopefully, that's just a bad memory now. I hope you never have to go through that again.

Silent pondering.

"Do you have a home?"

His short reply required many stuttered syllables. "Yes. My parents' house."

Hearing about involved parents shrunk Jake's radius of concerns for the man's welfare. "When you say they make you take your medicine, do you mean your parents?"

"I have to if I want to live with them. I have to swallow the meds in front of my mom. Why won't they believe me?"

"Believe you that you don't have paranoid schizophrenia?"

The young man nodded.

"Maybe they can't tell the difference, but they think that acting like you have it somehow helps you?"

"The meds don't help. They make things hazy."

"Can you handle things being hazy for a few weeks to see if it wears off?"

"Maybe. I guess." The man seemed uncomfortable, moved to the exit, and looked over his shoulder. "Can you pray for me?"

Unbalanced by the hasty retreat and request, Jake reacted positively. "Of course. A rosary before the end of the day."

"Thank you." The schizophrenic departed.

Driving home, Jake realized the unexpected encounter had brought an unexpected answer.

His wife, Linda, would be thrilled.

He texted Henri, who then called him from the south of France.

"Hello, Jake!"

"Henri, my friend! What's new with you?"

"Nothing, thankfully. I'm enjoying my free time, mostly volunteering to keep busy."

"Great!"

"But I suspect this chat will be about you?"

Jake stated his decision. "I'm leaving the fleet."

"Are you sure? That's a big decision."

"With the Church, I've got five more years of discernment before I'm ordained. But I promised Pierre an answer in one year."

"So, you'll be a priest?"

"Yeah. Sorry. I can't work for him anymore."

"Not to nitpick, but can you do this while being married?"

"Yep. It's uncommon, but it's less rare in the East, which is where I'm at, thanks to Linda."

"What does she think?"

"I haven't told her yet. But I know she'll be thrilled. She's tired of the deployments."

"I imagine midnight interruptions for your future parishioners' last rites will seem like child's play for her comparatively."

"Yeah. And, in case you're wondering, I'm twenty years older than my class, but middle-aged ordinations aren't unheard of."

"Sure. You still look young to me."

Jake chuckled.

Henri continued his questioning. "And…the language?"

"Are you trying to disqualify me?"

"No, just a curiosity."

"I'm learning Aramaic and Arabic. I need to master them. It's going to be hard enough for me as the only white priest."

"Huh. Interesting. Speaking of your identity, is the Church confident in your identity management protocols?"

Jake recalled his initial mission with Renard when the shady Frenchmen had offered vengeance in return for the nuclear warheads of a Trident missile submarine. "Wow, Henri. You remember what happened twenty years ago?"

"Your followers won't, but your enemies will."

"The identity management protocols have been working for two decades. Bishop Khalabat was willing to take his chances."

Henri sighed in acceptance. "So be it. Congratulations on your decision. May I ask what helped you to reach it?"

"I counseled a distressed man in need."

"In helping, you received help."

"I guess so."

"Someone familiar, or perhaps an angel prodding you along?

Jake snorted. "Who knows? Regardless, I'm taking myself off Pierre's bench. I'm going to give the Church my full attention."

"That's logical."

"And when I think of the *Specter* or ground combat, I feel empty, like someone else who looked like me made those memories. I've felt that way since Nigeria."

"Pierre and I noticed that. A changed man arose from your bed after your convalescence at his estate."

Jake reflected upon a schizophrenic's inner torment. "In speaking to that man today, I saw myself."

"You're mentally sound."

"I mean I recognized my brokenness, and I recognized my new battlefield. It's the invisible one, the one that matters."

"That's strange to hear from a combat hero."

"I've killed enough people, Henri. I can't kill another. I'd rather put away my weapons and do whatever I can to keep people from throwing themselves away."

## Epilog 5

Seated behind the desk of his study, Pierre Renard pondered ways he could oppose terrorists stealing humanitarian aid in the Gaza Strip, but Lieutenant Colonel Ariella Dahan had warned him that railgun rounds would bring more chaos than order.

Across the room, his closest friend examined a screen, searching for opportunities to bring relief to people in India.

"Henri?"

"Yes, my friend?"

"Any luck?"

The silver-haired assistant leaned back, folded his arms, and shook his head. "I can't find anything within reach."

"Very well." The navy's founder grunted. "Henri?"

"Yes, my friend?"

"I've sought your opinion on standing down the fleet for more than a year, and you have yet to advise me."

Henri shrugged.

"You don't want to answer, do you?"

Blushing, Henri confessed. "I may never."

His vessels stowed in the Naval Group's Toulon shipyard, mothballed and lacking enthusiasm from its commanders, Renard hoped something would reinvigorate his passion for running a mercenary navy.

A call from a nation in need.

An eruption of evil within maritime reach.

A chance to revive the fleet.

But nothing happened.

And unexpected relief in that nothingness provided his answer. "How fast can you bring the commanders to Lyon?"

Two weeks later, Renard entered the dining hall established for pilgrims atop Mont Sainte-Victoire, the mountain of his childhood he'd adopted as the fleet's unofficial retreat location.

Assembled before him, key players of the navy he'd spent two decades growing from nothing to global importance sat together for an emotional farewell.

Summiting the mountain had fatigued him worse than he could remember, and while his audience arranged meats, cheeses, breads, and produce on paper plates, he took rapid, shallow breaths. He hoped to calm himself after overcoming the anxiety of what he was about to say.

He wheezed while standing, and his head was fuzzy. He moved slowly to keep his balance. "May I have your attention?"

With uncharacteristic maturity, his key players and their families fell silent and paid attention.

"Wow. You must all be expecting something important."

The people he had mentored into better versions of themselves showed surprising restraint. The sarcastic greeting remained unchallenged until Danielle, rocking her twin infants in a cradle on the bench, replied. "Spit it out, Pierre. Get it over with."

Nervous laughter rose but died abruptly in anticipation.

"And so I shall get it over with. I'm dissolving the fleet. There. I said it. It's over. I quit."

Henri sighed and seemed to shed a mountain of stress. "I knew it had to happen. But to finally hear you say it. Thank God!"

Jake opined. "Yeah. We all knew it was coming. But it was worth coming together for you to say it. You'll always be our leader."

Pain blossomed in Renard's shoulder, and he recalled the other time in his life where he'd endured such intense suffering–two decades ago with a bullet wound in his shoulder aboard an abandoned boat off the coast of Russia.

He staggered.

Like lightning, his friends and family huddled around him and helped him to the dusty floor.

Jake muscled his way in and pushed back others. "Give him room. Jacques, run to the ranger's quarters. Tell him your father's having a heart attack. Ask for aspirin or nitroglycerin."

As familiar faces became murky in receding light, Renard replayed the worst moments, the biggest mistakes, and the ugliest embarrassments of his life. Like torment, memories flooded him. "My God, what have I done?"

Jake answered. "You gave us lives." Despite his cool crisis demeanor, the American let a tear escape down his cheek.

Using a weeping wife's strength, Marie brushed Jake aside and hugged her husband. "Pierre!"

After allowing tender moments, the American protested. "Marie, he needs air."

As she gave him room, Renard lifted a finger and pointed through the hall's rough ceiling. "The cross."

Jake understood. "Do you want me to carry you?"

"Yes."

Marie howled. "No! Don't give up, Pierre!"

Renard faced her. "Please."

Jake rationalized for Marie. "He'll get better air up there."

"Okay."

Arms of steel cradled Renard against Jake's chest as the American's legs bounded with impossible energy up an escarpment. Near the top, wind whipped, but the Frenchman heard his eighteen-year-old son yelling.

"We have aspirin."

With his failing strength, Renard shook his head. "No."

Jake carried him to the base of the nineteen-meter-high *Croix de Provence*. "How's this?"

The imposing cross filled Renard's sky. "Perfect."

As his family again crowded him, the blue sky became darkness.

Then light.

Then he was bodiless.

Then he found his bodiless self above his dying body, looking down and free of pain.

For moments, he hung there looking, admiring the compassion of people who grieved him.

Then a presence comforted him, speaking without words. "Welcome, Pierre."

Indescribable exhilaration overwhelmed Renard. He wanted

to ask the entity if it was from heaven, but his disembodied spirit, unencumbered by flawed flesh, knew.

Again, silent words. "Do you want to stay or go?"

Renard ingested a parting glance of people who had been his life. A supernatural desire to guide them from above overpowered his natural affinity to continue at their sides.

He also believed he was supposed to trust that desire, and that it was his destiny.

"Will I be reunited with them?"

"With the ones who stay true."

In his enlightened understanding, the answer seemed righter than a simple 'yes'. It was perfect. His interlocutor was perfect and offering him perfect counsel. "I know what I want. I'm so tired of this broken world."

"Then come with me."

"Yes, please. I want to go home."

## About the Author

*After graduating from the Naval Academy in 1991, John Monteith served on a nuclear ballistic missile submarine and as a top-rated instructor of combat tactics at the U.S. Naval Submarine School. He now works as an engineer when not writing.*

Join the Rogue Submarine fleet for bonus content!

# ROGUE SUBMARINE SERIES:

*ROGUE AVENGER (2005)*
*ROGUE BETRAYER (2007)*
*ROGUE CRUSADER (2010)*
*ROGUE DEFENDER (2013)*
*ROGUE ENFORCER (2014)*
*ROGUE FORTRESS (2015)*
*ROGUE GOLIATH (2015)*
*ROGUE HUNTER (2016)*
*ROGUE INVADER (2017)*
*ROGUE JUSTICE (2017)*
*ROGUE KINGDOM (2018)*
*ROGUE LIBERATOR (2018)*
*ROGUE MERCENARY (2019)*
*ROGUE NEPTUNE (2021)*
*ROGUE OUTLAWS (2021)*
*ROGUE POSEIDON (2022)*
*ROGUE QUEEN (2022)*
*ROGUE RAIDERS (2024)*

John Monteith recommends:
Jeff Edwards, author of Sword of Shiva.
Thomas Mays, author of A Sword into Darkness.
Kevin Miller, author of Raven One.

## ROGUE RAIDERS

Copyright © 2024 by John R. Monteith

All rights reserved. No part of this book may be used or reproduced by any means, graphic, electronic, or mechanical, including photocopying, recording, taping or by any information storage retrieval system without the written permission of the publisher except in the case of brief quotations embodied in critical articles and reviews.

## Braveship Books

www.braveshipbooks.com

The tactics described in this book do not represent actual U.S. Navy or NATO tactics past or present. Also, many of the code words and some of the equipment have been altered to prevent unauthorized disclosure of classified material.

ISBN-13: 978-1-64062-154-1
Published in the United States of America

Printed in Dunstable, United Kingdom